I0457701

ADMISSION OF GUILT

By T. V. LoCicero

TLC Media

Also By T.V. LoCicero

NOVELS
The Obsession (The Truth Beauty Trilogy, Book 1)
The Disappearance (The Truth Beauty Trilogy, Book 2)
The Car Bomb (The detroit im dyin Trilogy, Book 1)
Babytrick (The detroit im dyin Trilogy, Book 3)
When A Pretty Woman Smiles
Sicilian Quilt

NON-FICTION BOOKS
Murder in the Synagogue
Squelched: The Suppression of *Murder in the Synagogue*

COLLECTION
Coming Up Short

Praise for *Admission of Guilt*

"The depiction of the tragic milieu where children are neglected, exploited, corrupted, and even murdered, puts a good part of LoCicero's second work of the Detroit trilogy in the category of social realism, a distinguished literary tradition going back to Dickens and Balzac." — Patrick Frank

"...riveting and spellbinding and the pages will turn so quickly you will be sorry that it ended. Glad that this is only book two and knowing that this author has others that you can read." — Dee Gott

"Wow, another great story about crime in Detroit! The three books of 'The Detroit I'm Dying Trilogy' are must reads for any true crime readers out there...Exciting plot, excellent characters and an ending that pulls it all together. I definitely need to read more from T.V.LoCicero!!"--Kathi Defranc

"The characters find themselves making life and death decisions with moral, economic, and personal ramifications...lots of twists and turns to the plot that you just won't expect and a book you won't want to put down." — Linda Higgins

"Another gritty story involving the denizens of the Motor City; people who live in the same geoaphic area, but are worlds apart. Dialogue is as pithy as you'd expect it to be, and the descriptions, for one who has spent a lot of time in Detroit, are spot on. This is noir fiction at its best." — Charles Ray

"I tried and tried to put this book down and get on with some work, but to no avail...The pace is relentless - and the outcome is not certain until right at the end. This is a thrilling, compulsive story, so don't start it when you have important, time-sensitive tasks to complete. But when you are free, pick this book up and become mesmerized."--Rosemary Standeven

"John is flawed but he is trying to do the right thing. He really, truly cares. Which makes him one of the saddest, most likable characters whose adventures I've followed. The ticking-clock climax at the end nearly gave me a heart attack. But, as usual with this series, the most important part is the humans - good and bad - at the heart of the novel." — Elisa Rambacher

"...one man trying to make a difference in the lives of the kids of his city, a city besieged by drugs and organized crime. As with the first book in this series, The Car Bomb, all the characters were very well written to the point where you really care what happens to each of them." — Gary Hicks

"...you're set right into the middle of the fray with the first heart-stopping chapter. With a subject that is so prevalent in today's world and a writing style reminiscent of James Patterson, this one was a winner. The characters and scenes were so vivid that I felt like I could've been sitting right there. From the very beginning, this story was heart-wrenching and gripping. I couldn't put it down." — Becky Baldridge

"This book is fantastic! All of the characters are well-written and full of life, each one felt real. The plot is amazing! The details he worked out are fantastic! I will definitely be looking up more of his books!" — Kerry Gamble

"There are unexpected twists and turns that kept me wanting more. Even those parts of the plot that I had rather figured out and knew where he was going didn't wind up exactly where I expected them to. To me that is the sign of an excellent author. He puts out bait for me, letting me think I know what's going on and then trips an unexpected trap and I'm in a totally different place! I LOVE it!" — Teresa Collins

T. V. LoCicero

T.V. LoCicero has been writing both fiction and non-fiction across five decades. He's the author of the true crime books *Murder in the Synagogue* (Prentice-Hall), on the assassination of Rabbi Morris Adler, and *Squelched: The Suppression of Murder in the Synagogue*. His novels include the romance *When A Pretty Woman Smiles*, the coming-of-age literary novel *Sicilian Quilt*, and the crime thrillers *The Car Bomb, Admission of Guilt* and *Babytrick* (The *Detroit im dyin* Trilogy), and *The Obsession* and *The Disappearance* (the first two books in The Truth Beauty Trilogy. Eight of his shorter works are now available as ebooks. They are available as well (along wih several other short pieces) in *Coming Up Short,* a collection of fiction and non-fiction. LoCicero has also published stories and essays in various periodicals, including Commentary, Ms. and The University Review, and in the hard-cover collections *Best Magazine Articles, The Norton Reader* and *The Third Coast.*

ADMISSION OF GUILT

By T. V. LoCicero

The detroit im dyin Trilogy
Book 2

TLC Media

Admission of Guilt
by T. V. LoCicero
Copyright 2013 by T. V. LoCicero

This book is a work of fiction. Names, characters, businesses, organizations, places, events, and incidents either are the product of the author's imagination or are used fictitiously. Any resemblance to actual persons, living or dead, events or locales is entirely coincidental.

For more information on this and other works by T.V. LoCicero please visit:
www.tvlocicero.com

For Victoria

detroit im dyin
only come here on a dare
detroit im dyin
dont you even fuckin care

--Detroit Street Grafitti, early 1990s

Chapter 1

Spring leaves, already withering, scratched and whispered in the few Dutch Elms still standing on this dark, working-class street. Birds chirped and chattered on the pre-dawn breeze, and a worn-out Plymouth whined slowly to a stop in front of one of these decrepit wood-framed flats. A smallish figure slipped out, ran to a big front porch, then darted back to the street.

As the Plymouth's door opened, the dome light's yellow glow lit the black, care-lined, 38-year-old face of Joe Martino. Thirteen-year-old Lissa slid onto the front bench next to him and shut the door. In darkness again he moved the car forward.

"Your turn, Pappy." The girl reached to the backseat for a rolled-up Free Press in a thin rubber band.

"Pappy?" Martino's glance raised an eyebrow, and he made a face. "Where'd you get that? Pappy."

She shrugged, then smiled.

He said, "Okay, how about something that rhymes with table."

Her guess was quick: "A place to keep horses."

"No, it's not a stable."

Martino brought the car to a stop again, and Lissa opened the door. "How about the name of Mama's funky old aunt?"

He grinned. "No, it's not Aunt Mable."

Out of the car once more, the girl slammed the door, just the way he'd told her not to. He watched as she sprinted toward another porch. In the dome light her thin face and dancing eyes had so mimed her mother that he suddenly found it hard to swallow.

Tossing the paper up on the porch, Lissa ran back to the Plymouth, and Martino again sent it forward. This time she grabbed two papers from behind. "Is it the kind of fur coat that Mama always wanted?"

"No, it's not a sable. But that's pretty good for a kid." When he stopped the car, Lissa opened the door and eyed her father. He

1

reminded her: "Don't slam it."

"Right. For a kid? How about the kind of story that Aesop wrote?"

He laughed. "Yeah, it's a fable."

"Oh, Pappy, that was a good one!" In the darkness she moved quickly away, carrying the two papers. Her lean teen hips in the jeans he had bought the other day were hinting at the future.

At the front steps of the first house, Lissa flipped one paper up next to the door and ran quickly past the next two houses, glancing at the old Plymouth whining again slowly up the street and staying just behind her. They both knew every stop without thinking.

One more to run past. But as she moved through the overgrown yard in front of a low, crumbling porch, a loud, percussive crack seemed to explode right next to her ear. Terror bolted through her body. A sharp sting seared her right arm, and the rolled up paper fell from her hand. In a panic, she froze, then spun, unable to find the street.

Another explosive crack and with a high-pitched shriek she ran, finally glimpsing the Plymouth. Veering toward the street where the old car's door was swinging open, she screamed, "Daddy!" Another crack and, almost to the Plymouth, her legs stopped working properly. She saw her father yelling at her but couldn't hear him, the cracks now coming quickly one after another. Stumbling badly she threw herself at the car and somehow got her head to the seat and her left hand far enough in for her father to grab.

As Martino shoved the accelerator to the floor, there were more cracks and a side window exploded. The car lunged and squealed away, and, covered with shards and fragments and feeling his right arm go numb, he lost his grip on Lissa's hand.

The car careened weirdly across the street, jumped the curb and crashed into a front porch. The impact echoed for a moment, then faded into the whispers of the dying trees.

Back on the cracked pavement in the middle of the street Lissa was sprawled face down.

Chapter 2

Across the now silent street, in a darkened front room strewn with beer cans and candy wrappers, a 15-year-old boy named Marlon Maples, his heart still pounding wildly, leaned forward in a broken armchair shoved close to the sill of an open window. There was nothing moving out there now.

The muffled sound of a car door slamming at some distance had jolted him awake. Moving the tattered curtains covering the window, he had searched with fear in his throat the long porch, broken steps and weed infested front yard. With headlamp beams skewed, one low to the right, the other up to the left, a car had moved slowly in the street.

A sharp pain still wracked the base of his chin where he had slammed it against the sill, trying to duck when that figure in the dark had suddenly dashed toward the porch. His aching eyes felt the breeze that moved the curtains now. All he had seen was the figure and the car's lights, but that had been enough for his sweaty, nerve-wracked hands to squeeze the machine pistol until it was empty. He cradled it now in his lap,

The echoes of the car's collision with the house across the street had died away, and it was quiet enough to hear Marlon whimper.

Chapter 3

Two hours later John Giordano's eighth grade class at the Lincoln Middle School on Detroit's southwest side was starting its day. Twenty-five, with olive skin and dark, curly hair, John sat on a table at the front of the room, reading the roll for May 9, 1993. The walls and woodwork were dented and scraped, but the classroom was neat, colorful and decorated with posters and pictures cut from magazines. Magic Johnson urged the pleasures of reading. Denzel Washington hugged Oprah. A black man toiled in a surgeon's mask. A Latino woman presided in a judicial robe.

In desk chairs were 30 youngsters in their early teens, mostly black but with a few whites and Hispanics. As usual a half-dozen desks were empty.

"Shaun Dailey?"

No answer. Near the back a boy nudged Shaun, in pigtails and thick glasses, lost in a book.

"Shaun, are you here?" The teacher looked up.

The girl's hand waved. "Yes, Mr. Giordano."

"Are you sure?" She was one of his favorites. He noted the usual smiles, giggles, rolled eyes and smirks.

"Yes, Mr. Giordano."

"Eric Garner?"

Again no answer, and a few feet away he found Eric's small, black, beautiful face with a pursed smile.

"I wasn't sure, Mr. G," said Eric. The room filled with laughter and exaggerated guffaws.

John put his class list down on the table and stared at it to avoid smiling. When he got silence, he gave them a stern stare and said, "Very funny." And after a pause: "Look, folks, I don't like doing this any more than you do. It wastes my time and yours. And I figure if you want to be here because you get something valuable out of this class, then you'll be here. And if you don't, you won't. But it's the

4

law that we take attendance, and so we take attendance."

"If it's a dumb law," piped Eric, the smile impish now, "why don't we break it?"

"Because," said John, "if people go around breaking any law they think is dumb, we might as well be living in the jungle."

In the room's back row a lanky black boy named Mark Simpson stirred from his slouch. "What's wrong with that, man? Survival of the fittest."

John gazed at Mark, who was bright but usually said little in class. "Maybe nothing, if you're the fittest. But sooner or later you're gonna cross someone more fit."

"Yeah, maybe, but that's nature, man." As usual, Mark seemed to mix fatalism with a false bravado.

John picked up the class list. "Yeah, but what we're trying to do on this planet, usually without great success, is rise above the level of animals. Okay, enough of this. Rashad Jamal?"

"Here," said Rashad promptly.

"Jimmy Long?"

"Here."

"Lissa Martino?"

There was no answer, and the teacher lifted his gaze with a frown. "Lissa?"

"She ain't here," said Jimmy Long, a thin, quiet black boy with an obvious but hopeless crush on Lissa.

"She's *not* here," said John.

"It's what I said," said Jimmy.

John again dropped the class list. "No, Jimmy, you said 'ain't,' probably in an effort to prompt for the one hundredth time this year my speech on the importance of using standard English. Probably with the hope that I'd forget about the spelling test you're all gonna be taking in about one minute."

Laughter and groans filled the room.

"Okay, settle down." He returned to the roll. "Maria Mendez?"

"She ain't here neither," said Jimmy Long.

More laughter and this time their teacher joined in, flipping his pencil two feet in the air and grabbing before it fell on the table. When the room was almost quiet again, there was a knock on the door. Sara Whitaker, a pretty, beige-skinned young woman who worked in the principal's office, cracked the door and leaned in.

"Excuse me, Mr. Giordano. May I speak with you for a moment?"

"Sure." He got stiffly to his feet. "Okay, Mr. Simpson, since you're so fit, you come up here and keep order. There's a spelling test to study for, folks, so get to it."

In the grumbling commotion of students reaching for books, John joined the secretary in the hall.

Chapter 4

Standing next to the ancient metal lockers lining the hall, he continued to watch his class through the window in the door. In contrast to the relaxed, casual feeling he usually had with his students, he was immediately awkward and uncomfortable with this slim young woman. He couldn't even look her in the eye, but all it took was a glance to know she had nothing but bad news.

"John, something terrible's happened."

"Really, this couldn't wait?"

"No, I mean yes, it couldn't. Lissa Martino was shot and killed this morning."

For a couple of seconds, he did not move or speak. Finally he whispered a scream, "Oh, Jesus Fucking Christ!" And he slammed his palm against a locker door so hard it sounded like a bomb.

The secretary flinched badly, and knowing he had alarmed his students, he turned his back to the door and moved a few steps away.

Moving with him Sara said softly, "I know, it's horrible. Dr. Carter's been on the phone with the police since seven this morning."

"What the fuck happened?" He fought to control the fury in his voice and finally managed to say, "I'm sorry. It's just that..." He couldn't finish.

"No that's okay. She was delivering her newspapers, I guess, with her dad this morning. So she goes up to this one house, and this 15-year-old kid just starts shooting. Actually he used to go here, a boy named Marlon Maples. I think before you got here."

Shaking his head, he radiated so much anger that Sara moved a step away. Finally he stopped. "But why, for Chrissake? Why shoot a little girl?"

"Well, I don't really know, but the police have already got him. Apparently he was drinking all night and waiting for these other guys who were coming to fire bomb the house."

He shook his head again. "Fuck-ing dope."

"Yes, well they say this Marlon is with this with one crack gang, and it's in some kind of war with this other one."

"They're all shitheads!" He stared down the hall.

Sara moved another step away. "Really. But, John, Dr. Carter thinks we should wait until last period to tell the kids. Otherwise they'll be upset all day and won't get anything done."

He watched two tardy boys opening lockers at the other end of the hall. "That's ridiculous! Somebody's bound to come in late and know about it and tell everybody else. And that'll be worse. Tell Dr. Carter I have to talk to my class about it right now. Lissa was in my room, and I don't want them hearing about it from anyone else."

Sara looked uncertain. "Well, I'll tell her, but..."

"Good. Thanks."

He turned away abruptly, but stopped, trying to gather himself before getting to the door. When he walked back into the room, Mark Simpson got up from the table with his spelling book and sauntered back to his seat.

"Thanks, Mark. Okay, listen up, folks. We just got some very bad news."

"School's closed till next year," piped Eric with an arm thrust in the air. His classmates cheered and laughed.

John stood in front of the table and held up his hand. "All right, all of you, settle down! Sorry, but this is really bad news and really sad."

His students gave him worried looks and a few groans. He waited for silence before starting again.

Chapter 5

Late that afternoon in the cluttered living room of a cramped lower flat, a well-built black man sat in a frayed lounge chair reading the Detroit News. In jeans, athletic shoes and an old football jersey with a number, 34, matching his age, Charlie Watts lowered the paper a bit when he heard someone trying to unlock the front door.

Finally, after some extended fumbling, Susan Cole walked in with a large purse and a fat briefcase. Dressed in the plain but serviceable blouse-and-skirt outfit of a social worker, she was an attractive, light-skinned black woman with dark-rimmed glasses and a preoccupied frown.

She used an elbow to swing the door shut. "Charlie, have you tried to fix this lock? I told you it sticks, and it needs some oil or graphite or something."

He raised the newspaper again. It wasn't like her to whine before even saying hello. "No, I've been busy. I'll do it tomorrow."

On the couch Susan wearily dropped her purse and briefcase, and from behind the paper Charlie said, "Besides, what kind of greeting is that for your lover, chief cook and coach of your women's softball team?"

"Oh, damn, that's right, there's a game tonight."

"Indeed." Charlie put the News aside and looked closely at the unhappy woman in front of him. "What's wrong, baby?"

"Charlie, I've had the worst day of my life on this job. I just feel sick." Like a child, she sank to his lap and folded herself in his arms.

Having heard this line from her several times before, he kissed and hugged her warmly, then began unbuttoning her blouse. "I laid out your uniform for you."

"That was nice of you."

"But I think we got time for a quickie before the big game. How about it?"

She stopped his hand on her blouse. "Please, Charlie, I'm in no mood. I told you what happened today. This little girl had so much going for her. She was so bright and sweet and vivacious. And for this kid to just blow her away like that while she's delivering newspapers? When they told me I thought I was going to throw up."

Charlie ended his effort with the blouse. "Crack or smack?"

"What's the difference? The kid's with the gang that calls itself America's Team."

Charlie nodded. "In a war with the Vices, and she got caught in the crossfire."

"You make it sound like it's just, 'Sorry, that's life in the big city.'"

He gave her an impassive look. "Yeah, well, that's pretty much what it is. Crack is just too damn big, and now smack is back with a vengeance. We just lost the damn war, that's all. Ain't nobody gonna stop 'em. And lots of kids are getting messed up big time. You know that, but you just take all this shit way too much to heart."

Stiff with anger, she was up from his lap to pace the room, re-buttoning her blouse. "You wouldn't be so goddamn blasé, if you had to do what I did today. I told you about this family. Joe Martino's wife died of a brain tumor right after giving birth to Lissa's sister. He's been laid off from the plant for about a year. And he's been barely able to care for his daughters and make ends meet by taking welfare and doing odd jobs. Last month his sister, who's about his only relative here, got married and moved to Texas. So I spent the day trying to reach the sister and find care for the two-year-old, making funeral arrangements and visiting Joe in the hospital where I had to tell him his daughter was dead."

From his chair Charlie moved to Susan and took her in his arms. "That's awful rough, baby. I'm really sorry."

"There's nothing to be sorry about. It's just my job." Apparently soothed, she paused, pressing her cheek against his chest. "So how was your day?"

"Same old petty shit. This fat ugly old guy wants me to tail his fat ugly wife. Thinks she's getting it from the minister at their church."

Susan smiled for the first time. "Is she?"

"I hope so for her sake." Charlie raised her chin a bit and kissed her softly on the lips.

Chapter 6

At nine the following morning, through lush trees guarding the rear of the property, bright sunlight dappled the cedar deck in the beautifully landscaped backyard of a large Tudor home in exclusive Grosse Pointe Park. At a glass-top table sat three members of the Monelli family. Blond and fair-skinned, in a pink dressing gown, 35-year-old Catherine was reading the Free Press. Her husband Steven, 38, dark and impeccable in well-cut navy pin stripes, bantered with their 12-year-old daughter Megan in tight jeans and a tube top. Anna, an older Italian woman, served breakfast and was more or less obsequious to each of them.

Finished with her Frosted Flakes, Megan said, "Com'on, Daddy, it's Saturday. I'm going to grow up all warped and twisted if my father doesn't maintain a warm and loving relationship with his only child. And today that means taking her out on his 47-foot cruiser."

"I wonder," said Monelli, "how you're going to look all warped and twisted."

"Like this!" The girl contorted her face and body with an effort both vigorous and amusing.

"Pretty ugly!" Monelli laughed. "But I guess we'll just have to live with it, because I've got meetings at the office all day."

Out of her chair, Megan moved to her father and somehow snuggled into his lap. "Daddy, what's the point of having all this money, if you have to go out and work all the time?"

Monelli nuzzled her. "I'm going to pretend I didn't hear that. Catherine, did you hear that?"

Catherine behind the newspaper: "I heard it."

"I mean, what's happening to the great American work ethic? With kids saying things like that?"

"I say a lot worse things," said Megan.

"I bet you do," said Monelli. "Anna?"

"*Signore?*"

11

"Tell Robert I'll use the BMW this morning, and he'll drive Vampira here to the Yacht Club."

"*Si, signore.*" The woman was promptly off the deck and into the house.

Megan was still snuggling in her father's lap. "You're gonna send me off with that child molester?"

"The way you're dressed, Robert's the one in trouble. Look at this sexy little outfit." Monelli finally moved her down from his lap.

"This? Sexy?"

"Yes, sexy. Now go find Robert. I'll try to finish at the office early and get to the club by two. Then we can take a run out to the island."

"Daddy, you're the baddest man I know." Megan's dark eyes, her father's eyes, beamed with pleasure as she gave him a big kiss and hug.

"You're pretty bad yourself," said Monelli.

"Bye, Mom!" Lowering the paper, Catherine also got a hug.

"Bye, baby. I'll see you later. Don't forget to use the sun screen."

"I won't." Megan was dancing off the deck. "Where's my favorite child molester?"

Shaking his head with a smile, Monelli watched his daughter leave the patio.

"She's growing up too fast."

"Not fast enough for her." Catherine moved her gaze from daughter to husband.

"At that age we were the same way."

"No, I liked being a child."

"Well, you had a doting father."

"And she doesn't?" Catherine picked up the paper again. "By the way, did you see this awful story about the little girl who was shot and killed delivering the Free Press?"

"Yeah, I saw it. A lousy shame."

"Disgusting is what it is. And people just let this kind of thing happen?"

"Honey, they don't let it happen. It just happens. Dope's an ugly business, and the people in those neighborhoods have been killing each other over it for a long time."

"Well, but still..."

"The problem is most of them are animals."

"Steven, my God, how can you say something like that?"

"Because it's true. I've dealt with those people. You haven't. Just about all of them are into cocaine or heroin or some kind of new dope of the month. It's just a question of a slow death or fast. Actually it might have been a blessing for that girl. Down the road, maybe, probably, she gets hooked, then prostitution to get her fix, and then God-knows-what."

She glared at him. "Yes, well, what if it were *your* daughter?"

"If it were *my* daughter? Without a doubt I'd find some way to get her out of that rotten world, no matter what it took. Period." Monelli stared hard at his wife.

She lowered her gaze to the paper on the table and did not speak for a few seconds. When her eyes moved to her husband's hands, it was as if she were seeing them for the first time. She had always thought of them as attractive in a sensitive, handsome way. Now they seemed bony, cruel and forbidding.

Finally, she said, "Well, I feel like I should go to that little girl's funeral."

"Why in God's name would you do something like that?"

Catherine looked up at him again. "Just to show those people there's someone else who cares."

"Catherine, that is just plain ridiculous."

"Well, it may be ridiculous, but that's exactly what I'm going to do."

Chapter 7

"Ma, I know he wasn't an educated man. He could barely read or write. But Pa grew up in a very different world. When he came to this country, there were still lots of jobs for guys who worked hard. There's just nothing out there for these kids unless they get a half-way decent education."

In a dark suit and tie John Giordano clamped the phone between his ear and shoulder. He sat at a small kitchen table in the cold light of his basement apartment. The kitchenette was one end of the dingy room, and at the other a single bed was rumpled and unmade. In between an old armchair, split in a few places with the stuffing exposed, held a stack of eighth-grade English papers. Sitting at the table, he continued to jot in red ink on the one he'd been correcting when the phone rang.

"No, Ma, I'm not giving them that. I'm only one teacher. And some of them are lost before they ever get to me. Listen, this is from a theme I had them write on who was responsible for Lissa Martino's murder."

Putting the ballpoint down, he picked up the paper he'd been marking. "Yeah, she's the one on the news, and whose funeral I've got to go to in about one minute. But listen to this: 'I do not *thank* no body are *responsibull* for the *merder*.' And just figure, Ma, every other word is misspelled, even though I wrote some of the key words on the board—like responsible, and he still spells it with b-u-l-l at the end. Anyway, 'I do not thank no body are responsibull for the merder. It were accident ceptin them fire bomers who be comin to off that dude with the uzzi. Uzzi be one fine masheen gun. It cut a man into peaces and it be very quite. If fire bomers done mine they bizniz no body get hert.'"

He paused again.

"Yeah, it's sad all right, and this was after we discussed the whole thing in class."

14

He picked up the pen. "Yeah, well, I gotta go, Ma."

Up from the table he began pacing a few steps, back and forth. "I know it's the anniversary of Pa's death. I was the one who found him, for chrissake!"

With the ballpoint John conducted an imaginary orchestra that needed to pick up its pace.

"Yeah, I know. So is Harry home?" Pause. "Because if he were on the road, I'd come by and say hello."

His mouth pursed in a smirk, he shook his head.

"Because he loves his truck more than he loves you, Ma. And because we just don't get along. We're all adults. We should be able to accept that. Look, Ma, I'm gonna be late for the funeral. I'll talk to you soon." Pause. "Okay, bye."

John pushed a button on the phone and looked at his watch.

"Shit!"

Tossing the phone on the table and grabbing his keys, he headed for the door.

Chapter 8

Outside a light rain was falling. He ran up several steps to the sidewalk and around to the driver's side of a new red Camaro parked on the street in front of his old brown-brick building. Inside the car he revved it up, did a quick U on wet, slippery pavement and fishtailed up the dismal street.

The quickest route to the funeral home? Uncertain he swung onto Fort and headed downtown. From there maybe pick up Jefferson going east until he hit the Boulevard at the Belle Isle Bridge. From the inside pocket of his suit coat he pulled a clipping from yesterday's Free Press. At a red light he unfolded the clip, noting again the headline: "Ritual of Grief Stabs Another City Family." At the bottom in italics he read the funeral information.

"A family hour for Lissa Martino will be held from 7 to 8 tonight at the Swanson Funeral Home at 806 E. Grand Blvd. A funeral service will be at 2 pm tomorrow at the funeral home. Burial will be at Woodmere Cemetery."

At another red, he scanned two paragraphs he had underlined near the end of the story.

"O'Neil Swanson, a funeral director in the city for 30 years, is infuriated that violence has become so much a part of life for some young people.

"'What's happening today is unconscionable,' he said. 'There's a total disregard for human life. What we're doing to one another is so senseless. Things have become barbaric and animalistic. No, I take that back. Not even animals kill one another the way we do.'"

He slipped the clip back into his pocket.

Finally rolling through the downtown canyons, he turned off Fort at Washington and headed for the river. Two towering construction cranes loomed on his right: a huge addition to the convention center, $250 million dollars, but who'd want their convention in this damn town? And more construction on his left: a new high-rise going up, the first new office space downtown since the Renaissance Center, which was what, more than 20 years old? Ahead, the mirrored walls of Center's towers glistened with a gun-metal silver in the rain. He passed under the cement trestle of the People Mover, another three hundred million plus with all the over-runs for a little three mile loop of downtown, weaving in and out of buildings and surely intended to give this small downtown corner a few vistas that might pass for futuristic. In fact, he had to admit, with all the millions pumped into this area along the river, it looked almost viable. At the expense, of course, of all the neighborhoods across this crime-infested jungle that called itself a city, and with a school system that was a hopeless disgrace, run by crooks and incompetents stealing and squandering resources that were woefully inadequate to begin with.

In the rain there were few people on the streets around the City-County Building and even fewer moving with any pace or purpose. Most had the look of those struggling with, if not defeated, by what life in this city had brought them, whites and blacks in about equal numbers, though at day's end most of the whites would jump on the freeways and head out to their homes in the suburbs. Most white people had long since fled, and now the black middle class was hot on their heels. What could possibly keep this pathetic place from becoming a kind of blighted reservation for the old, the poor and the desperate?

At Grand Boulevard he headed north away from the bridge and found the Swanson Funeral Home within a few blocks. But it was nearly 2:50 when he pulled into the parking lot and asked a solemn young black kid in an attendant's black suit and tie about the Martino funeral.

"They already on their way to the cemetery, sir."

John immediately wheeled out of the lot and onto the Boulevard, heading back to where he'd just come from. The cemetery was deep on the city's southwest side.

"Fuck my life!" he screamed and pounded the steering wheel. "I'll be late for my own goddamn funeral."

Chapter 9

In a corner of the old cemetery, it was raining harder as two-dozen people in dark clothes and holding black umbrellas huddled together for a graveside service. Joe Martino sat in a wheelchair, his right arm in a sling and his two-year-old daughter in his lap. At his side were his sister and brother-in-law flanked by friends and neighbors. All of them were African-American, along with Susan Cole, who stood with a small red umbrella to one side.

Walking to a spot close to her, Channel 5 anchor Frank DeFauw and his producer Fay Banks, a young black woman, shared a large green and white golf umbrella. Frank looked around at the only other white person in the group, a blond woman standing by herself in a tailored black trench coat and holding a small black umbrella several feet behind the other mourners.

As the minister stepped forward to begin, Joe Martino tugged on his sister's sleeve, and she leaned close to him. Glancing at Frank, he whispered a few words, and the woman moved quickly to Frank.

"Mr. DeFauw, Melissa's father, Joe Martino, would like you to join him at the gravesite."

Frank looked at Fay, who nodded firmly and then moved with him, carrying their umbrella to the spot where the sister had been standing. The others stared as Frank leaned down, took Joe's left hand and shook his head in sympathy.

"Almighty God," intoned the minister in a deep rumbling voice, "in Your infinite wisdom, we beg You please to help us find a way to lift this terrible scourge of drugs and guns afflicting our city and especially our young people."

"Please, Lord!" exclaimed a woman nodding next to the freshly dug hole.

"Say it, Reverend!" wailed the man next to her.

"Please, God," chanted the minister, "help us to give our children lives filled with meaning and purpose, love and truthfulness."

"Yes, Jesus!" sang a small woman with a wizened face, standing in front of the blond woman.

Catherine Monelli, with her eyes closed, opened them in time to see a young white man running through the rain to join the group.

Without an umbrella John was already drenched, but when Susan Cole noticed him stopping nearby, she motioned for him to share hers. With a tight, embarrassed smile he moved next to her, and she covered them both.

"Let this tragic event resolve the spirit in each of us to re-double our efforts to save our community and our children, so the cruel and vicious death of this innocent young girl shall not be in vain."

"Teach us, Jesus!" sobbed the woman in front of Catherine Monelli. John glanced at Susan Cole, who, like many of the others, was weeping.

"With this fervent hope, Almighty God, we render the spirit of Thy good and faithful servant Lissa unto the bosom of Thy loving embrace for all eternity, Amen."

Several others echoed the minister's "Amen."

A few minutes later, two workmen in muddy clothes, who had been standing under a nearby tree, were at the graveside and prepared to lower the plain wooden casket. Joe Martino, hugging his two-year-old daughter in the wheelchair, moaned with bitter anguish.

"No, Lissa!"

The two-year-old began to wail, and Joe's sister took the child from him to soothe and quiet her. His brother-in-law, holding a single red rose, handed it now to Joe to place on the casket. Joe struggled to get up from the chair, but, even as Frank tried to help him with a hand supporting his elbow, the grieving father finally thought better of it. He settled back into the chair and handed Frank the rose.

As their eyes met, both men had tears on their cheeks. Frank placed the rose on the casket, then folded his hands and bowed his head as the casket sank slowly into the grave.

With the service complete, the brother-in-law moved behind the wheelchair to roll Joe away, and the others were walking now over wet grass toward a line of cars on the cemetery road.

John and Susan were moving also, still sharing her umbrella, but they stopped to watch and listen as Catherine Monelli walked up to

Joe, as the brother-in-law stopped the chair.

"Mr. Martino, I just want you to know," said the blond woman, bending stiffly to place a hand on the black man's arm and look into his reddened eyes, "there are many of us in the community who share your grief."

Joe stared at the woman seemingly without comprehension but finally nodded. His sister, holding both the two-year-old and an umbrella, offered a puzzled frown and said, "Thank you."

Taking advantage of the awkward moment that followed, Frank move up to hold Joe's hand one more time. "Joe, I know what it's like to lose a child. There's nothing worse. My heart goes out to you and your family. Please let me know if there's anything I can do for you."

Joe nodded and closed his eyes. When he opened them, he managed to say, "Thank you for coming."

His sister added, "Frank, you bein' here means a lot to us. Thank you for the kindness in your heart."

Frank looked at her and then at the 2-year-old who was staring at him with wide eyes. He touched the child's cheek. "Thank you. But seriously, please get in touch if I can help in any way."

The sister thanked Frank one more time before turning to follow her brother in the wheelchair as everybody headed for their cars. Catherine Monelli watched for a moment as the group moved away, then she walked toward a large gray BMW.

Frank and Fay were walking next to John and Susan. The four exchanged glances and nods. Drying her eyes with a tissue, Susan asked John, "Did you know her?"

"Lissa? Yes, I was her homeroom teacher. How about you?"

Susan nodded. "I work with the family for Social Services. She was one of the sweetest, brightest little girls I've ever met."

"She was probably the best student I've had. That preacher said the right words, but it all seems so damn hopeless."

"I know."

"I have 13- and 14-year old boys and girls who sell crack and heroin on the street and who some days make more money than I do. How can I tell them to keep their noses clean so that one day they can get a job at McDonald's?"

From the corners of his eyes he glared at her and added, "It's a fucking plague on this city."

Susan simply nodded, and Frank entered the silence that

followed. "Hi, I'm Frank DeFauw with Channel 5, and this is my special projects producer Fay Banks."

The four of them stopped walking. "Hi, Frank, I'm Susan Cole."

"John Giordano."

Frank shook hands with each. "We're working on a special, a documentary really, on kids and dope in this town, and we'd love to talk to you about the problem. I think your perspectives on it would be really valuable. Don't you, Fay?"

"Absolutely."

"So how about giving us your phone numbers, and we'll get back in touch and set something up?"

Susan asked, "You mean on camera?"

Fay said, "Well, we'd talk first, and then if you're comfortable, we'll do it on camera."

"I work for the county, so I'd have to clear anything on camera, but I'll talk to my boss."

Frank said, "Great. How about you, John?"

John turned his gaze away but said, "Yeah, probably."

Frank took the umbrella from Fay. "Okay, good."

Fay pulled a pen and reporter's notebook from her purse and took their phone numbers.

A minute later, when John and Susan stopped in front of the Camaro, he asked, "You think he's serious?"

"Frank? Probably. He seemed genuine about it."

"I guess." He gestured toward the car. "This is mine. Thanks for sharing the umbrella."

Susan smiled. "Nice ride."

John shook his head. "I can't afford it. I live in a dump so I can make the payments on it. But I wanted those kids to see that somebody besides a pimp or a pusher can drive a nice car. I must be an idiot."

"I don't think so." She smiled again.

"Well, see ya. Thanks again." John ducked from under the umbrella, dodged quickly through the rain to his car and climbed in.

She gazed after him as he drove away, then moved toward her Rabbit. Joe Martino's brother-in-law was struggling to get him from the wheelchair to the backseat of an old black Buick. With one last glance back at the gravesite, she saw the workmen filling the hole where Lissa's body had been placed.

Chapter 10

On the large studio camera pointed at Frank DeFauw, the words he had pounded out earlier in the evening were scrolling on the mirror that sent them across the lens and allowed the anchor to look straight at his million-souled audience and speak as if he were just now formulating these sad and angry thoughts. Next to the sign-off goodbyes, this was the last item in the teleprompter and had been teased throughout the newscast.

"I went to a funeral today," said Frank, "the funeral of a beautiful young girl just 13-years-old and with her whole life in front of her. And what a promising young life it was. She had these bright almond eyes and a smile that lit up the world. Smart as a whip and an excellent student, she was loving to her father and her baby sister, and warm-hearted to all her friends at the Lincoln Middle School in southwest Detroit.

"But as Lissa Martino grew up brimming with hopes and dreams in one of this city's many troubled neighborhoods, she had no idea her days were numbered. And a few mornings ago, as she was delivering the Free Press with her dad, she was brutally cut down in a hail of bullets and died in the street.

"Now no parent, but especially one as caring and devoted as Joe Martino has been with his two little girls in the wake of his wife's death from cancer last year, should have to attend such a funeral. And no city, certainly not one with the proud and remarkable history of Detroit in the most prosperous and powerful nation on earth, should have to bury a lovely young child it failed to nurture and protect.

"So who was responsible for the cruel and pointless murder of Lissa Martino? Who do we blame, so that, at least for some of us, the intolerable becomes somehow more acceptable, or more easily forgotten?

"Well, of course, there's the kid who pulled the trigger, barely two years older than Lissa herself, and already sent through Juvenile Court no less than three times.

"The boy was on assignment, folks, just doing his job, protecting what neighbors all knew to be a busy dope pad, guarding it from members of a rival drug gang, who were reportedly coming to fire bomb the place. Don't leave, not even for a second, he was told, or you'll end up with your head full of holes. And so after killing little Lissa, thinking she was carrying not a Free Press but a bomb, he was still cowering in a corner when the cops arrived.

"So maybe blame the gang who put that boy in the house? Or the gang who threatened to burn it down? Or their big-time suppliers living no doubt posh and comfortable lives in one of our safe and beautiful burbs?

"Or how about our under-funded and over-stretched police force who can't seem to wage an effective war even when everyone on the block knows where the enemy is?

"Of course the cops take their cue from our city's politicians who have for so long turned a blind eye to the corruption and corrosion of illicit narcotics. As it destroys the social and moral fabric of this town, their motto seems to be, 'To hell with the public trust. Just let me get mine.'

"Then we have those state leaders who seem happy to look the other way and leave this poor, debt-ridden place, once revered and respected as the Paris of America, to its own collapsed tax base and hopelessly inadequate resources.

"Count in all those suburbanites who wouldn't be caught dead setting foot south of Eight Mile or those who only hop into town to cop a quick fix.

"And, yes, certainly add our auto execs, those erstwhile captains of an industry that helped to create the most potent economic engine the world has ever seen, and who then allowed their thinking to become so hide-bound, timid and stale that they let the Europeans and the Japenese waltz right in here and eat our lunch.

"Let's see, who am I missing? Well, surely our desperately inadequate city schools, run by administrators who care not a whit about the future of our children, sacrificing their education to a bureaucratic order that protects the jobs of incompetents, passes over talented and devoted young teachers, and lines their own pockets while they sit around and push paper.

"And what about this city's church leaders who, instead of pushing for change, spend most of their time finding sweet words to mollify their suffering congregants while sidling up to their political brothers for some mutual advantage.

"Oh, yes, and how about all those gun advocate idiots who are perfectly pleased with a system that ends up putting a .9mm killing machine in the hands of any 15-year-old who wants one.

"Finally, you didn't think I'd let all of us in the news media off the hook, did you? Without question, newspapers, TV, radio, you name it, we have all too often covered these tragic stories, less to shine a light than to exploit the sensational, as a way to run up our numbers.

"Yes, folks, for the senseless, heartbreaking murder of Lissa Martino there seems to be more than enough blame to go around. And, from where I sit, none of us gets a pass.

"We can all share the blame for the terrible loss of this beautiful little girl's hopes and dreams. The bloody fact is, we should all be ashamed of ourselves."

Chapter 11

On a warm afternoon after school he climbed the steps of a large frame house, its dirty gray paint badly flaking, its porch in serious disrepair. He carried a file folder and checked the address against a slip of paper in the folder one more time before he pushed the doorbell button. No sound came from inside the house. He pushed the button again with no response and finally knocked loudly on the broken screen door. After another wait, the inside door opened, and a small Hispanic girl appeared holding a baby about six months old sucking on a nippled bottle half-filled with water.

"Hey, Maria, how you doing?" A smell came at him from inside. Maybe mildew?

"Okay, fine." Maria was clearly surprised and nervous about finding her teacher at the door.

"We missed you at school today." He smiled, trying to seem less threatening.

"Yeah, I had to take care of my little brother." She nodded toward the boy she was holding on her hip. He watched John with large brown eyes, the nipple still in his slack mouth.

"So what's this guy's name?"

"Alex."

"Hey, Alex, *com'esta*?" John winked at the baby, whose expression didn't change. Finally, he asked, "Maria, is your mom home?"

Maria hesitated. "Uh, yeah."

"Could I come in? I just need to talk to her for a couple minutes."

"Well..." More hesitation. "I guess."

"Great, it'll only be a couple minutes." John opened the screen door and stepped inside. The smell was now a stench — urine, he decided — that filled the large front room. The place was a mess. A dirty brown rug littered with popcorn and taco chips, torn magazines strewn about, soiled, thread-bare furniture. In one corner, though, a new 30-inch Panasonic offered cartoons. Carrying the baby, Maria moved to a closed door off the front room and knocked.

"Mama?"

No answer. She finally turned the knob and opened the door. What John saw through the doorway made him want to turn away. Instead, he stared at a stick-thin black man nodding on a bare mattress on the floor and, on a filthy couch, Maria's mother about to use a syringe on a white woman in her 20s and obviously pregnant.

"Maria, what you want?" snapped her mother, who then caught a glimpse of John standing in the front room. "Close the door! I come out."

Maria pulled the door shut. She and John glanced at each other but said nothing. The baby dropped his bottle on the dirty carpet, and Maria picked it up and put it back in his mouth. She stood with John in front of the TV. With no idea what to say to his student, he watched the Smurfs.

Finally, the door opened. Maria's mother slipped into the room, closing the door quickly behind her. A heavy-set woman in an old dress ripped at the seams, she ignored John and moved directly to Maria, taking the baby to hold him as she dealt with her daughter.

"How many time I told you, don't bother me when I workin'? And don't never let nobody in this house less you know 'em."

"Mama, this is my teacher, Mr. Giordano."

John spoke up quickly. "Hi, Mrs. Mendez. I have Maria in home room over at Lincoln."

"I don't care who," said Mrs. Mendez, still ignoring John. "You don't let nobody in this house without my lookin' at 'em first." Finally she turned to John. "Now, what you want?"

"Well, Mrs. Mendez, I haven't seen you at Lincoln for any of the parent-teacher conferences, so I thought I'd stop by and talk to you for just a few minutes about Maria's progress in school. I can come back again if this isn't a good time."

"Have no time for no conference. Report card say she do okay."

"Yes, but lately she's missed so many days of school that I'm afraid she's going to have to attend summer school in order to catch up. Now Maria is a very bright girl, as I'm sure you know. And I've brought along some of the papers she's written for me in English class, just to show you what a fine writer she can be."

"If she so good, why she need more school?"

"Well, she's just missed so many days and so many assignments.

26

She's just not going to be ready to start high school next fall, if she doesn't go to summer school. Here, let me show you some of these themes, and you'll see she's got real potential."

Mrs. Mendez hiked the baby on her hip. "I don't have no time to read. You say they good, I believe. Then why she need summer school? And she don't really miss that many days. I workin' all the time. I need help with the baby some days, and she stay home."

"But Mrs. Mendez, I..."

"No." She shook her head. "I ain't gonna talk to you about this now, cause I ain't got time. I talk to principal. He understand."

He smiled. "The principal, Dr. Carter, is a woman, and she's likely to be less understanding than I am."

"Whatever she be. I got business goin' now, so you leave."

She moved toward the front door, and he followed. "All right, Mrs. Mendez, I hope we'll see you at school for a visit real soon."

"You see me okay." Mrs. Mendez pushed the screen door open for him. "Real soon."

"Bye, Maria." He waved back at the girl standing alone in the front room. "See you tomorrow."

Walking to the Camaro, he thought of the beautifully-kept bungalow he grew up in just across the city, but worlds apart from this horrid excuse for a home. A happy childhood for him with a five-minute walk to his grade school at St. Clare's and all his friends close by in the neighborhood.

Until the day when his warm, indulgent mother had turned into something akin to the fierce Mrs. Mendez on the subject of where he would go to high school. Somehow she had decided that her very smart son would have nothing less than the best, a Jesuit education, and that meant a daily 40-minute bus ride to and from the male-only University of Detroit High School on the other side of the city. God, four years of those interminable bus rides, while all his buddies were riding a few minutes up Mack avenue to Austin Catholic Prep.

He would spend much of his time on the bus watching for kids walking to and from school in the many neighborhoods along the way. Looking for the same kids everyday and fantasizing about their lives, trying to imagine the homes they lived in.

Nothing he had thought up had ever come close to Maria Mendez's home.

Chapter 12

"'You see me okay. Real soon.'" John mimicked Mrs. Mendez as he urged the Camaro past several decayed and ravaged homes. "Fuck!"

Leaving the residential street, he turned onto Fort, a wide old thoroughfare that offered a view of the tall gray office buildings downtown a few miles to the east. Actually, though they could see it, he knew that some of his students had never even been downtown. They had never been out of out their own neighborhood. This was their whole world — a tough, ugly, depressing strip with lots of boarded up storefronts, a number of burned out buildings and a few small stores painted in gaudy colors and struggling to stay alive.

After a few blocks he spotted two familiar youngsters, along with a third boy who looked a bit older, hanging on a corner on the opposite side of the street. They were in front of a party store that stood alone next to a large overgrown vacant lot. John slowed as he watched a late-model Olds pulling to a stop in front of the boys. The older kid leaned into the passenger-side window.

Eric Garner and Jimmy Long were searching the street up and down as the older kid serviced the car.

"You got boy today?" asked the man in the Olds.

"Hey, Renaldo the Fish!" said Darnell, the older kid. "The best, man, Safety Blitz."

"How much?"

"The usual, man, dime and two. Cause you a regular, dime and one."

Spotting John's Camaro, Eric nudged Jimmy, and the two watched their homeroom teacher do a slow u-turn and park in front of the vacant lot a hundred feet from the party store.

They could see him watching carefully as Darnell went into his pocket, pulled out something small and white and handed it into the

28

car. He came out with cash in hand, and, as the car drove away, he stood there counting it. Eric flicked a look at Jimmy that said the older boy was a dumb shit, flashing it out in the open like that. Then with a big smile he and Jimmy, who was all business, sauntered up to the Camaro's open passenger-side window.

"Mr. G., how you be?" Eric's favorite greeting.

"Hey, Eric. What's happenin', Jimmy?"

"Hey, Mr. G."

"So what are you guys doing?"

"Just hangin'," said Eric.

"Looks to me," said John, "like you and your friend on the corner are doing business."

"We might be," said Eric, still smiling.

"What happens when the cops come by?"

"Nothin'," said Eric. "We don't do nothin', and when they leave we back in business."

"Cops don't mess with us," added Jimmy. "We run faster'n them. And even if they catch us, we got mostly only a pack or two on us, and Juvenile say, 'Don't do that again,' and turn us loose. I been there four times. Nothin' happen."

"Mr. G.," said Eric, "You got some nice ride. How about can I sit in it?"

"You clean or dirty?"

"I'm clean, man. I almost never got it on me. I keep my stash back in the field there, near the alley."

"Okay then, hop in."

With an even bigger smile Eric opened the door and climbed into the passenger seat. With the door closed again Jimmy leaned in at the window. Eric ran his hands over the leather dash.

"Real fine," he said. "Gonna get me one of these here real quick."

"These things cost big time," said John.

"That's okay. I'm savin' up. I give some to my ma, and the rest I'm savin'."

Jimmy looked up at an old Toyota passing slowly. "Here come Too Fat in the Rice Rocket. Catch you later, Mr. G." Jimmy moved away from the Camaro and headed for the dirty Camry that was stopping now in front of the party store.

"Who's Too Fat?" asked John.

"One a his regulars. You got to do good for the regulars. Keep 'em happy and comin' back."

As John watched, Jimmy gave a series of hand signals as he approached the car, then turned away and headed back into the vacant lot.

"Where's he going?" asked John.

"His stash in the alley. He keep his shit like me back there, case he get stopped."

John watched as Jimmy leaned over briefly at the back of the field, then headed back toward the Camry.

"So how do you feel selling shit to these poor dumb junkies?"

"Hey, we providin' a service," said Eric. "We can't help if they dumb junkies. They need it, we sell it."

John looked at him squarely. "No guilt over what you're doing to them?"

"What do you mean, man? What we sell 'em make 'em happy."

"Sometimes it kills 'em."

"No, not our shit, man. We only sell good, clean shit."

By now Jimmy, finished with his transaction, was walking back towards the Camaro, shoving his wad of cash deep in a pocket.

"But what you're doing is against the law," said John.

"The law is dumb, man," said Eric without his smile. "Shouldn't be no damn law."

"Tell me this, Eric. What do you want to be doing in ten years? What kind of a future do you want?"

"Me? I wanna run some big deal like this, man. Make *me* two, three grand a day, like this one dude I know. Not just five, six bills a week like we make now."

"You make five or six hundred dollars a week?"

Back at the window again Jimmy said, "Easy, man, no problem."

"So what about you, Jimmy? What are you gonna be doing in ten years?"

Before answering, Jimmy gazed up toward the corner as a man staggered coming out of the party store carrying a bottle in a paper bag.

"Tell you one thing," said Jimmy, "I ain't never gonna turn into one them dumb-ass winos, go beg me some nickels, buy a two dollar wine and stay drunk all day. Me? Always gonna have me enough money to live good, whatever it take."

"Well, from what I hear," said John, "if you guys stay in this business, sooner or later the law's gonna lock you away or somebody's gonna blow your head off. One or the other."

Eric's response was quick. "Not if you do it smart, like us. Besides, we got protection, man. Anybody mess with us on the corner, here come the 'Fearsome Foursome.' With bats and guns. They are some mean motherfuckers." He stopped to pull a fat wad of tens and twenties out of his jeans. "Besides, where else I'm gonna roll this much in a couple hours?"

Shaking his head with no answer, John gazed up the street at a lanky young boy talking to the older kid doing business on the corner. Finally he asked, "Isn't that Mark Simpson? From class?"

"Yeah," said Jimmy, looking up the street, "that's the Simp. He always hangin' around here. He want to do what we doin', but he tryin' to get up the balls."

Eric opened the car door and climbed out. "Gotta get back to work, Mr. G. Catch you later."

"See you in class," said John, watching the two boys walk back to the corner, nudging each other and laughing. He put the Camaro in gear, did another u-turn and sped away in the opposite direction.

Digging his elbow into Eric's side as they headed for the corner, Jimmy said, "How about we tell the Simp that was the heat, and they got his name?"

Eric giggled and dug back with an elbow. "Naw, man, he know Mr. G's ride."

"Man, he be shakin' too much to notice."

By the time they reached Darnell on the corner, Mark Simpson had disappeared. Jimmy asked, "Hey, Darn, what the Simp want?"

"The usual. Want me to give him some to sell. I told him you got to talk to Andre, man. They no other way."

"He scared to see Andre," said Jimmy. "The Simp's all mouth and no balls."

"Maybe he be better off not rollin'," said Eric searching the street intently up and down. "Once you start, you get used to that wad in your pocket, you ain't gonna stop"

"Yeah, so why you wanna stop?" Darnell had menace in his voice.

"Don't say I wanna stop. Just say it ain't as much fun out here with the heat on us like now. Them motherfucks drivin' by and shootin' the other day, was lucky they missed one of us."

31

"Wasn't no luck," said Darnell. "They ain't shoot for shit. Beside, what you need be a heater. They old equalizer, man. Need to pop for one and pack it on you."

"Naw, man." Eric folded his arms, trying to look both smart and tough. "You got it on you, some cop stop to talk on the corner, he already got your ass. You already caught a case."

"It don't matter, man," said Jimmy. "Juvenile don't do shit, man."

Jimmy felt the bulge under his shirt. "Hey, Darn, know where I can get me somethin' bigger? I wanna get me somethin' bigger."

"Sure, man, Andre say he know a cop'll get you anything you want, man. Cheap too. They get 'em for nothin', you know, man, when they take 'em off them dudes they bust. They got anythin', man, .44s, .357s, Uzis."

"No way I'm like dealin' with no cop," said Eric, his arms still folded.

"Hey, Andre say this cop doin' more than we doin'. He got two crack shacks he runnin'. And he always be rippin' off these other places he find out about doin' his cop work. Andre say he don't care about nothin' but money. You got the bread, you good with him."

Chapter 13

Later Jimmy and Eric walked home down a blighted residential street replete with weed-infested lots, boarded up houses and burned-out hulks.

"You ever want to work a crack shack?" asked Eric as they passed a dilapidated house they knew to be one. Ripped and dirty shades were drawn over the front windows.

"Sure, man, why not? You make more'n we do, and nobody see what you doin'. You not out there in the wide open like we is on the corner."

"Wide open be better to me. Least you can run when the heat come or somebody try to rip you. There ain't nowhere to run in a shack like that."

"No, inside still be better. You got the gun by the door, and you don't let nobody in you don't know. And in between you do anythin' you want—play poker, watch tube, do dick-a-chick. You got so many cunts comin' to your door and half of 'em don't have no bread, so they beggin' to suck you off or whatever, so they can get what they want. They love that crack, man."

"Yeah, but..."

"You hear that story Andre tellin' at the club the other night? About this one place he know where this dude has him some dogs, like a German sheep dog or somethin'. And when some cunt come beggin' for it, he say, 'Okay, bitch, you want some smoke, you fuck my dog.' And she do it. They got dogs doin' these cunts every day."

Eric stopped, turned back against the direction they'd been walking and stood there with his arms folded. "That is bullshit, man. You can't get no dog to do no bitch. They don't want no bitch."

"Oh, man. Andre say he seen it his self. More than once. He say everybody come and watch and laugh they asses off. And he gonna take us there anytime we want, so we can see them dumb cunts doin' them dogs."

Eric unfolded his arms, turned and yelled at his friend, "Andre full of shit, man."

"You full of shit," Jimmy yelled back. "Andre been there, man. He seen it his self. You see when he take us there."

"I ain't goin'."

"So you miss it, you dumb nigger."

The boys walked on in sullen silence for a while.

Eric finally asked quietly, "You ever think about what Mr. G be saying?"

"Like about what?"

"Like about how there ain't no future in this shit. Like how you either gonna end up dead or busted."

"I don't never think about that stuff. Too busy makin' cash."

"Mr. G. be a smart dude. He know about a lot of things."

"Yeah, if he so smart, why he a sorry-ass teacher? Why ain't he doin' somethin' where you can make the big bucks?"

"He like teachin'."

"That be what I'm saying, if he like teachin', he ain't be all that smart."

They walked for another dismal block before Eric spoke again. "You ma know you rollin'?"

"She know."

"You tell her?"

"Don't have to. She seen me on the corner. She know what we doin'. She ain't working', so they ain't no other bread comin' in. So when I give her some, she just say, 'Thank you, you the man of the house now.' What about your ma?"

"She don't know. Least she act like she don't know."

"Where she think all that bread you give her come from?"

"She don't know. Last time I told her I just found it."

"And she believe that shit?"

Eric shrugged and said nothing.

"What about your pa? What's he say?"

"He ain't been around," said Eric.

"How long?"

"A year, maybe two. We don't never see him. He left right when my littlest sister was born. She's two now, I think."

They arrived in front of Eric's house, an old two-family flat in filthy yellow brick. The cement steps to the two front doors were cracked and crumbling. Eric ran up the steps saying, "I still think Andre's full of shit about them dogs."

"I still think you a dumb nigger," yelled Jimmy.

"Catch you later."

Chapter 14

Inside the lower flat Eric found his mother sitting in the dark watching a Superheroes cartoon with his three younger sisters. They all had their feet tucked up on the old sofa right below the huge jigsaw puzzle of a dinosaur that he had put together a while back. His mother had been so proud of him that she had taped the puzzle to the wall above the couch like a fine painting.

"Hi, Ma. Got somethin' for you."

"Hey, Ricky." His mother got up and followed him into the kitchen. She was wearing her gray nightgown, and he knew she wasn't feeling well again.

"I got somethin' good, Ma."

"What is it, Ricky? Would you like a glass of milk?"

"Yeah." Eric pulled a carefully folded wad of five twenties from the pocket of his jeans. "I got lucky again, Ma."

He handed the wad to his mother who placed a half-glass of milk on the sink, then unfolded and counted the twenties. With both wonder and suspicion, she said, "Ricky, where did this come from?"

"I found it, Ma, like the other one."

"Ricky, how could you just find this much money?"

"I just found it. I don't go just lookin' all over. I go where people might be droppin' their money and not findin' it. Like that parkin' lot over near to the supermarket. I looked for a long time for that money."

"Well, all I can say is you sure got you some sharp eyes. And we sure can use this here money. Now I can buy some groceries tomorrow. We was all outta stamps."

Eric took a swallow of milk and wiped his mouth on the sleeve of his T-shirt. "Ma, can I ask you a question?"

"'Bout what?"

"'Bout dogs."

"Dogs? We can't keep no dog, Ricky. I told you that."

Eric took another swig of milk. "No, I'm askin' would a dog, like say maybe a German sheep dog, ever like do it with some woman?"

"Ricky, whatever you talkin' 'bout?"

"Like do it, Ma. Could you make a dog like do it with some woman?"

Eric watched his mother's eyes widen in her deeply lined face. "Oh my God, Ricky. No, that don't never happen. Wherever did you hear about such ugly things?"

"From Jimmy. He say it happen."

"Well, Jimmy don't know what he talkin' 'bout. And I told you I don't want you hangin' round with that damn Jimmy after school. He ain't good for nothin'. And he gonna turn out just like his pa who been in prison as long as I been knowin' his ma. That boy act like he ain't responsible for nothin'. He father a child last year, and I hear he ain't given that baby or the mother one penny for support. He just no good, Ricky, and I don't want you spendin' no time with him no how."

Eric took one last sip of milk and watched his mother nervously fingering the twenties.

Chapter 15

Until about ten years back when it went topless, the Oldies Paradise, on Livery near Fort, had been a typical neighborhood bar in one of the city's many struggling neighborhoods. Now in a garish red light on a raised platform on one side of the large square room, a bare-breasted young woman in a red g-string and red heels worked her number while Bob Seger wailed on the juke box, "We were makin' Thunderbirds."

Two waitresses, one thin and one plump, each looking like she was wearing the other's black leotards, were serving a slow weeknight crowd. They moved between the bar and a half-dozen tables, each with one or two men watching, drinking or talking with one of the other scantily clad dancers.

The song ended, and there was distinctly modest applause for Sally as she moved from the stage, down three steps to a nearby table where one of the few men clapping was wearing her flimsy red top on his bald head. With a smiling smirk she picked off the bra and sauntered toward the back of the room. Still bare-breasted but slowly beginning to put the bra in place, she stopped at a table where John was talking earnestly with a tough-looking, cocoa-skinned fellow in a black T-shirt, jeans and vest.

"Johnny G!" crooned Sally. "How ya doin', honey?"

"Lookin' good up there, Sal." John glanced at her only briefly.

"You weren't even watchin'. Too busy talkin' to Sergeant Wolfman here." Sally mugged at the black man and slid into a movie-moll moan: "How they hangin', copper?"

George Wolf offered a cop's pleasant contempt. "Wouldn't you like to know, sweetmeat?"

"Why bother with this creep?" she asked John. "He just causes trouble."

"Hey, he's a good guy," said John. "You just gotta get to know him. Sit down and join us for a while." Unlike the discomfort he usually felt around women, John always seemed more relaxed with the dancers at the Oldies Paradise.

"In a few. I gotta powder my nose." Sally winked at George, tousled John's hair, and walked away. Another dancer, a thin redhead, punched a button on a box next to the stage, changed the lighting to blue and then climbed up to start her routine to Billy Joel's "Second Wind."

George watched Sally leave. "Nice ass," he said, "and the tits ain't bad either."

John turned to look as if he'd never noticed. "You're right." Swinging back he picked up where he left off. "So the kid pulls out this wad and says where's he gonna make this much, you know, doin' what? And what am I gonna say? I mean, he's right. Given the economic realities of this city and the likelihood that he'll drop out of school within the next couple years, what's he gonna do?"

"You know what."

"Still, can't you guys put some fear into these kids? I mean they're doin' it right out there on Fort. Broad daylight."

"They're doin' it right out there in lots of places. And they just don't worry about us. We're spread so damn thin, for one thing. And they know us. We bust 'em once, and they know us."

"What about this big crack down the mayor talked about, all these new cops added to narcotics? I thought you guys were sweeping all these corners, hitting all these crack houses, eight a night or something like that."

"Yeah, so we're doin' that, all it amounts to is a little harassment. On the corners, if we do catch 'em when they run, mostly all we do is give 'em BFD tickets."

"What's that?"

"That's what the kids call 'em, 'Big Fuckin' Deal.' They're loitering tickets. And with the houses, half the ones we hit are dry cause we're movin' so fast we can't get good intel. And all these new guys don't help much cause they don't know what they're doin' and half their cases get tossed anyway. Even when we do put the fuckers away, it doesn't matter much. There's so much money, six kids are waitin' in line for every new spot that opens up."

"So what can we do?"

"Not much. Not now when every little kid on the block grows up wanting to be the dope man and knows exactly how to do it. Maybe if we'd done this ten years ago, after we took Young Boys down, we mighta had a chance. When all this crack started pourin' in, with all these new asshole groups who learned how to do it from Y.B.I. Everybody learned from Y.B.I. They were the fuckin' model. But our illustrious mayor didn't want to do it then, cause he didn't want to call it an emergency that would make the city look bad. As if the fuckin' image coulda been much worse. So he lets it go completely outta hand, and now his own niece is all cracked up and hitched to one of the biggest rollers in town. The feds finally got him for offin' somebody, the dumb shit, but his outfit's still going strong. Yeah, it's frustrating as hell. Like sticking your finger in a leaky dike."

"What about the kids? Can't Juvenile Court do something?"

"Oh, Jesus, Juvenile's a joke, afraid to tap these little fuckers on the wrist, afraid they're gonna scar their little psyches."

"They are kids, George."

"Kids, my ass! You should see 'em, blowin' each other away on the street, like it was nothin'. No emotion whatsoever. Cold as ice. Anyway, the big guys, the importers are the whole game, and we never get close to 'em. They're too insulated. They only deal with people they know. And they don't ever use the phone."

"Like who? Who's one of the big guys?"

"Oh, Christ, there's so much of this shit comin' in. Just talkin' coke, the feds say two and a half tons the past year. You know how much two and a half tons is? They say that's a 'conservative estimate.' And with a glut on the market the cost is way down. Maybe fifteen or twenty grand a key wholesale. So all kinda jerks are bringin' it. Black assholes running their own rings here, makin' their own scores in Miami or right down in Bogata. Straight-lookin' types in the burbs, doctors, lawyers, business guys just underwriting deals, like bankers. Big time guys fly it up here in their own plane, smaller guys drive it up in a rent-a-wreck. One guy we busted awhile back had it mailed to him by UPS.

"There's big time athletes and boxers doin' it. There's Jamaicans with their posses. And there's the old Mafia guys still doin' it. Too much money for them not to. I remember we did this posh high rise condo with the feds. Belonged to one of the top black assholes. He wasn't there, but we found like eight hundred thou in fives, tens and twenties in a garbage bag. And so the feds tap him again, and they hear him saying to somebody he's not worried about us, he's worried about the dagos. So you know."

John was sitting forward, listening intently. This stuff about the Mafia had him even more interested. "You know the names of any of these Italian guys?"

George leaned back and gazed at the naked redhead on stage. "Oh, like Monelli. Steven 'The Bank' Monelli."

"The Bank?"

"Yeah, the way he dresses, the way he lives, in this mansion in Grosse Pointe Park, he looks like a banker. Has a number of supposedly legit things goin'. But his father is old Cigar Mike Monelli, one of the old mob guys, and they been importing smack from the labs in Sicily for years. Then we heard they got some connection in Colombia."

"So if you know all this, why can't you get him?"

"It's like I said, he stays insulated. Never gets near the stuff, and neither will his top people. He's always careful what he says on the phone, and it's pretty much impossible to hook him up with anything. We know what he's doin', we got nothin'll stand up in court."

John shook his head and said nothing for a few seconds, staring at old scratches in the tabletop. George continued to gaze at the redhead. Finally, John looked up.

"You think I could come along with you guys sometime on a raid or something? I'd like to see how you work."

George turned his tired brown eyes on John. "Why the fuck would you wanna do that?"

"I told you, this shitty business is eating up my kids, my students. I'd like to see it from the inside, maybe write something about it." He was thinking about what the TV guy DeFauw had said about a documentary but thought he shouldn't mention that yet.

George shrugged. "Yeah, maybe if I tell the super you're doing some kinda magazine piece or something. He likes that kind of thing."

"Sure. Exactly what I was thinking."

"Well, let me ask him about it and get back to you. But you take all this way too serious, John Boy. What you need to do is get into old Sally there." He nodded toward the dancer standing now in a new yellow costume talking with a customer at a nearby table. "Take her up north and spend a week screwing your brains out."

John glanced at Sally. "You're probably right, but in the meantime I got school to teach in the morning."

Getting to his feet, he extended his hand to the sergeant who gave it a pump. "Take care, John, and cool out a little."

"Yeah, you're right. I'll see ya."

Heading for the front door, he passed the stage, and a black dancer who had just started her routine with a back flip called to him over J. Giels doing Hard Drivin' Man. "Hey, Johnny Gumba, where you goin', honey? You haven't even seen my yum-yums."

Laughs and snickers as he called back, "I know they're lovely, Doris. I'll be back."

"Okay, baby, don't trip on your sword."

More laughs as John left the Oldies Paradise, thinking somehow of "Father Mountie."

Maybe the hint of derision in that laughter reminded him of the way other boys at U. of D. had talked about Fr. Paul Montgomery as a kind of "Dudley Do-Right" type. The young priest had burned with a social zeal he was always trying to pass on to his charges, touting the "inestimable value of a life devoted to others," Christ's call to serve the less fortunate, and the almost sacred role of the teacher who could literally change, even save the lives of his students.

Father Paul had taken a special interest in him as a freshman, recognizing his writing skills and quickly assigning him to the school newspaper and the yearbook. And with his father's death during John's freshman year and his mother's re-marriage two years later to a man he could not abide, the priest's influence on him had been powerful.

The way those intense brown eyes would bore into him was inspiring, almost thrilling, and in his junior year when Father Paul began talking about a possible call to the priesthood, John had seriously considered it. Finally, one afternoon as they walked a hall together, he had said, "Father, I think I like girls too much." Even he thought that was a bit odd to say, since he had never even touched one at that point. But the priest had simply clapped him on the back and said, "Well, John, you're going to make some girl very lucky."

On the way home that day on the bus, his fantasy had included a scene in which he proudly presided over a classroom full of underprivileged kids.

Chapter 16

"Hey, Mr. G, watch this one. Tell us what you think."

"Yeah, give us your *critique!*"

With classes over for the day at Lincoln, a group of six girls in rag-tag, handed-down cheerleader outfits, were practicing in the parking lot as John left the building. Shifting his old brief case jammed with themes to correct, he stopped to watch. "Okay, lay it on me."

The girls started their cheer, an elaborate, high-energy, syncopated number with much hand-clapping, jitterbugging and some of the same sexy moves, he noticed, that were standard fare with his topless dancer friends. As he watched, Sara Whitaker, from the principal's office, joined him. When the girls finished, they both offered enthusiastic applause.

"Fantastic, ladies. You're terrific!"

"Thanks, Mr. G," said one of the girls, nearly out of breath. "We practicin' already for high school."

"Hey, you'll knock 'em dead."

As the girls ran off, squealing with excitement, Sara gave John a warm smile, and they began walking together toward their cars in the parking lot. "How you doin', John?"

As usual shy and awkward, John avoided her bright hazel eyes. "Not bad. How about you? How's things in the office?"

"Okay, I guess. Dr. Carter's really concerned about all this talk about layoffs. She thinks with all the pressure on the superintendent and the board to deal with this $60 million deficit they keep talking about, there really are going to be layoffs. She thinks the superintendent is really going to have to do something dramatic. You know, with lots of teachers laid off and half days and all the rest."

"What they really need to do is get rid of all those fat-cat, do-nothing administrators downtown. They'd save a bundle."

"Yeah, but Dr. Carter thinks they're serious about cutting teachers this time."

"Well, I just can't believe people would stand for that. I can't believe with everything in the papers and on TV that people in this city don't understand that we're on the verge of losing a whole generation of kids."

"Well, I hope you're right. Listen, how about coming over for dinner tonight? I make a great carbonara sauce."

They stopped in front of Sara's car. John stared at his shoes. "That sounds nice, but I can't, though. I promised one of the kids I'd take him to the Palace tonight for the play-off game."

"Oh, that's too bad." Sara sounded not surprised but still disappointed. "I mean, it's nice for him, but...maybe another time."

"Sure. Well, see ya. "

John moved to the Camaro wondering why it had taken him so long to see that Sara Whitaker was interested in him.

From his first days at Lincoln three years ago he had noticed the girl's good looks. He liked those light-colored eyes with their soft, firm gaze, even though he could barely look at them for more than a second or two. And he liked the way she moved with a kind of nonchalant grace that seemed to say she was perfectly at home in her body.

But for those first two years she and the science teacher Ray Willowby were clearly an item. And when Ray was transferred to another school, John had not heard until recently about their split.

Whenever he thought about his awkward shyness with women, he always blamed "the humiliation" in his last year at Notre Dame. It was the night he had lost his virginity to Mauve, the South Bend "townie" who had come on to him so hard in a record store that he had thought maybe she was a pro looking for a trick. Back at her apartment she had turned him on so fast that he had lost it before she could even put the damn thing in. Actually she had been okay about it, but he had definitely not been okay.

Of course, the gals at the Paradise were the exception. His first time at the bar, with Sally up there doing her naked best for all those gaping guys, he had felt sick to his stomach and nearly left. But when he came back a second time, he had felt much better, calm almost and, and most importantly, in control. He had liked that feeling and the idea that he could walk into or out of these intimate moments with these sexy, smiling women any time he liked. Quite simply it made him happy to watch them dance naked for him in this safe, no-touch place. And when he got to know some of the girls, sitting there talking about everything from dirty city politics to problem parents, he usually found them to be sweet and nice to him in a completely unthreatening way.

It was almost enough to convince him he didn't have a problem with women.

Chapter 17

At the Palace of Auburn Hills, deep in the northern suburbs, 14 seconds from the end of this NBA playoff game's frenzied first half, an absurdly tall, amazingly lithe, teenaged multi-millionaire, who two years ago to the day had been wearing a high school graduation gown that reached only six inches below his knees, dribbled the ball off one of those knees and watched with stunned mortification as the coveted sphere skittered out of bounds.

"Shoulda stayed in school!" barked John to young Mark Simpson in the nose-bleed seats he had saved for weeks to purchase. He got to his feet and said, "Com'on, I'll buy you a pop."

"Oh, man, it ain't over."

"It's *not* over. You can watch while we beat the crowd. Com'on."

Reluctantly, with frequent glances at the action from the steep steps they were descending, Mark followed John. In the circular cement hallway behind the stands they moved to a counter with only two customers ahead of them.

"He's not flashy," John was saying, "but he does the little things that help you win. Boxes out, keeps his man off the boards, gets lots of rebounds. He plays good, tough defense, like you just saw, and he sets great picks. You gotta have someone like that if you're consistently gonna win."

"But you gotta have a superstar shooter too," said Mark.

At the counter, John told the girl, "Two large Cokes" and turned back to Mark. "Well, maybe so, but what I'm saying is that everybody's gotta fill their role if you're gonna have a winning ball club."

"That'll be five dollars," said the counter girl.

"Five bucks! For two Cokes? Un-be-lievable!" But John reached into his pocket for a thin wad, peeled off five bills and dropped them on the counter. With the Cokes he and Mark moved through the surging crowd of fans and almost immediately encountered Eric

Garner and Jimmy Long.

"Yo," cried Eric, "look who it is!"

"Mr. G and the Simp." Jimmy offered his sly smile.

"Guys!" said John, shocked to see them. "What's up?" The four moved off to the side, out of the crowd's heavy flow and favored each other with various mock-elaborate handshakes, high fives and hip bumps to celebrate this unexpected meeting.

"How about that Michael?" asked John.

"Yeah," said Eric, "they gonna shut him down now."

John playfully cuffed Eric's head. "I hope you're right. So who'd you come with? You got family here?"

Eric shook his head. "Naw, we come with Andre. Sittin' in a private box with one of them windows on it."

"Who's Andre?"

"Dude we work for," said Jimmy. "Take us here, concerts, lotta stuff. We sell the most, we get the perks."

"Man," said Eric, "you gotta check out the ride we got tonight. Big white-ass limo."

"Stretch Caddy," added Jimmy.

"Yeah, stretch, with TV, CD, bar with every kinda drink."

"And some bad bar girl. Andre say we go to the club later."

"What club?" asked John.

"Our club," said Eric. "Private club. Got pool tables, foosball, video games, booze, weed, women, anything you want, man."

Jimmy called over John's shoulder, "Hey, Andre, over here, man."

John turned to find a slim young black man, about his own age and dressed in black leather, nodding at them and taking leave of another black fellow dripping in gold.

Andre headed for Eric and Jimmy. "Where you dudes been?"

"Right here," said Eric, "hangin' with the Simp and Mr. G."

Andre paid attention first to the boy. "Hey, Mark, what's happenin'? You lookin' good." They did the ritual handgrab and hug. Mark smiled and looked embarrassed.

Finally, Andre turned to John. "Mr. G.?"

"Hi, John Giordano." He extended an uncertain hand, and Andre took it briefly with a mock limp wrist.

"Andre Phelps, man. How you doin'?"

"I'm doin' fine."

"Well, good for you, man." Mockery, scorn and sarcasm dripped from Andre's sidelong smile at the boys.

John told himself to stand up to this leather-clad local hero as Eric tried to shift the focus. "Hey, Andre, when we goin' to Vegas?"

"Soon, man, soon. I got some things to take care of and then we gonna hit old Caesar's Palace. You comin' with us, Mark?"

Mark stared at the floor. "Maybe."

"Maybe," repeated Andre. "That's a real strong answer, Mark, real strong."

Mark said nothing, and John answered for him. "Maybe he doesn't figure a measly trip to Vegas is worth getting his head bashed in with a bat."

Andre stared hard at John. "My boys don't get they heads bashed. We the ones do the bashin'."

John looked away, knowing this meant he was backing down. Still, he tried to salvage the moment. "You don't say."

Andre only came on stronger. "I do say, man. For a teacher, man, you don't know shit."

John said nothing and shook his head, hoping for disgust beyond words.

Andre stepped up closer, leaning down a bit to look him in the eye and talk into his face from inches away. "You don't agree? You think you know somethin' I don't?"

John hesitated, looking past the guy's angry black face. Finally he said, "Maybe. But I know what I know."

Andre turned to the boys with a wide-eyed sneer. "There's that fuckin' maybe again. Real strong! Where you dudes get this whimpo-fag? He can't learn you nothin'."

Eric eyed Jimmy, and they moved to Andre's side, each taking an arm. "Com'on, man," said Eric, "leave him alone. The game gonna start again."

As they tried to move him away, Andre freed his arms with a flourish. "Mark, why you hangin' around with this white turd? You come and see me tomorrow. I got somethin' for you."

Mark looked up from the floor. "Okay."

With a vehement nod, Andre said, "All right, later, man."

He began to move away with Eric and Jimmy but stopped to glare back at John. "Dumb, limp-ass cocksucker!"

John said nothing, and within seconds he had lost Andre, with arms around his boys, in the crowd.

Chapter 18

An old black woman with a three-year-old boy by her side picked up a Free Press from the stack on the stand near the counter. Shaking her head slowly, she scanned the front-page headlines. One said: "Gang Warfare: The Toll Rises." And another: "400 Teachers to be Laid Off."

Taking the boy by the hand, she moved to the bulletproof, plexi-glass enclosed counter, opened a small door and placed a dime and a quarter on the turntable arrangement operated by the young Chaldean behind the counter. Folding the paper into her cloth shopping bag and taking a firmer hold of the little boy's hand, she walked to the door.

Emerging from the Party Hearty, the woman and the boy were on the same street corner that Eric Garner and Jimmy Long had been working. Today three different 13- and 14-year-old boys were selling on the corner. One of them had his head inside an old Saab stopped at the curb. The other two were straining to look nonchalant as they gazed up and down the street.

"Hey, how about Safety Blitz?" asked the Saab's fat white driver.

"Fuck no," said the boy with his head in the window. "We the Vices, man. We got better shit, and this here's our corner now."

As the woman and the boy rounded the corner, they moved too slowly to avoid getting bumped heavily against the wall of the store and nearly knocked to the sidewalk by four well-pumped older teens carrying baseball bats on their shoulders. They were laughing as if they were headed for a ball field in the neighborhood.

"Hey, watch out, Grandma!" said one of the four amid more laughter.

Turning the corner and without hesitation, they set upon the three youngsters who were selling. The boy with his head in the Saab uttered a weird high-pitch scream when he was smashed in the back with a bat. The second youngster fell quickly from a blow to the head, and the third, in a bright yellow windbreaker and yellow gym shoes, took off running into the field next to the Party Hearty. Two bat-wielding enforcers were in swift pursuit.

The Saab at the curb squealed off with the first boy lodged in its window and still screaming. When the car screeched to a halt, the boy fell to the street and was immediately attacked by the muscular fellow who had cracked his back and who now delivered a number of vicious blows to the kid's legs, arms and head. As the Saab again screamed away, the old woman limped fast down the walk, nearly dragging the small boy, who had turned to watch the mayhem with large frightened eyes.

Chapter 19

The principal's outer office at Lincoln was bustling at the start of another school day. Teachers burdened with papers and supplies stopped in quickly to pick up their mail. One secretary loudly admonished a sullen boy who had again failed to deliver a permission slip. Another tried to calm an irate parent on the phone. Sara Whitaker was working at a filing cabinet when John walked in carrying his overloaded briefcase.

Sara gave him a half-hearted smile. "Morning, John. She's waiting for you. Go right in."

He told himself not worry about the smile. "Thanks."

At the open door to an inner office he looked in and knocked lightly on the jamb. Dr. Eunice Carter, a large, handsome black woman, looked up from behind her desk, smiled, rose and motioned John into the room. The wall behind her was covered with framed certificates, plaques and other mementos of a long, successful career in education.

"How are you, John?" Dr. Carter's smile quickly faded as she moved to close the office door and pointed to a chair in front of her desk. "Please sit down."

Nervous now, he sat and said, "Thank you."

The principal returned to her desk. "I know you have a class to meet, so I'm not going to drag this out. I just didn't want you to hear this from anyone else, before I talked with you."

He nodded stiffly with the briefcase in his lap. Some kind of dread seemed to be forming in his stomach.

Dr. Carter held his gaze for a second, then looked down at her desk. "As I'm sure you've seen in the news, because of the sorry financial state of this school district, on Tuesday the Board sent out four hundred layoff notices. It grieves me to tell you that your name is on one of them."

Despite the nerves and the dread, John was stunned. "Mine? I

51

have...but this is my third year. I have three years in. I..."

He stopped, bewildered, feeling his heart pound.

Dr. Carter continued in a voice that was tired, kind and tinged with anger. "The cuts went deeper than anyone expected. And there's nothing fair about this. You're a superb teacher, John, absolutely wonderful with these children. If our all teachers were like you, this system would have no problems. But there's simply not enough money. And I guess the Board and the Superintendent wanted to demonstrate what they hope will be seen as fiscal responsibility."

"But why don't they call another millage election? Once people understand..."

Dr. Carter interrupted. "Look, John, with all the accusations in the papers of mismanagement and incompetence, some of which, I have to say, are well-founded, they're not going to try again for another millage increase until at least November, until people have a chance to see the impact of these cuts."

"But what am I gonna do?" He leaned forward in the chair, trying to control the whine in his voice. "Teaching is everything to me. I'm a teacher, and these kids need me."

"Of course they need you." Dr. Carter's tone was both soothing and implacable. "But because of seniority they're going to have someone else next fall. The fact is that things are tight all over this state. And you may have to relocate at some considerable distance if you want to keep teaching."

"Keep teaching!" His voice was nearly cracking. "What else would I do?"

"You're a very talented young man, John. There are lots of things you could do."

John screamed, "Like what!" Then startled and shamed by his loss of control, he dropped his head and stared at his briefcase.

Dr. Carter said nothing. After a few seconds he got to his feet and spoke softly. "I'm sorry, Dr. Carter. I'm just losing it here. Thanks for your kind words. I've got a class waiting for me." He turned and left the room before Dr. Carter could say anything else.

In the outer office he moved quickly past Sara Whitaker. "John?"

He said nothing and emerged from the office with his legs feeling almost numb. Turning a corner he moved up a stairway and grabbed the railing, wondering if he would make it to the top. Two students were running up the steps ahead of him and passed old Marlowe, the famously incompetent math teacher, who was heading down.

"Hey, John, how's it going?"

He acknowledged the greeting with barely a nod.

So why did the despair he was feeling now make him think of Notre Dame? Of course, it was the fiasco with Gala.

The university had gone coed more than a decade earlier, and so there were more than a few females walking around this former male bastion. But the odds still favored the girls, and he had felt especially fortunate in his sophomore year when he met Gala Simone. Even the name had enthralled him, and the speed with which he had won the heart of this lively, dark-eyed beauty had made him feel 10 feet tall.

For his major he had wavered between journalism and education, but Gala was headed for the ed school, so that settled the matter. During that summer he had visited the girl and her family at their home outside Indianapolis and hit it off beautifully with everyone. As they started their junior year in many of the same classes together, a life full of love and meaning seemed to be unfurling with the girl of his dreams.

That she was a good Catholic girl in a day when such creatures were increasingly hard to find had only made her an object of greater appeal. And at the same time, that she had allowed him to touch her breast over her blouse and bra as they were necking on that warm early October night had seemed astonishingly generous.

And then came the unmitigated disaster of Robert Birch.

A tackle on the football team, Robert was also in their classes, an almost absurdly large fellow with a big handsome head, and John watched as his own beautiful future had slowly crumbled into dust. The official end had come one sunny spring day with the banal words, "John, I'm sorry. Robert and I have decided to be a couple."

In their senior year he'd been treated to the gut-wrenching spectacle of Gala and Robert in love. Robert was the starting right tackle that fall, Gala graduated with honors and John was invited to their wedding in June.

Along with the humiliating loss of his virginity, his senior year had also marked the loss of his faith. Among many other reasons, life with no God seemed to make much more sense than one with a God who dabbled in betrayal.

Chapter 20

A happy din filled the room, with a number of students out of their seats and talking loudly, as John walked in and dropped the briefcase on his desk.

"All right, settle down. Everybody in their seats."

This rare, sharply angry tone stopped the noise quickly, and within seconds everyone was seated quietly at their desks. With a quick sweep of the room he found Eric Garner's desk and three or four others empty. Trying to re-compose his face to get through this class, he walked to one of the big, old wood-cased windows and stared down at the schoolyard.

"Okay," he said with his back to the class, "get out your grammars. In about five minutes, after I take roll, you'll have that quiz on subordinate clauses I promised you yesterday."

There was some grumbling, but it stoppped when he turned with a scowl. Turning back he gazed out the window again. With his navy Tigers cap twisted to one side, its brim tilted up, Eric Garner was running diagonally across the large playground toward the school building. As he approached a rusted old backboard and bare-rimmed basket he took a couple of phantom dribbles, tossed up an imaginary hook shot and shoved his fist in the air. Then he trotted into the narrow parking lot immediately behind the school.

Having tracked Eric's progress across the yard, he only now he spotted another kid in the lot, a boy in a bright yellow windbreaker and yellow gym shoes, crouching behind a large black Chrysler two cars down from his Camaro. The boy was obviously marking Eric's route toward the school. When John finally saw something glint in the crouching boy's hand, Eric was almost up to the Chrysler.

John moved suddenly to lift the big old schoolroom window and screamed, "Eric, watch out!"

Eric stopped, looked up at John in the window and then down at the boy who was standing now a few feet away, holding a gun rigidly in both hands and pointing it directly at Eric's chest.

Eric spun and dashed away, but there was only a moment's pause before the boy in yellow pulled the trigger, and a loud crack echoed in the schoolyard. Eric was slammed against the fender of the Camaro and slumped to the ground. John watched the boy in yellow race out of the parking lot and disappear around a corner of the school building.

Chapter 21

On one of the Detroit's many hopeless commercial strips — empty storefronts, dilapidated one-and two-story office buildings in desperate need of tenants, and boarded-up gas stations with tall weeds sprouting from cracked cement — Susan Cole parked her four-year-old VW Rabbit in front of a building that looked like it once housed medical offices. Now it served a few small, mostly failing businesses. Carrying a McDonald's bag, she entered the building.

Inside she wrinkled her nose at a strong urine smell and walked quickly through it down a hallway lit badly and in need of paint. She stopped at a door with a sign that said, "Charles Watts, Private Investigator." Opening the door she entered a small, bare reception area with a couple of chairs and a coffee table covered with magazines — People, Sports Illustrated, Time, Woman's Day — all at least six months old.

"Charlie?"

His voice came from the inner office: "Yeah, I'm here."

She moved to the office door and looked in. This room at least had a few framed photos on the wall: Charlie a dozen years younger in shoulder pads and the number thirty-four on his football jersey; Charlie in a police uniform standing with his hands on his hips in front of police headquarters; Charlie with two other narcotics officers posing behind a table with white powder and drug paraphernalia.

There were two chairs in front of an old metal desk, behind which Charlie sat pouring over a file folder.

"Busy?"

He looked up. "Not really. Just faking it."

She moved to give him a warm kiss and put the McDonald's bag on the desk. "Well, it's looking a little better." She gazed around the room. "The pictures help. Of course, if you spent less on all your electronic gadgets, you could afford a more impressive office."

"They're not gadgets, they're tools, and they help me do my job." Charlie looked in the bag. "Where's yours?"

"I ate in the car. I have a meeting at 2."

"You have too many meetings."

"All part of the job."

Charlie frowned. "The thing is, what I need is not a more impressive office. Just a break from one of those big insurance companies. You know, I told you about those worker's comp cases where the guy says working on the line ruined his back, and they want to know if he goes bowling at night or whatever. If I had somebody at one of those companies throwing me cases..."

He stopped and listened to the sound of the outer-office door opening and closing. Nodding at Susan, he got up from the desk. "Well, Miss Cole, I'll get on this right away. I should have a full report for you tomorrow afternoon."

She smiled, then put on a mock serious air. "Thank you, Mr. Watts. I can't tell you how impressed I am with the quality of your work."

He walked her out of the office. "I'll be in touch shortly. Goodbye now."

"Goodbye, Mr. Watts." As Susan moved through the reception room to the door, she passed a white man in his late 20s, wearing the rough clothes of a construction worker. He stood by the door unmoving and looking uncomfortable.

"Mr. Baker?" asked Charlie.

"Yes, I'm Marv, ah..." The man was already at a loss for words, but Charlie with a friendly smile reached to shake his hand and usher him into the office.

"Charlie Watts. Come on in and have a seat, and we'll find out how I can help you."

Marv Baker ducked his head nervously and took a chair in front of the desk. Charlie sat behind it, opened the McDonald's bag and removed a Quarterpounder, fries and a diet Coke. "Would you mind," he asked, "if I ate my lunch while we talk? I'm so jammed up with work at the moment, this is all I have time for."

"No, go right ahead." Marv seemed pleased to have something he could say without groping for a word.

"Probably buying myself a heart attack here with all this red meat, fat and grease. Now you said on the phone you're concerned about your wife?"

"Yeah, she's, eh... Well, Cherry's a beautiful girl and, eh...Well, here, I have a picture of her." He stopped, pulled out a wallet and fumbled a while before finally extracting the small photo. "I'm not really sure how to talk about this. Here, that's Cherry."

Charlie reached across the desk, took it by the edges so as not to stain it with burger grease and looked at it closely. "Yes, she's very attractive." He placed the picture on the desk next to the Quarterpounder box.

"Yeah, well, as I say, I'm not sure anything's going on, really. Maybe I'm just imagining things."

"What kind of things, Marv?" Charlie spoke between bites of the burger. "Do you mind if I call you Marv?"

"Oh, no, that's okay."

"Good. So what kind of things we talkin' about, Marv?"

"Well, I'm not really sure, but she's been goin' out a lot at night lately, and even in the afternoon, when I call she's never there. And..." He faltered again.

"And you're concerned," said Charlie, "that she might be seeing someone else."

"Yeah, I'm concerned." Marv Baker looked thoroughly defeated.

Chapter 22

The good-looking blond in her early 20s slammed the front door of the bungalow shut, let the aluminum screen float closed behind her as she moved quickly down the porch steps and front walk. On this hot, hazy June day, the woman wore backless heels, a tight, white short skirt and a thin, sexy top. With a stride that would grab any male eye, she walked to a middle-aged green Ford Escort parked on the street and got in.

As she closed the car door, Charlie in a rusted white Nova several houses away, moved his hand to the ignition. When the woman started the Escort, Charlie turned the key, and when the Escort pulled away, the white Nova followed.

He kept a discreet distance as the woman rolled out of her postwar northeast side Detroit neighborhood and turned right onto the broad and busy lanes of Gratiot Avenue. She was headed toward the suburbs.

Driving fast now and often changing lanes, she raced through an amber light at 7 Mile Road and had Charlie wondering if she had somehow made him, as he half-ran a red to stay with her.

No, he decided, she was just in a hurry, and now she had him talking to himself. "Jesus Christ, lady, he ain't gonna start without you." And when she cut off another car in her haste to change lanes: "Watch it, fella. We got one bitch in heat."

At 8 Mile they crossed the city limits, passing an American flag hanging limp on a wide grassy island that now separated the traffic flow, going and coming. "Welcome to Eastpointe" said the sign under the flagpole. Except for this broad traffic island filled with large old trees, he thought there was nothing special about this strip: a banquet hall, an old neighborhood theater (still hanging on in this age of the multiplex), Tubby Submarines, a bowling alley, a Chevy dealer, an Italian restaurant. Lots of wops out this way. He knew Susan would disapprove the slang, but he liked the sound of "Lots of wops."

Yeah, the commercial enterprise was doing a little better than what they had just cruised through on the city-side of 8 Mile. But there was nothing all that impressive here, nothing to set it really apart beyond the fact that it was lily-white, and you just stopped seeing black folks on the street. A few in cars driving someplace, probably with a much better idea of destination than he had, following this hot-looking broad so anxious to get out of her skirt. She had been forced to slow down for the moment behind three side-by-side cars doing no more than the speed limit.

So Eastpointe. Actually East Detroit until last year when some enterprising, image-conscious leaders got a referendum passed that incorporated the mellifluous new name, borrowing from their high-tone neighbors along the lake, to seem more separate and apart from the cursed city with which it shared a common border, a city whose dope, crime, corruption, poverty, entrenched unemployment, incompetent schools, inadequate services and racial polarization had made it seem the epitome of American urban despair. Really, he couldn't blame them.

The gal in the green Escort finally managed to dodge between two of the slower moving cars and was on her way again, racing across I-696 into Roseville. Charlie stepped on it to split the same two cars and hit the intersection just before the light changed. For a while Roseville seemed a copy of Eastpointe, both older suburbs without room for new development, but generally the farther you got from Detroit, the greater dedication to commercial consumption.

More auto dealerships now, a good-sized shopping center and a plethora of restaurants and fast food emporiums — Taco Bell, Burger King, Little Caesar's, Long John Silver's, Church's Chicken. Finally, the Escort slowed as it neared a large, well-kept, two-story building. The big sign in front said Eastbrook Manor Motel. The car's right turn signal began flashing.

He slowed as the woman turned into the motel lot, moved all the way to the back, and stopped in front of the main building. The motel was well back from the street and, sheltered by several large elms, had a secluded air.

Pulling into a second driveway, he parked next to the office. From there he could see the woman get out of her car, walk to a first-floor room in the building's center, and knock on the door. Her entry came so quickly that he got his binoculars up in time only to see the door close with the number 15 on it.

Leaving the Nova he walked to the office. Inside he found a young man dressed neatly in shirt and tie, reading a book with a yellow marker in hand. The young clerk seemed surprised to see the well-built black man in a white short-sleeve shirt over beige slacks moving to the counter. He put down the book (*Small Business Fundamentals*) and got to his feet.

"Can I help you, sir?"

"Yeah, I'd like a room."

"Fine, sir. How many will there be?

"Two of us. Actually, I'd like a specific room, if that's possible. Number 15. It's got kind of a sentimental value for us. If you know what I mean." Charlie winked.

The clerk grinned politely, looking down at his computer screen and fingering the keyboard a few times. "Oh, I sure do, sir. But I'm afraid 15 is already occupied."

"Really? Say, what's the name on that? Maybe my friend's already here."

"Is your friend a gentleman, sir?"

"Ah, no, she's not."

"Then I'm sure it's not your friend, sir."

"Too bad," said Charlie. "Well, how about one of those right next to it, fourteen or sixteen. At least we'd be close."

The young man looked down at his computer screen again. "No, I'm sorry, sir, but those are taken as well."

"Well, damn." Charlie turned and looked out the window at the rooms in question. "Some lucky day. How about right above it? Room 25?"

The clerk answered this time without even looking at his computer. "No, sir. I was thinking of that one too, but it's also taken."

Charlie tried looking puzzled and annoyed. "I can't believe this. It's two in the afternoon, there's two cars in your lot, and all these rooms are taken."

"I'm very sorry, sir." The clerk paused, then raised one finger as if he'd just thought of something. "Sir, let me check just one thing on 25. I'll be back in a moment."

He turned and left through a door behind the reception desk, closing it firmly. Charlie leaned across the counter, hoping to make sense of what he saw on the computer screen, but it contained only a photo of the motel.

Turning, he gazed out the window at 15. The clerk was back in about a minute.

"We're in luck, sir. There was a cancellation on 25."

Charlie knew there was something not right about this, but as he stood there nodding, he also knew the only alternative was to walk away. "Okay. I'll take it."

Chapter 23

He imagined her eyes closed, her body naked and glistening in the misty spray, Cherry Baker luxuriating in a warm shower, with a man's hand reaching to soap and fondle her tits. He did not have to imagine her moan, or the fervent words that followed.

"Oh, baby, when you touch me, I get so excited my knees feel like water. It's like I'm just gonna fall on the floor."

With earphones on, Charlie sat cross-legged on the tile floor of the bathroom in room 25. With two of what Susan called his toys—a highly sensitive listening device he had dropped down an air duct and a micro-cassette tape recorder—he monitored the conversation, such as it was, in the shower below.

At the moment, over the hissing spray, Cherry was saying, "I've never felt like this before with anybody. Not ever. Here, can I do this for you?"

The hiss increased until a man groaned, and her voice asked, "Do you like that?"

Listening intently, he watched the cassette wheels turn on the floor next to him. And then suddenly he saw the barrel of a large black automatic move directly to his left temple. The earphones were ripped off his head, a man's foot clad in a fancy-cut dress shoe stomped on the recorder, stopping it permanently, and a powerful hand grabbed his shirt and the back of his neck.

"Get up, motherfuck!"

On his feet, the hand still clamped tight on his neck and the nose of the automatic stabbing his back, he silently cursed his own reckless stupidity. It was not like he hadn't warned himself. Forced out of the bathroom and up against the nearest wall, he got a brief look at a second man—white, fat and dressed in a business suit—holding another automatic on him.

"Okay, nigger boy," said the man with the hand on his neck, "hands on the wall and spread out down here."

He kicked Charlie's ankles apart so that he was spread-eagled against the wall and, apparently putting his gun someplace, began to frisk Charlie with both hands. He quickly found and removed the .357 from a holster under the white shirt at the small of his back.

"Well, nigger boy packs heavy." The fellow behind him stepped back.

"You know, nigger boy," said the second guy in a strange, high-pitched voice, "you look tired to me. I think you need a little nap. Spread out on the bed face down."

After hesitating for a second, Charlie straightened up, turned from the wall and got his first good look at his captors. The fat man holding the gun on him now was about his own age. The other prick, shoving the .357 into his waistband next to the black automatic, was younger, about six-three, and so muscular he looked as if he might burst the seams of his navy blue suit with any substantial move. Both were dark complected, maybe Italian.

Charlie stared at the fellow with the squeaky voice for a moment, then said, "I'm not sleepy, you wop asshole."

"Oh, cute!" said the fat man, surprised and angry. "Very cute, nigger boy. But I said get on the fuckin' bed or I'll make you so fuckin' sleepy, you'll never fuckin' wake up."

Charlie stared again without moving. "That's a limited vocabulary you got there, wop boy."

The guy's small dark eyes narrowed. "You fuckin' piece of shit!" he said moving toward Charlie, who waited just long enough to slap the gun so hard that it flew across the room. He buried a vicious left hook in that sloppy gut and without pause threw a powerful right into the muscle man's face as he reached for one of the items in his waistband. Then he kicked him cleanly in the groin.

One more kick to wop boy's head, and he was reaching for his Magnum when the door to the room opened, and another well-dressed thug was moving in, gun-in-hand, trying to make sense of the room's disarray. Charlie bum-rushed the 10 feet between them in about a second, grabbed the guy's gun hand with his left and delivered his right to the point of the chin, knocking him back through the doorway and over the balcony railing to fall from the second floor and land flat on the Nova's roof.

Glancing back in the room, Charlie saw the muscle guy stirring. On the balcony he bolted to his right for the nearest stairway, but another gunman was heading up. Sprinting back to his left toward a stairway at the far end of the building, he got about halfway before spotting still another armed fellow nearing the top of those stairs.

He stopped, swung over the railing, dangled for a second, then dropped to the ground just as someone on the balcony opened up with several rounds from something silenced. Landing well, he ducked under the balcony, dashed 20 yards to an opening between buildings and raced through the passageway toward the back end of the complex.

With a surge of his old confidence he was in the process of telling himself he still had it and was home free. Then two more high-fashioned gun-toters suddenly appeared from around a corner 15 yards in front of him. He whirled to find no exit from this passageway except for where he had entered, and that was being filled at the moment by two more of these armed assholes in suits and ties. So, yeah, game over.

Chapter 24

At first the room had only a few fuzzy lights, but gradually vague shapes appeared, slowly resolved themselves and finally came into some woozy focus. After a while he decided he was probably in a motel room, but, if so, it was one set up for someone's special pleasure. A king-sized bed, a well-stocked bar, and a furniture grouping that included a projection TV, two armchairs and the couch on which he currently resided. Sitting on the edge of the bed and standing next to the door were the fat guy and the hulk.

Seated in the chair across from him was a man he recognized as Steven Monelli.

Bruises burned on Charlie's face, and he winced a bit from the pain in his side as he shifted on the couch. He'd been beaten and maybe also drugged. Monelli was reading through a file-folder on his lap, but he finally looked up at Charlie.

"Feeling better?"

He stared at Monelli for a while. "No."

"You will shortly. The drug they used is very safe."

"Thanks so much."

"Good, Charlie. That's the attitude."

"The fuck am I doing here?"

"You tell me, Charlie."

With considerable discomfort he moved to a sitting position on the couch. "I told your assholes. It was a simple wandering wife case. I followed her here and walked into a war."

Monelli offered something that resembled both a smile and smirk. "It's not nice to invade other people's privacy, Charlie."

"I can't help that. I do it for a living."

"That's what I understand. In fact while you were resting, I had a little profile run, so now I know all kinds of interesting things about one Charlie Watts." Monelli gave him a full-fledged smile this time and held up the folder.

Charlie said nothing.

"It says here you're thirty-four, a former college football star, former cop in the narcotics unit, currently a down-on-his-luck private detective. You share a flat on the westside with an attractive girlfriend, a social worker named Susan Cole."

Monelli paused. Charlie said, "Pretty boring."

"It gets better. Twelve years ago, it says here, you fucked up a very promising career in pro football by getting involved in a betting scandal at a university in California. Some years later you fucked up again, Charlie, getting yourself bounced off the police force here for holding on to a little too much drug raid cash. Thereafter you bounced through a number of jobs—garbage man, hospital orderly, factory worker—suffered the break-up of your marriage and saw your ex-wife and two sons move off to California."

Charlie didn't like the way his life sounded in brief review. "So what's the point?"

"The point is," said Monelli, speaking slowly and with a steady stare, "I could use someone with your background and skills."

Charlie leaned back on the couch. "I got a job."

"Now don't be bullheaded, Charlie, just because my staff was a little unpleasant with you. One on seven, and from what I hear, you gave just as good as you got."

"I told you, I got a job."

"Some chicken-shit job." Steven Monelli's voice remained pleasant. "Spying on frustrated young women."

"Hey, we can't all contribute handsome threads to the social fabric of our time."

Monelli smiled again. "So you're verbally gifted as well. You could do well with me, Charlie."

Charlie glared at the man. "Steven 'The Bank' Monelli. Only surviving son of old-line mob boss, Michael 'Cigar Mike' Monelli."

Monelli's smile held its wattage. "How about it? Come work for me."

"Sorry, I just like running my own show."

Monelli paused and looked like he'd decided something. "Well, that's understandable. You ever change your mind, just give me a call." Rising from the armchair, he offered Charlie his hand.

Eying him for a while, Charlie got up slowly from the couch and finally shook the man's hand. Then he walked slowly to the door, glancing with no interest at the fat guy sitting on the bed with a smirk.

Monelli called after him. "Oh, Charlie, one more thing. It would really put young Mr. Baker's mind at ease to learn that his wife is in fact spending her time volunteering down at the church."

Charlie stopped and turned. "There's one thing I don't understand."

"What's that, Charlie?"

"Why a guy like you, who could have any kind of place you wanted — romantic cottage on a lake or anything — why you come to this fuckin' motel."

"I come to this fuckin' motel, Charlie, because I own it. It comes in handy in all kinds of ways, and it keeps things anonymous. I like that."

Charlie moved again for the door.

"See, you could learn things from me, Charlie."

"Yeah," said Charlie, his hand on the doorknob, his eyes on the young muscle guy standing next to it and trying to stare him down. "I'll let you know if I ever want to learn them."

Outside room 15 he walked into the cool night air and headed for his old white Nova parked close by. Getting in, he stopped to gauge the new dents in his roof and tried to calculate the cost of having them fixed.

Chapter 25

There was still no marker on the grave, just the bald dirt cover and, at the head, a small discolored teddy bear and a clear glass vase filled with dead flowers that had toppled onto the bear. On the monitor, propped up on the grass with a tape box, John was positioned so you could see the gravesite over his left shoulder. It was fuzzy, but you could tell what it was back there.

With considerable respect for her judgment and skills as a producer, Frank could not recall his last serious disagreement with Fay. But they had actually argued earlier when he arrived and, with the crew setting up in front of the grave, found her carrying a fist full of wildflowers she had picked from a patch nearby to replace the dead stalks in the vase.

"Fay, you can't do that," he had said.

"Of course I can."

"No, really, you can't."

"Frank, what's wrong with it? Anybody might have come along and put these here. I'm just doing it first."

"But anybody hasn't come along, and you're doing it for your own reasons — to make the picture look better."

"No, it just looks so damn sad this way, and it'll look bad for the family. I talked to the father yesterday, and he's still completely broken up. He was in tears on the phone with me. Said he can't bring himself to come here. Came once and that was it."

"Hey, it *is* so damn sad, and that's the way it should look, just the way it is. Am I right, fellas?" He had turned to Marty, standing next to the camera and James, the pudgy, black audio tech, fussing with the wireless mike equipment.

Marty: "Frank's right, Fay."

She had opened her mouth wide before responding. "Marty, you agreed with me completely. You said, 'Let's do it.'"

"Yeah, but now that I hear what Frank's saying, I think he's

69

right."

James had said, "Give it up, Fay."

And so she had, and now, with the wildflowers on the grass at her feet, she stood behind Frank, who sat with John a yard away, both of them on folding chairs. She was watching the monitor, jotting his questions on a clipboard and noting the time code from the camera.

Frank was in a crisp beige suit, but it was 92 with no breeze and humid, and he had discarded the coat and tie and rolled up the sleeves of his light blue shirt. John was in a plaid short sleeve shirt and well-worn jeans. Four days of black stubble covered his frowning face.

"So John, we've talked about how bad it is on the street, how the lives of the kids you teach are impacted by the drug trade..."

"Taught."

"I'm sorry?"

"Taught. I used to teach. I don't anymore. I was laid off."

"Oh, right, I want to talk to you about that in a few minutes. But right now I want to get into what you think needs to be done. What can we do to turn this thing around, to save this whole generation of underclass kids from a terrible fate that seems almost inevitable?"

"For most them it is inevitable. And it isn't just the so-called underclass kids. I have kids, well, I used to have kids, who come from what you'd say are decent working class, even middle class families, where both parents are working. And whether they're too busy, or they just give their kids too much freedom, or whatever, these kids are practically raising themselves, and way too often they're picking up on the same model for success we were talking about earlier. You know, the down and dirty, quick and easy road to the big bucks, the gold chains and the designer sneakers."

"Okay, so what do we do? What's the answer?"

"I don't know that there are any answers."

"But, John, there's got to be answers. Give us your thoughts on what needs to be done."

John pouted his mouth and shook his head. "I really don't know. I've heard cops say maybe if they had cracked down 10 years ago, when it was starting to get really bad, maybe they could have put a dent in it then. But the politicians didn't want to admit there was a problem and soil the city's image. As if this sad sack city hasn't been a mess for more than two decades."

"What about today, John, what can we do today?"

"Today? I'd even go for legalization like in Britain. Take the profit out of it. But there's no way this straight-laced, cash-crazed society would ever go for that. Besides, these are mostly black and Hispanic kids. They're worthless, they scare us and we'd be better off without 'em. That's what too many people think, so the powers-that-be simply don't give a damn. Let 'em kill each other off and ruin their lives, the faster the better."

"You really believe that?"

"Of course, I really believe that. We won't even fund education enough to help them get out of this hellhole they're in. Look, maybe if they really went after the big guys, the importers, the guys who drop tons of this poison on our neighborhoods, maybe if they really started slamming those guys, it could have an impact. But it's a huge business and the biggest players are just so well protected, and connected. The cops know who they are. They know this mafia guy Steven Monelli is doing it, for example. They just aren't given what they need to get him."

Frank glanced back at Fay. "We should try to interview Monelli."

As she nodded and scribbled a note, John actually laughed. "He'll never talk to you. I mean, why should he? He'll never do it."

Chapter 26

Still in his shirtsleeves, his coat and tie in the Mercedes' trunk, Frank raced up I-75 and back to the station. Fay was riding with him, air conditioning blowing in her face, her short coral skirt hiked high on her pretty brown thighs. Normally that sight would engender some serious erotic notions, but as usual Frank reminded himself that he'd be proud to call her his daughter. In typical cryptic fashion she said, "Pretty good."

"Who, Giordano? No, he was great. We got a ton of great bites there."

"He's a little over the top."

"Yeah, a little maybe, but I probably agree with most of what he said."

"Well, you're always over the top." Used to her banter—she was never afraid to give it to him—he simply smiled and shook his head. She added, "By the way, I already tried Monelli. I talked to a secretary last week. She said they would take our request under consideration and get back to us."

"So we'll never hear from them again."

"Probably, but I'll try him again in a week or two."

"It'll be a total waste of time."

"I'm not sure. There's a big spread on him and his family in the new issue of Metropolitan, with pictures and lots of quotes from him and his wife. So maybe he's decided to use the media for his own purposes."

Chapter 27

On a steamy evening in front of the Oldies Paradise, a tall, thin, jheri-curled black man named Rico carried a small suitcase across the sidewalk, pried open the door and pimp-walked in.

The pumped-up sound system inside the smoky old bar offered Aretha Franklin singing "Freeway of Love" while on stage JoJo, a buxom, red-haired, beige-skinned woman, made less-than-energetic moves for a typically sparse weeknight crowd. As Rico searched through the haze, he found three other dancers—Sally, Doris and Tina, a petite brunet—sitting at tables with customers.

JoJo spotted Rico first. From the stage she called over the music, "Hey, Rico! Baby! Lookie here, ladies, it's the Bon Bon Man!"

Rico waved with a gap-toothed smile, and Sally called from a table in the middle of the bar, "Rico, where you been? Long time, no la-dee-da."

Bopping slowly toward the back of the bar, Rico spoke with a hint of the islands in his effeminate lisp: "I been off to find the best for you. Come off like a dream, make you feel like dyn-o-mite. Come back, ladies, have a look."

"Rico, you talkin' costumes or candy?" asked black, round-faced Doris.

Rico kept moving. "Whatever you want, baby. I got all kinda goodies. Make you feel like the sexiest thing on two legs."

"Whooee!" Doris popped to her feet. "I'm comin', honey."

Leaving her customer Sally joined Doris to follow Rico to the back of the bar. At a table near the rear, little Tina sat with a young man in a baseball shirt with the sleeves cut off, ragged jeans and dirty old gym shoes. Lots of unkempt black hair and a heavy beard frame intense dark eyes.

Rico passed their table and paused. "Tina, baby, do I have something special for you! Miss Sweet-and-Petite, you gonna love it."

"Oh, I'm comin', Rico!" Tina quickly got to her feet.

"What's he got?" asked the bearded fellow.

"Costumes, honey. The best."

"Costumes for dancing?"

"Yeah!" Tina was anxious to follow Rico. "And other things make you feel good as you look." She smiled and winked. "Come on back and tell me what you think."

"Yeah," said Sally, "Com'on, Johnny. Hey, ladies, Johnny G. gonna be our fuckin' fashion advisor!"

"All right," cried Doris, "Johnny Gumba!"

With the others leaving through a door to a back room, John hesitated at the table. Tina moved back quickly to take his hand and pull him with her.

The back room served as a lounge and changing room for the dancers, and as Tina and John entered, Rico had already opened his suitcase on a single bed against one wall. On another wall was a full-length mirror along with hooks and hangers for the dancers' street clothes and costumes. In the room also were a couch, a floor lamp, a chair and a small table stacked high with dog-eared magazines.

Chattering with excitement, the dancers held up items from Rico's case, stripped off old costumes and tried on new. Not wanting to stare at the mostly naked women, John moved to the chair in the corner and picked up a magazine from the table. Sally pranced up to preen in a tiny yellow sequined outfit. She kept looking back and forth between John and the mirror.

"Mr. Gumba," she cried finally, "How 'bout it?"

John looked up. "Very sexy, very pretty. You look great."

"Ah, yes! Thank you, Mr. Gumba!" Sally turned from the mirror and moved back to Rico's treasure trove. "Okay, Bon Bon Boy, I'm taking this one. What else you got?"

The black man's mouth lit up with gold. "Got somethin' pure as the driven snow!"

"All right! I'll take some of that too!"

Amidst more chatter across the room, cash, costumes, small cellophane packets and tiny manila envelopes were changing hands. Tina came to John holding up to her small, lean, naked body a bright red number with lots of fringe. She was also clutching four tiny envelopes that John figured were filled with heroin.

"How 'bout it, baby?" she asked. "Is it me? You like?"

"I like. Should look great."

"If it fits. They never make these things small enough for me." Tina put her envelopes down on the couch next to John and began to slip into the new red bra and g-string. He glanced down at the magazine in his lap to find a glossy local publication called Metropolitan, its cover featuring a stark black-and-white photo of a calmly smiling Steven Monelli. The heading read, "Crime King or Model Citizen?" He opened the magazine to find the cover story.

"You read that?" asked Tina.

"The article on Monelli? No, I don't normally look at this magazine."

Tina was standing in front of him with only the filmy bra in place. "It's a good story. Got pictures of his house, his family, everything. You want it, keep it."

He glanced up for a second to find Tina' tiny bush right in front of his face. "Thanks. Monelli's a favorite subject of mine. So what's in the little envelopes?" He gestured toward the couch.

"That's my smack-a-doo. The big H, baby." Tina was stepping into the new red-fringed g-string.

"That stuff'll kill you."

"Oh, shit, it's the best bliss that is. And Rico gets the best of the best. Probably from that guy." She pointed to the magazine. Adjusting her bra, she posed now for John. "Well, how about it?"

"Very pretty, Tina. Fits like a glove."

"Yeah, it does." She yelled across the room, "Hey, Rico, I'll take it. You got another one?"

Out of the case came another fringe affair, this one in black. "Try this one, baby. Should be the same size." Rico tossed it across the room, and Tina caught it on the fly. "So," she said, starting to change again, "what do you do with yourself, Johnny? I mean with school out."

"School may be out permanently for me." He continued to stare at the magazine in his lap.

"What's that mean?"

"I was pink-slipped when they laid off all those teachers because the school system's broke."

"But you love teaching, baby. And they need good teachers. You just gotta find another place to teach." Tina was already half into the black outfit.

"I'm trying. It's not that simple."

Into the busy room bopped the full-figured JoJo calling, "Hey, who's up? I'm history. Rico, you sweet thing, what you got for me?"

Tina hooked her bra. "Oh, that's me. Gotta work. Good luck, baby."

Checking herself briefly in the mirror, Tina grabbed her costumes and her smack, stuffed it all into a canvas bag, and ran out of the room. John continued to sit in the corner, reading the magazine.

Chapter 28

On the four corners were an abandoned gas station, an empty field, a boarded-up store and a former flower shop that was now, according to its hand-painted sign, "The African Missionary Evangelical Church of Jesus Christ."

In front of the empty gas station Jimmy Long and Mark Simpson worked the corner with business brisk. Mark had his head inside the cab of a Chevy pickup at the curb, while Jimmy stood watch. Another car pulled up, an old, rusted-out black Ford. Through the open passenger-side window, Jimmy failed to recognize the bearded man as his former teacher.

"Hey, man!" Jimmy eyes danced in a way John hadn't seen before. "You lookin' for somethin' hot? I got the hottest. Like three women doin' you in the same bed."

"How you doin', Jimmy?"

"Who's that?" Jimmy cocked his head, staring at the man in the decrepit car. Finally he asked, "Mr. G?"

"Yeah, man, how you been?"

"Mr. G, man, that beard, man. And this here junker." He stepped back for a moment and looked it over, then leaned back in the window. "What happen to your ride, man?"

Before he could answer, the pickup in front pulled away from the curb, and counting his cash, Mark walked back to Jimmy.

"Hey, Simp, look who's in this here ride. You never guess who's in this here, man."

Mark stared blankly in the window for a moment.

"Hey, Mark," said John, "how you doin?"

A large smile covered the boy's long face. "Mr. G, what's happenin', man? How you doin'?"

"I'm okay. How you guys doin'?"

"We're good," said Jimmy. "How come you do the beard?"

"Oh, just letting it grow. Got tired of shaving. But the car I had to sell. You know, I lost my job, and I just couldn't afford the payments anymore. That's the way it is. You can't afford something, you do without, or get something less expensive."

"Man," said Jimmy, "that's a drag."

"It's all right. Hey, how about you guys take a break? Is there a place around here I can buy you a pop?"

Jimmy and Mark looked at each other, uncertain, then down the street a half block at what looks like a girl, Hispanic, maybe, or mulatto, standing with a casual slouch but watching traffic closely. "Mickey D's a couple blocks down," said Jimmy finally.

"Well, good. Com'on, hop in. I'll take you down there, and we'll get something to drink."

Jimmy looked at Mark. "You wanna? Chink be coverin' for us."

"I guess, man, but I got regulars comin'. We can't be doin' it long."

John asked, "Whose Chink?"

Jimmy flapped his hand at the girl down the street. "She workin' with us. For a hot minute or two, she can take care a business."

"Well, this won't take long," said John. "Your customers can wait a little."

Jimmy opened the Ford's squeaky, rusted-out door. "That's the thing, man," he said once they were settled in, "don't nobody wait for nothin' these days. We sellin' crack and smack, and it don't matter which, they always want it *now*. If they don't see you or you ain't got it, they gone someplace else. Cause it's all over, man. Crack be the hottest thing that ever was, but smack be comin' back now too."

John moved the noisy Ford away from the curb. "So now we got this god-forsaken town going nuts over both poisons."

As they passed the girl, Jimmy gave her a quick hand signal before saying, "Yeah, but crack still be bigger'n smack ever be. Peoples can't get enough of this crack. Best buzz that was. You ever tried it, Mr. G?"

"Me? I'd never touch that shit. It'll kill you." He turned into the McDonald's lot.

"Man, just use the drive-through," said Mark. "Get back there quick."

Jimmy said, "That's bullshit it'll kill ya. We smoke it all the time, and it don't do nothin' but make you feel wicked awesome."

"You smoke it?" John pulled up to the order board.

"Damn straight, man. Right in this here pretty little pipe." Jimmy pulled a small glass tube from the pocket of his running suit and held it up for John to admire.

John shook his head with a frown. "What do you guys want to drink?"

"Coke," said Mark.

"Me too." Jimmy put the pipe back in his pocket.

"Three medium Cokes," John told the order girl and moved the noisy Ford forward.

"Man, you should try it," said Jimmy. "You won't hardly believe what it do to you."

John gave the girl at the window four crumpled dollar bills and handed out the cokes. "I know what it does to you. It'll give you a heart attack, stop you breathing. Don't you guys read the newspaper or watch TV, for Chrissake?"

"Man, that stuff all total bullshit." said Jimmy. "Even that Zigman Fraud guy smoked crack, man. I know lotsa peoples do it, and none of 'em have heart attacks, man. Me and Mark smoke it all the time, and it just make you smarter and more awesome. And when that first rush come, man, it be better'n sex."

John stared at the boy. "Yeah, you're gonna feel real awesome on a slab at the morgue some day."

"Man, that ain't gonna happen."

Stopping off to the side of the lot, John decided he would not take these delusional boys back to their corner any sooner than he had to. Looking up at the street he saw a smallish figure in a wheelchair moving on the sidewalk near the lot entrance. There was something familiar about the figure wheeling the chair.

"Hey, man," piped Jimmy, "there go Ricky."

John was jolted with recognition. "Jesus, that *is* Eric. Let's go say hi."

"No, man." Jimmy spoke sharply. "He don't talk to us no more."

"What do you mean? You guys were best friends."

Mark slouched in the backseat. "No, not now, man. Not since the chair. Say he won't talk to us no more 'less we stop dealin'."

"Well, good for him." John caught Mark's eye in the mirror, and the boy turned away.

Jimmy with a dismissive wave: "Well, he can't do nothin' in that chair, and he gotta be there for the rest of his life, man. He shit outta luck, man. But I'm gonna keep on makin' the big bucks, man, and if he don't talk to us, too fuckin' bad, man."

Having rolled past, Eric turned a corner. John put it in gear, and the Ford growled back onto the street.

"Well, I guess it doesn't surprise me that you're still in this asshole racket, Jimmy. But, Mark, what are you doing? I thought you had more sense than this thick-headed friend of yours."

Mark's handsome black face frowned in the mirror. "I need cash, Mr. G."

"Cash? Whatta you need with this filthy rotten cash?"

Mark stared out a side window. "Hey, I'm livin' on my own now. My mother and me is always fightin', so I just moved out. I'm livin' with my cousin over to his place now."

"What were you fighting with your mom about?"

"About this here." Mark glanced for only a second in the mirror.

"You mean rollin' dope."

"Yeah, but she really just tryin' to keep me in a damn closet, man. And I ain't gonna live like that. I got too much to do."

"You're only fifteen. What do you have to do? Except go to school and get a damn education, which you're not doin' either. I can't believe you're still out here after what happened to Eric." John turned into the abandoned gas station and stopped.

"That ain't gonna happen again," said Jimmy. "Vices got a truce."

"And that'll last until the next get-down on the corner. You guys really piss me off. I got better things to do than wasting my time on a couple losers. See you around."

The two boys looked at each other, then climbed out of the Ford. Turning in his seat, he watched them walk back to the corner. The girl had her head in a car down the block. Jimmy flagged another to the curb.

Chapter 29

He drove back to the street Eric had turned on and for a long time looked for the boy in the chair, driving up and down these sweltering residential streets on the southwest side. Small groups of black people sat on stoops and steps, looking for a breath of air. On top of everything else this summer, the city has been hit with the worst heat wave and drought in recent memory, lawns withered and brown, leaves on bushes turning yellow. That devastating Dutch Elm disease afflicting the city had left only a few sheltering trees, standing on this street, and these old homes and flats without air conditioning were surely like ovens. On some days when the temperature had moved over 100 and was still close to 90 after sundown, he had seen families take the mattresses from their beds and toss them in their front yards to sleep on during the night.

He thought of the shooting gallery at Maria Mendez's house with the mattress on the floor. The house was only a few blocks away, and he wondered if he should stop by to see if Maria was going to summer school. Instead he asked himself aloud, "What's the use?"

Having driven aimlessly for a while, he found himself passing Lincoln's old redbrick facade. At the entrance to the parking lot he turned in and drove to the rear of the building. With the playground entirely deserted, he moved the Ford past the spot where Eric had been shot and through an opening in the fence to park next to the rusted old jungle gym. Getting out of the car, he walked under the gym, gauged the height of one of the bars, and began doing chin-ups. For a while he moved smoothly, up and down, but soon began to sweat and struggle, his strength giving out. Finally, he dropped heavily to the ground.

On his back, breathing hard and flexing his hands to relieve the painful ache in his arms, he told himself he was a fucking weakling. He gazed at the windows of the second-floor room where he used to teach and wondered if he had the balls to do what he was thinking.

Chapter 30

In his ill-kept kitchenette, next to the sink full of food-caked dishes, he made himself a glass of instant ice tea. Stirring the brew a few strokes with his last clean spoon, he carried the tea to his tattered old armchair.

With the glass on the dusty linoleum floor, he slumped down in the chair and took a large red spiral notebook from the ottoman in front of him. The bulb glaring from the adjacent floor lamp was the only light in the room.

On the notebook's first page, he gazed at the photo of Monelli cut from the cover of the magazine. The guy looked as if he had tried for pride and conviction, and yet around the dark, wide-set eyes a slightly bemused quality turned the total effect into cruel arrogance. Taped to subsequent pages, as he leafed slowly through the notebook, were the other clipped photos.

A family portrait with Catherine Monelli — the face still somehow vaguely familiar — standing to the side and behind her husband, who was seated with a proud, possessive arm around the waist of their daughter Megan. An exterior of the Monellis' large home in Grosse Pointe Park. An old news photo of Michael "Cigar Mike" Monelli testifying before a senate subcommittee on organized crime. A shot of Steven and Catherine with friends around a table at a social gala at the Bayside Yacht Club. And a picture of a fleet of garbage disposal trucks, each with the Monelli Sanitation logo.

Another page turn and there was the body of the article, also cut from the magazine and taped here. A yellow marker highlighted several passages and in the margins were little notes scribbled to himself. Again his gaze moved to the highlighted passage that opened the piece.

> He sits there in his handsomely appointed
> office, offering you his impeccable three-piece

suit, his calm brown eyes and engaging smile, and says quietly: "Look, I run the day-to-day operations of three successful companies. I'm a husband and father, a pretty good one, I think. I'm a member of the Symphony Society and a Friend of the Zoo. I belong to the Bayside Yacht Club and the Detroit Country Club. I spend a lot of my time with my family on our 47-foot cruiser and playing golf with my friends, who are car dealers, judges and successful businessmen. So how in the world would I even have the time to be involved with organized crime?"

And you find yourself nodding in agreement and wanting to say, "Well, yes, of course. It's out of the question."

But then you remember the retired Strike Force Commander Thomas Terranova telling you, "Old Cigar Mike, his father, used to run the outfit with an iron fist, and then for awhile, after the old man's heart attack, it was the older brother Vince until that suspicious car accident. Now this kid is younger, smoother maybe and better educated, but he's just as crooked and just as ruthless as his father and his brother were."

His eye skipped back and forth across the pages as he read and re-read the passages in yellow.

Steven Monelli has a younger sister, Felice, who lives with her husband Sam Cotaldo, the son of a prominent Chicago Mafia figure, in suburban Phoenix, not far from her parents' ranch. But Cigar Mike's only surviving son has always been the apple of his father's eye. Born December 18, 1955, he grew up in the Fifties, when the family was heavily involved in traditional Mafia activity, gambling, loan-sharking, prostitution, and the Sixties, when Cigar Mike began to add narcotics and a number of legitimate-looking businesses.

~ ~ ~

Ask Steven Monelli what is most important to him, and he'll look you straight in the eye and answer quickly, as if he has been waiting for the question, "Two things: respect and my family."

Ten years ago, at the age of sixty-two, Michael Monelli suffered a heart attack and was reportedly told by his physician that if he wished to have any reasonable chance at a ripe old age, he must retire to a warmer climate. So Cigar Mike bought a small ranch in Arizona and left the reins to his businesses — of whatever legitimacy — in the hands of his oldest son Vincent.

Thirty-one at the time, Vincent had been running the family's restaurant, bar and home delivery orange juice company, while sitting at his father's right hand, according to one source, learning about all of the family's various enterprises.

For the next five years Vincent Monelli ran things pretty much as his father had, with his younger brother Steven keeping a low profile, running his own accounting office and handling the family's books. Then came the accident in Colorado in which Vincent and his wife Emily were killed when their rented BMW plunged off the side of a mountain road. Police were never able to establish a cause for the accident. All the family businesses were now in the hands of Steven Monelli.

~ ~ ~

At DePaul University as an accounting major, Steven, according to some, was not a particularly dedicated or serious student. "I always thought he was quite bright," said business law professor George Armbruster. "But he seemed unwilling to put forth anything but the minimum effort."

It was at a party in September of his senior year at DePaul that he met a pretty, blond Irish-Catholic coed named Catherine O'Brien, and a whirlwind courtship promptly followed. "Cathy's family were working-class," recalled a mutual friend. "And of course she wasn't Italian, and Steve's family were pretty much opposed to it. But Steve was bound and determined. I heard he even threatened to elope, and he finally got his way."

"I thought he was the brightest, most attractive man I'd ever met," says Catherine Monelli today. And she is adamant about reports of the family's Mafia connections. "Steve told me his father did some rum running back in the old days when everybody else was doing it. And that and because he was Italian is the reason the police have always given the family a hard time. It's been sixteen years now, and I still can't believe how awful the police and the media have been to this absolutely wonderful family."

~ ~ ~

Five years ago Steven Monelli embarked on a bold new plan that, according to police and DEA sources, eliminated the family's lame and ailing traditional activities, such as gambling and loan-sharking, and established a world-class cocaine connection with a carefully arranged and apparently impenetrable buffer between himself and his sources and distributors.

Also part of the new approach was the liquidation of the family's losing businesses, including the home juice operation, and the purchase of a number of legitimate companies — lucrative and stable — in trucking, waste disposal and linen supply.

~ ~ ~

"He's a wonderful father," said Catherine Monelli, sitting on the back deck of their beautiful Tudor home in fashionable Grosse Pointe Park. She gestured at her husband and 12-year-old daughter Megan cavorting with a frisbee in the large backyard. "He absolutely adores her, and she thinks he's the greatest thing since rock'n roll. I don't know what he would do if anything happened to that child, God forbid. We wanted to have more, but after Megan, I wasn't able, unfortunately."

Finally, flipping a page, he came to his hand-written entries. At the top of the first page was his heading in large printed caps: THE PLAN.

Below, his tight, neat handwriting covered the next four pages. When he arrived at the final sentence, he pulled a ballpoint from the breast pocket of his shirt, paused for a moment, then continued his writing.

Chapter 31

The lawn glistened as the morning sun lit the elaborately landscaped Monelli home. Down the drive from behind the house came a gleaming black Cadillac, quietly, nose first. Inside, with Robert driving, Steven lounged in the backseat and spoke into a phone. "Yeah, Pa, everybody's fine here. How's Ma?"

He gazed out the window at his front lawn and decided the new landscaper was finally getting it right. "So, she read it too?" He listened, then shook his head. "Look, Pa, I was given certain assurances by that magazine, and now I'm gonna sue their ass."

After listening again with a frown: "Yeah, well, Pa, you're behind the time. In your day, yes, stonewalling and the low profile, no doubt about it. But today's different. They've been takin' pot shots for thirty years, Pa, and I finally decided it's time to whack back. Do a little PR work for myself. Show I'm not afraid of the light. And that's why I'm gonna sue."

He glanced out the window as they passed an old black clunker parked at the curb, a guy with a beard, black T-shirt and jeans at the rear just finishing with a tire change. Obviously not a neighbor, probably a refugee from the wrong side of the city limits at Alter Road, just a half-dozen blocks away.

As they rolled on, the guy seemed to have no interest in the Cadillac or its contents. With the trunk lid up, he moved deliberately, picking up and stowing the old tire, with the jack and tire iron to follow.

Back at the Monelli home a gray BMW sedan was in the driveway now, Catherine waiting behind the wheel as the front door of the large house opened, and Megan in a yellow top and white shorts bounded out. She was still stuffing a red bathing suit into a beach bag as she climbed into the passenger side. Her mother moved the car down the drive and turned away from the Ford.

Chapter 32

The large pool at the Bayside Yacht Club was a popular place on this already hot and humid morning, the scene dominated by teens, the boys showing off, the girls flirting. Although a little younger than most of the kids in the group and just beginning to fill out her red swim suit, Megan seemed to be holding her own.

The club and its grounds occupied a small sprit of land jutting into a bay on Lake St. Clair. The pool and its large patio sat between the clubhouse, and the extensive docking facilities, accommodating an array of expensive pleasure craft. Tennis courts lined one side of the drive from the clubhouse to the gatehouse guarding entry to the private club from Grosse Pointe's Lake Shore Drive.

At a spot on the shoreline maybe a hundred yards from the club's entrance, John sat on the down slope of a grassy berm at the lake's edge, tending a fishing rod. Placing it in a holder stuck in the grass next to him, he trained a pair of high-powered binoculars on the pool and patio adjacent to the clubhouse. With a mostly unobstructed view, he scanned slowly across the kids playing in and around the pool, stopped when he centered on Megan in her red suit and then followed wherever she moved.

From the high board, slim, good-looking, 16-year-old Danny Welland laid out in a well-executed half gainer. Climbing out of the pool he was treated to fetching smiles from two precocious 15-year-olds in bikinis walking past. He followed the girls to a group of a dozen kids hanging out together, spread out on deck loungers and towels. Megan was one of them.

Danny grabbed a towel and waved it. "Listen up, space cadets. Time to blow this pop stand. My breeders are cruisin' the Greek Isles, and we can have ourselves a nice little party."

"All right! Party at Danny's!" A boy snapped a towel at Danny's dripping rear end. Others whooped and hollered as everyone except Megan began to collect belongings.

One of the bikini girls called back on the way out, "Hey, Meg, you coming?"

"Yeah, I gotta go do something first."

"Well, com'on, space girl. Go do!"

From his spot on the shore, his binoculars followed Megan's red swimsuit as she moved away from the pool. She was walking quickly now toward the docks closest to him, and he watched carefully as she began to run past a number of large cruisers. When she reached the access for one of the largest, she turned in, and he lost her for a time. Then there she was again, stepping onto the back deck where her mother and three other women were playing cards.

Megan on board: "Mom, Danny Welland is having a party at his house, and I've been invited." Trying to anticipate her mother's response, she sounded as if the invitation held no urgent interest.

Catherine Monelli discarded. "That's nice, dear."

"So can I go?"

Her mother looked up. "When, now?"

"Of course, why do you think I'm asking?"

"Well, I didn't understand." Catherine raised an eyebrow at her partner across the card table. "Are his parents home?"

"Ah, I think so," said Megan and immediately knew she'd blown it.

"I don't think it's a good idea," said Catherine, shaking her head. "The answer is no."

Megan whined, "Mom!"

Watching this back-deck scene from a distance, he saw the girl gesticulating with both hands and feet, obviously not giving up without a fight. Just as obviously, her mother was saying absolutely not. Finally, defeated, Megan stomped off the boat and walked dejectedly back toward the pool area. He followed the red suit until she moved behind a line of people near the clubhouse.

Giving up on the binoculars, he faked fishing for a while, reeling in and casting a few times, then leaned back against the grassy bank and closed his eyes for a while, letting the sun heat up his face. After some time he sensed he'd been dozing and popped his eyes open. Something told him to gaze back at the yacht club guardhouse near Lake Shore Drive. And there was Megan, walking quickly in her yellow top and white shorts, carrying her beach bag and glancing back furtively at the clubhouse and the docks. Grabbing his binoculars, he watched as she passed the guardhouse, crossed Lake Shore's divided lanes and headed up the side street on which he had parked the Ford. He quickly reeled in, collected his gear and moved across the road to his car, still watching Megan walk up the street.

Chapter 33

In Danny Welland's backyard the gaggle of teens from the club had reassembled. A few were drinking pop; most had beer or mixed drinks. Whitney Houston's "Saving All My Love For You" blared from an outdoor sound system, and several of the youngsters had paired off and were either dancing cheek-to-cheek or were curled up on lounges, necking.

The Welland's spacious backyard was quite secluded, but with the house on a corner lot, there was a spot up the street a bit that offered, between two large flowering bushes, a narrow view of the patio. On that spot the old Ford was parked.

Inside, slumped low in the front seat, he stared through the binoculars. One of the shorter boys was dancing very seriously with Megan, his hands planted firmly on the white shorts covering her 12-year-old buttocks.

Watching, he felt a strange kind of elation. But that was quickly followed by something disturbing. Why could he almost feel those hands on his own ass? The sensation was suddenly so upsetting that he lowered the binoculars and squirmed on the seat.

Then came the memory he had always tried to stifle and will away. Usually it seemed buried so deep it would never surface again, but then without warning it would come flooding over him, as it was now. That night late in May in his senior year at U. of D., on the camping trip to Stratford. He and six other boys and Father Paul had just seen Much Ado About Nothing and then sat around a fire roasting marshmallows and chewing over the play.

Later, sharing a tent, he and Father Paul had gone off to sleep, until sometime in the middle of the night when he woke in the dark to a hand fondling his buttocks. When a finger slid softly across his anus, he turned slowly, and the hand moved to his penis, which was hard within seconds. Now he was wide awake with a confusion of pleasure and rage, his thought not of Father Paul but of some intruder. But when he finally swept back his fist, it struck an ear, and it was the priest who gasped softly, "Oh." And when he had turned far enough to see the man's face, barely visible in the dark, it was covered with both hands in shame.

Chapter 34

Late that afternoon, most of the small basement apartment was dingy, with only the reading lamp lit over his shoulder, as he sat in the armchair, feet propped on the ottoman, writing fast in his red notebook.

The 12-inch portable TV on a small table nearby showed shape-shifting computer graphics flowing across the screen with insistent staccato music to announce "the Channel 5 News Live at 5." As the music softened, he stopped writing and looked up at a familiar face.

"Hello, everybody, I'm Frank DeFauw. Tonight at 5 on our Up-Front segment: Michigan State University professor Carl Taylor, who has literally written the book on urban gangs, is here to give us his take on the epidemic of illicit narcotics and related crime that seems to be over-running our city."

After the interruption, he did not go immediately back to the notebook. Instead he stared off at nothing, thinking again about why he had never told a soul about what had happened in the tent. It was not because he had felt sorry for the priest who had tearfully whispered his apologies over and over, until John had finally turned his back and pretended to sleep. In fact, he had not slept again that night, stewing in anger and regret that Father Paul had not managed to fight off or control his own demons with just two weeks left before graduation.

He had spent most of the following day in fear that one of the other boys had over heard those whispers in the night and guessed at what had happened. But none of them had showed any hint of suspicion, and he was finally left to admit that he would never say a word about it to anyone out of his own guilt and shame. Guilt that he'd been completely clueless about what Father Paul had been going through for the past four years. And shame over the pleasure he had felt from the priest's gentle and loving hand.

Chapter 35

Olive-skinned, bright-eyed, verging on plump yet light on her feet, Mrs. Harry Green walked into her large kitchen, handed a set of keys to her son and sat down with him again at a table that showed the remains of a heavy Italian meal.

"Fifteen years," she said, slightly out of breath. "I been holding on to it, hoping the land at least might become valuable to these guys who make these subdivisions all over the place. Then at least I would have something of value I could pass along to my son. Honey, have another cannoli."

John pushed his dessert plate away. "No way, I'm stuffed, Ma. The thing is, I just thought since I'm not doing anything right now, I'd go out there, look the place over, see maybe I could clean it up a little. And then possibly try renting it out to somebody. Or even sell it. Not as a cheese factory probably, but maybe somebody would have some other use for it."

"It's a wonderful idea." Mrs. Green used a knife to cut herself a third of a cannoli. "I'm just saying, whatever you can make from it, it's yours, that's all."

At age 15, after his father's death, he had asked his mother one day why she hadn't sold the business, and she had said simply that she didn't need the money. Now he asked again.

"Look, honey, I've told you, the money I didn't need. Your father was a great one for saving. He really put it away. And he also bought a lot of life insurance. I always thought it was because his father, your grandfather, had died of a heart attack as a young man, in his 40s."

Fingering the keys, he said, "And he figured the same thing might happen to him."

"He was right, poor guy. But I still blame those thugs for what happened. Putting all that pressure on him, trying to buy into the plant, really trying to take over the business is what they wanted. I swear to God if I had that old man Monelli here right now, I'd still scratch his eyes out. Johnny, don't play with those keys. Makes me nervous."

He puts the keys down. "Cigar Mike."

"Cigar Mike. I swear to God. That's why I didn't do anything with it when your father died. There was no way they were gonna get their hands on it." Mrs. Green took a bite of the cannoli. "Honey, have the other half of this."

"It's not half, Ma, and I can't. I'm too full. Did you see the story on Monelli's son and his family in the magazine that's out right now?"

"I saw it, but I won't read it. I'm sick of hearing about those people. The police always talk like they know so much, but they never do a thing. It's been that way since I was a little girl."

He picked up the keys. "Ma, I gotta go. I want to go out and look at the place while it's still light."

Mother and son got to their feet. "If you're gonna clean it up," she said, "you'll have to get the water and the electricity turned on."

"I know, Ma. I'll take care of it."

She leaned close and whispered, "Please, Johnny, for once try to be nice to Harry."

"Ma, please." He swallowed with quiet exasperation.

She led him out of the kitchen and into the dining room where his stepfather was cleaning a gun collection. Harry Green was a large man with a self-satisfied air, an independent trucker with his own rig. Sitting at a dining room table covered with newspaper and a variety of long guns and side arms, he looked up as his wife and stepson came into the room.

"Going already, John?"

"Yeah, I gotta go."

"Well, remember what I told ya." Harry always sounded sure of himself. "There's a lotta worse ways to make a living than driving a truck."

"Yeah," said John, telling himself to keep it light, "I'll remember. So which one of these handguns is the easiest to use?"

"The easiest?" Harry smiled indulgently. "They're all easy if you know what you're doing. For the beginner I guess this little .22 would be the easiest." He picked up the gun and sighted it at a picture of John Kennedy on the wall. "It's not that heavy, has a nice smooth action, and it won't kick you all over the place. Here, try it."

He handed the gun to John, who looked it over and then pointed it at the wall. "So when you go up North, will you take these with you and do some hunting?"

Harry shook his head in mild disbelief. "Hunting season's in the fall, John. No, your mother and I are just gonna go up and relax. Now if you want me to call that guy I mentioned about the truck, let me know so I can do it before we go."

John handed back the gun. "Harry, no way I'm gonna drive a truck."

Harry looked at him from under his brows. "Too good for the job, huh?"

"That's not what I mean." John caught a look from his mother.

Rubbing a cloth over the gun John had just handled, Harry said, "But it's what you feel, ain't it."

"Oh, fuck it! Ma, I'm leaving."

As John walked out, Harry said, "Nice language in front of your mother."

He kept moving. "She's heard a lot more from your garbage mouth."

"Basically," Harry called after him, "you're just a spoiled, smart-assed punk."

John left his mother's bungalow from the side door onto the driveway where the Ford was parked behind his mother's late model Topaz. In the garage was Harry's Aerostar.

Mrs. Green followed her son out of the house. "Nice. For the life of me, I've never understood why the two of you can't get along."

"Just leave it, Ma."

"But why, Johnny?"

"Because he's an asshole, Ma. And I have no idea how you can share your life with him."

"Johnny, you've never, ever given him a chance, even when you were a boy."

"When I was a boy he was hardly ever around. Which was just fine with me. I only had a problem when he came home." John opened the Ford's driver's side door with a loud squeak.

"Your car looks like it's gonna die."

"It serves the purpose."

"Why don't you use mine when we go up north? We're taking Harry's van, and the car's just gonna sit there in the garage."

"I'll see, Ma." He got into the Ford.

"Well, you have the house key and you know where the car keys hang inside. So you're welcome to it."

John slammed the car door and said, "Thanks, Ma."

Mrs. Green leaned in the open window to kiss his cheek. "Do me one favor, honey."

"What's that, Ma?"

"Please get yourself a haircut and shave off this beard. I don't know my own son this way."

John started the car. "I just might do that, Ma. I'll see you later." He backed the Ford loudly down the drive as his mother gave him a worried wave.

Chapter 36

It was surprising he remembered this area at all, a mostly rural stretch off I-94, beyond Mt. Clemens, northeast of the city. Nearly 15 years since he'd been down this road, and yet there were still a few landmarks he recalled. Like the old weathered barn with the two silos. He remembered that because he had asked his father on one of their trips to the plant—he must have been eight or nine—why that farm had two silos instead of one like all the other farms on this road. And his father had given him a look and said in his raspy voice, "Cause they need one more than the other ones."

He remembered feeling embarrassed by his stupid question, asked probably because he felt, as he often did with his father in the silence between them, awkward and uncomfortable. "Because," he had added quickly, trying to recoup his father's respect, "they have more grain or corn to store."

"*Si*," his father had said and drove on, as usual, in silence. Having arrived here from Sicily at 13, Joe Giordano had learned to speak his accented English quite well, but at least around his son he was a man of few words. Hard-working to the point of obsession, he often missed dinner and arrived home after John had gone off to bed. And even in the time they spent together, on their Saturday visits to the plant, for instance, the man would be using every available moment, it seemed, to work on ways his small factory could produce more cheese.

But then, according to John's mother, his father had always been that way: driven, obsessive, at age 15 working incredibly long hours for the old man who owned the cheese company, scrimping, saving everything, and of course learning every facet of the business. In less than a dozen years, before he reached 27, he had saved enough to buy out the old man. And then he had worked even harder. For three years he had come into an Italian grocery store on the eastside to deliver his cheese and to flirt shyly with the owner's daughter, a full-figured young woman who worked behind the counter. It had been three years before he felt successful enough to ask her for a date. By then they were both in their late 20s, and on that first date he had asked her to marry him.

Of course, much on this road had changed substantially, and there was much that John did not remember. Most of the farms were no longer worked. In fact, most appeared abandoned, their fields overgrown, their pastures empty. There were a few newer homes and a store or two John could not recall, and the mottled gray of the highway itself, little used and never repaved, seemed much darker. So why had this area remained rural and undeveloped with so much sprawl in almost every other direction beyond the city's close-in suburbs?

The front of the cheese factory property was so overgrown with trees and bushes that the building, set well back off the road, was barely visible. He passed the entrance twice before finding it. Finally, he pulled the Ford off the quiet highway and stopped in front of the rusty gate. Out of the car he walked through low weeds to the gate, fumbled with the keys his mother had given him and eventually found one that opened the heavy padlock. With some effort he shoved the gate through thick underbrush.

Moving the Ford slowly up the dirt road heavily overgrown with huge weeds and bushes, John watched the old plant finally come into view, a long, two-story cement block building with a badly faded sign on the front that said "Giordano Cheese." He followed the road as it crossed in front of the building to a spot where he could park near a door with a small rusted "Office" sign attached.

There was still a lot of light left, but crickets were already chirping loudly as John got out of the car, looked over the unpainted block exterior of the plant and walked to the office door. Again he had to try several keys before finding one that worked. He pushed the door open with a loud creak and stepped inside.

There was just enough light coming from two dingy windows for John to see and recall a good-sized room, large enough to accommodate two desks and two filing cabinets, a small refrigerator, a couple of chairs and a couch. Everything was covered with a heavy layer of dust, and many generations of spiders had obviously been busy in this room.

On the wall above the larger of the two desks was a calendar with a curled picture of a scantily-clad young woman milking a cow. The month was June. Standing in the middle of the room, he wondered about the year. It had to be '77. He hadn't been in this room in more than 14 years. Perhaps no one had. Something small made scurrying noises in one corner, and he decided he'd need to buy some mousetraps.

Another door, in the back wall, led out of the office, and he moved to it. Before leaving, he turned back and tried to imagine the room the way it had looked 15 years before. In his memory it was bright and cheerful. A smilimg young secretary was typing at the smaller desk, and at the larger one John himself, at age 10 maybe, added up a long list of numbers with the help of an old hand-cranked adding machine.

As the reverie continued, a dark little man about 40 came up behind the boy and playfully placed an empty perforated tin cheese container upside down on the youngster's head as if it were a helmet. The boy looked around and saluted his smiling father, and John recalled with both pain and fondness how rare that carefree moment had been. He turned back to the door, tried the handle and left the office.

Now he was in a dimly lit storeroom with an open area to his left and aisles of shelves to his right. Looking left he saw what was left of burlap bags with their contents eaten away. Better make it rat traps, he thought. When he turned back he saw the room as it once was: clean and bright, shelves filled with cheese tins, cans, boxes and other items used when the plant was a going concern.

He also saw himself, again at age ten, moving quietly and alone down an aisle toward a corner of the storeroom. He recalled vividly what the boy had found there one summer afternoon: his father and the young secretary from the office locked in an unmistakably carnal embrace. He remembered being stunned by the sight, almost gasping with the confusion of his feelings, but watching unseen for awhile, not making a sound, then backing away quietly and leaving the store room by another door that stood open and led to the main production room. Now he did the same.

Enough early evening light came through several dirty windows to see a number of large vats as he moved into the plant's biggest room. For awhile he stared into one of the dusty, empty vats and remembered what this room had looked and smelled like when he was a child, the milky liquid being stirred in the gleaming vats, the workers in white overalls seeming never to notice the slightly sour dairy odor that always filled the plant.

He also thought of the cigar. And the day he had pushed between the white pant legs of two workers to come upon a frightening scene in which his father was speaking vigorously in Italian to three burley, tough-looking men across one of the vats. His father had been beet-red in the face when he pointed to the door, and the three men began to leave. But one of them had stopped, turned and flipped his fat cigar into the white liquid being stirred mechanically in the vat between them, the long gray ash being quickly folded into what soon would have been the region's best ricotta cheese. Laughing raucously the three men had walked out of the plant, and John turned from the empty vat now reeling with the anger he had felt as a 10-year-old.

Starting to move back toward the storeroom, he noticed the large airtight door to the adjacent refrigeration room standing wide open. He headed for that instead, knowing full well what his memory would call up there.

In the open doorway he peered in and felt again the chill on his face and hands from that day at age 11, when he also found the door open and looked into the large, well-lit refrigerator, its shelves lined with freshly-made cheese. There on the floor his father had been sprawled on his back, his eyes wide open in a death stare the boy would never forget. Now he turned and walked away from the dark empty room.

In the office again he moved to a door at the far end of the room. Opening it, he found the small, dark, windowless bathroom pretty much as he remembered it. After he closed the door, his hand rested on the knob, then moved up to a spot on the door and its jam where he knew it would be a simple matter to attach a latch and a lock.

Chapter 37

At dusk a dark green van rolled to a stop at the curb on a street lined with old clapboard two-story homes in the city's southwest corner. Inside the van were four men wearing bulletproof vests. Three of them also wore baseball caps that said "Narco."

In the front passenger seat George Wolf was particularly interested in the house on the corner about a half-block away. As the sergeant watched through binoculars, a young black man, with a peculiar shambling gait, left the house.

"There's Thomas." Putting down the binoculars, George picked up a radio mike hanging on the dash. "Wolfman to Red Rider."

The radio crackled once before offering a response. "Yeah, Wolfie, I see him. Back in a minute."

"Copy." George put the mike back.

"Who's Thomas?" asked John in the backseat behind the driver.

"Informant." George used his binoculars again. "He found this place last week."

John strained to see the house that George was trained on. "And what is this place?"

"Supposed to be a crack house for America's Team. The place where they take delivery, cook it up and package it for distribution."

With all the houses on this block looking the same to him, John leaned back in the seat. "So what's happening now?"

George continued to stare at the house on the corner. "Guy I talked to on the radio is picking up Thomas and getting the scoop about what's happening inside. Then he'll call me." George reached into a pocket and pulled out a blackjack. "Here," he said. "Anybody comes at you, hit 'em with this."

"Thanks," said John, half-smiling and holding up the small black club for a closer look.

"Just be sure you you're the last one in. In fact, don't come in 'till I tell you."

"Okay."

The radio crackled again. "Wolfie."

George picked up the mike. "Come on, this is Wolfman."

"C.I. said he thinks we missed it. They moved their start time up, so the big bag is already gone. He says they're all in the living room, in front, smokin' and watchin' porn on the VCR."

"How many?"

"Maybe eight or nine. The works is still all set up in the dining room and kitchen. Also, Wolfie, he says there's a kid in the basement. Thought he had sticky fingers, so they poled him."

"Shit," said George quietly before pushing the button again on the mike. "All right, we gotta go in whether the bag is there or not. Okay, everybody, let's move. Have a good one."

The driver moved the van away from the curb, heading for the house on the corner. Two other unmarked cars along with a scout car were also converging on the corner.

John leaned forward in his seat. "Poled him?"

"You don't want to know," said George.

"Yes, I do."

"They tortured him. Made him an example. If he's lucky, he's dead."

"What did he mean, poled him?"

The sergeant did not have time to answer. As the van screeched to stop in front of the corner house, George and the officer in the seat behind him jumped out first. With a small battering ram in hand George sprinted for the front door with the cop next to him carrying a shotgun. Other officers, all with guns at the ready, were in close pursuit or running to cover the sides and rear of the house. Up on the front porch the cop with the shotgun grabbed the screen door open, and George screamed, "Police," as he slammed the battering ram into the front door.

Other officers were also screaming, "Police," as George delivered one more blow, and the door gave way. Dropping the ram, George pulled his revolver and charged into the house behind the officer with the shotgun. From the front hall they could see figures ducking into the kitchen at the rear. The cop with the shotgun moved straight for them shouting, "Police! Halt right there!"

In the hall George turned to his right in time to see two young black males and one black female scrambling out of the living room toward the back of the house. Another black male, slouched in an armchair facing the hall, did not move except to raise a revolver at George's chest. The man fired immediately, and the cop took the bullet on the right side of his flack jacket. Stunned and off-balance, he still managed to fire twice, hitting the gunman in the right arm and leg.

The young man screamed as he dropped the gun and writhed in the chair. The cop with the shotgun charged in, leveled it at him and fired just after George tipped the barrel with his forearm. The shot smashed high into the living room wall.

"Hold your fire, everybody," screamed George. "Hold your fire! All of you, up against the wall." He gestured to three others — two males and a female — cowering now on the floor near the wounded man.

"Com'on, assholes," yelled the cop with the shotgun, "on your feet and against the wall."

"Somebody help me," whined the young man who'd been shot. "I'm bleedin', man."

Two more officers were in the room now. One of them said, "No shit, you stupid fuck."

From the rear of the house came the sound of glass breaking. An officer screamed, "Where the fuck you goin', assholes? Everybody back inside."

With the wounded man still slouched in the chair and pleading for help, his three companions were spread-eagled against a wall as officers patted them down. Two more cops entered and paused to watch the porn film still running on the big screen TV in the corner.

"Turn that fuckin' thing off," yelled George.

"Aw, Sarge, you're just no fun," said one of the younger cops gazing at the TV.

George yelled, "Who's got the second floor?"

"Secure up here, Sarge," shouted a voice from upstairs.

"How about the basement?"

"Basement secure," screamed a female officer from below.

George moved out of the living room, through the front hall and stuck his head out the door. "Johnboy?"

Two feet from George on the porch, pressed against the wall next to the door, John gripped the blackjack next to his ear. "Yeah, you okay?"

104

"There you are. Yeah, com'on in."

John followed as George walked back into a putrid smell in the living room. "Asshole here got off a shot, but the vest took it." George fingered the damage to his flack jacket. "Probably so high on the stuff they're smokin', thought he's in a movie. Still so much in the air, we'll all be flyin'."

"All right!" piped one of the cops still watching the porn.

The wounded man quickly locked on John. "Please, man, help me. I'm dyin' here."

George barked at the cops watching the TV, "Get him outta here."

A black female officer walked into the room, glancing quickly at the porn, three white women working on hugely endowed black man. "Sarge, you want to look at the basement?"

"No, but I guess I have to."

"It ain't pretty." The female cop led the way.

Leaving, George turned to the TV watchers. "I said turn that fuckin' thing off."

John followed him through the dining room where packaging paraphernalia covered a large table—trays, scales, envelopes, rubber bands, tiny plastic bags and a sealer. Against two filthy walls three people were being frisked and handcuffed. And in the kitchen—like the other rooms dirty and littered with trash—boxes of baking powder and a bottle of ether sit on the counter while the old gas stove was covered with blackened baby bottles used to cook the coke. Two young men who had tried to flee out the back were also up against a wall.

Still following George and the female officer, John, negotiated a darkened staircase to a filthy basement with a stench even more disgusting than on first floor and with the broken discards of a lifetime littering the stained cement floor. The light from one bare bulb in the middle of the room showed them two red-smeared baseball bats abandoned next to a black youngster about fifteen, lying face down in a pool of blood. He was naked, his body badly bruised and lacerated. His legs were spread, and three feet of a broom handle extended from his bloody rectum.

"Jesus Christ," said George quietly.

"They sharpen a broom handle," said the female officer, "and shove it up as a kind of coup de gras, while the others all stand around and watch and learn the lesson."

"Oh, my god!" said John moving to get a better look at the side of the boy's face.

"Just hope he croaked before they did that, " said George.

"Yeah, for sure," said the female cop.

John was close to the boy now, staring down at his face. "Oh, Christ! No! Mark!"

"Shit," said George. "You know him?"

John turned away, his head swimming, his voice choked with tears. "Yeah, I know him."

Chapter 38

Fay moved some scripts to sit on the cluttered couch. "I talked to John Giordano this afternoon."

"Who?"

"You know, the ex-teacher we interviewed for the doc."

Frank finally looked up from the Times. "Oh, yeah, how's he doing?"

"Still no teaching job. I wanted him to introduce us to some of his former students who are working the streets, but he wouldn't do it. Said we'd just give them a big head, make them think they're something special, just make their sad little lives seem glamorous."

"He's probably right."

"But he did tell me where to stake out and shoot some dealing on the street in broad daylight. Said if we picked out one or two of the kids and paid them for their time they'd probably talk to us if we did them in silhouette."

"Good."

"But he was disappointed we haven't finished the doc yet. I told him these things take time, and we'd have it on asap."

Frank looked up from the paper. "You know, I've been thinking. I bet we could take his interview and just string together some bites. Call it "Personal Perspective" or "My Turn" or something like that. With the right intro it could be effective. Maybe run it on the 5 or the 11?"

She nodded. "Might be good. And a tease for the doc. I'll work on it."

Chapter 39

"Can you move a little closer together?"

Fay glanced between the small monitor propped up next to her and the two kids sitting several inches apart on the van's back bench. On the second bench with her were the curly-haired Marty and his Betacam, and, with his headset in place, burly James was somehow folded on the floor, the tape deck and its meters sitting next to him. Behind the kids was a large white card about 4 feet square, blasted with the light from a sun gun. The result on the monitor: the kids' normally dark faces were rendered in black silhouette.

Jimmy shook his head. "She don't like to be touched."

The girl, maybe half Hispanic, slid on the bench until she was up against him. "Don't matter long as you keepin' your hands still."

"That's better," said Fay. "Okay for you, Marty?"

"It's good. We're all set."

Finally. She was always impatient with their set-ups, but on this one, the identity of these kids was at stake. She held up the monitor to show them. "See, we can't really tell what you look like. This is how it'll be at home."

Jimmy frowned. "That's ugly. Can't tell nothin'."

"Well, Batman, that's the point." They had decided she should call them Batman and Chink. Fay lowered the monitor. "You didn't want to be identified and, I think, with good reason. So this way we can see and hear you, but people won't know it's you."

Chink said, "What about voices?"

Fay: "I told you, you got my promise we'll change 'em."

Chink: "Let's hear 'em."

James: "We can't do that here. We'd have to do it back at the station."

Chink shrugs. "Then let's do this here. We losin' cash big time with the little bit you payin'."

Fay nodded at Marty. "Okay, then, let's roll."

Marty said, "We already are."

"Okay, let me start with you, Chink. How old are you?"

"Fourteen."

"What school do you go to?"

"Don't go to no school."

"Why not?"

"Don't like school." She shook her head, and the ends of her cornrows vibrated.

"Why do they call you Chink?"

"Don't know. Cause they say I squint all the time, like a Chinese."

Jimmy: "She do look Chinese."

Fay ignored him. "So how long have you been selling on the street?"

"Along about two year."

"Two years, that's a long time. Selling what?"

"Boy, Girl. Mostly.

"You're talking about heroin and cocaine?"

"Yeah, smack, crack."

"Now these things are illegal."

Jimmy: "The people buy 'em."

"Why do people buy them?"

Chink: "Cause they love it."

Jimmy: "They addicts, man. They gotta have it. We providin' a service."

"Batman, I want to talk to you about this, but right now I'm talking to Chink. Okay?"

Jimmy shrugged. She'd been fascinated by the girl's role in this from the beginning of their stake out but decided to interview them together to help make them a little less nervous.

"So, Chink, why do you sell it?"

"Cause I like makin' the cash."

"And how much do you make in a typical week."

"Typical?

"Yeah, what do you usually make?"

Jimmy again: "In a week, maybe 600. I usually make 6 –7 bills."

"And you, Chink?"

"About like that, maybe 600."

"Chink, do you like this work?"

"It's okay. Bettern' sellin', you know, your thang."

109

"Are those the options you see for yourself, illicit drugs or prostitution?"

"Ain't never been a ho, ain't never gonna be. Don't do no kina drugs."

"Where do you live?"

"Lotta different places."

"So you're on the street a lot? How long has it been?"

"Couple years."

"Where were you before that?"

"Foster home."

"What happened to that?"

The girl paused, then said, "Man there was feelin' me up. So I run away."

Jimmy said, "I told yous she don't like no touchin'."

"Did either of you know the young man who was found tortured and murdered in a dope house last week?"

Jimmy: "Yeah, Mark, I know'd him."

Chink: "Yeah."

"Why did that happen to him? Do either of you know?"

Chink looked at Jimmy who said nothing. "He done some stupid ass thang."

"Like what?"

"Like I can't be sayin'."

"Was he holding on to too much money?"

"Could be. I don't know nothin'."

"Chink, in five years, what do you see yourself doing?"

"Five years?" The girl seemed dumbfounded.

"Yeah, in five years. What are your dreams? What do you want for yourself?"

She stirred and moved slightly away from Jimmy. "For me? I wanna run the deal. Like that bitch worked it before Rick."

"Rick? You mean Maserati Rick?"

"Yeah, Rick."

"Chink, a lot of smart people say one of two things will happen to someone like you. Either you'll go to prison or you'll end up dead. What do you think about that?"

The girl's brown eyes were blank. Fay glanced at the monitor's inscrutable silhouette, then back at the stoic face.

"Don't matter."

"What do you mean it doesn't matter? This is about your life."

"Don't matter. Nothin' for me to do 'bout that."

"No options, Chink? No other possibilities in life for you?"

"Fate gonna take care a that."

"So you just leave things up to fate?"

A shrug and a nod. "Ain't nothin' nobody can do 'bout livin' and dyin', 'cept fate."

Chapter 40

At the far end of a large, loaded parking lot serving the Lakeside Mall, a two-year-old red Topaz moved slowly down one aisle and up the next. Clean-shaven, his hair neatly trimmed, and dressed in a dark suit and tie, John in his mother's car was looking for the right empty parking space. Finally, he rolled up on one that fit his needs: the car in front had been backed in. He turned in and shifted into park.

The Topaz idling, he was out quickly, his eyes sweeping the area, darting over and between cars, searching for any kind of movement. With no one nearby, he carried a screwdriver to the back end of the car in front. Looking around one last time, he ducked and quickly removed the screws securing its plate.

His third in three days. He was becoming an old hand at this.

Chapter 41

On the backyard patio at Danny Welland's house there was another party well under way. As on previous occasions, several teens were drinking, smoking, dancing and necking. Under a large tree to one side of the patio, three girls were chatting and passing a joint. One of them said, "If my mother found me doing this, she'd chain me in a closet and toss the key."

Her friends giggled as she pulled a drag.

On the street nearby John slowed the Topaz and parked on the spot that gave him that open view of the backyard. With the binoculars he slipped low behind the wheel and scoped the patio. His slow pan across two couples necking on lounge chairs stopped on a group of young girls.

His heart jumped.

This was fate. Too incredible to be anything else. Fully prepared, fully *expecting*, to wait and watch for at least a week, he was only on day three. His first stop after checking the yacht club, and he was watching one of the girls hand Megan a joint.

Putting down the binoculars, his heart still pounding, he reached under the seat to retrieve Harry's .22. The revolver still looked and felt strange in his hand, and he put it back under the seat. He picked up the binoculars again. As if on cue, Megan had her small purse now on a strap over her shoulder and looked to be taking her leave. She waved to her host and moved off the patio. John quickly shoved the binoculars under the seat, put the car in gear and, grateful for the engine's quiet purr, drove away.

In his rear view mirror a half-block away he saw Megan reach the sidewalk and head in the opposite direction. Turning right at the next corner, he upped his speed on the long block toward the lake. At Lake Shore Drive he stopped and turned right, passed the yacht club entrance on his left and turned right again at the next side street.

He had driven around the block, with the expectation that he would meet the girl on this street, halfway between the party house and the club. Now he searched up the street on the sidewalk ahead of him, and, yes, there she was, walking his way.

As he approached, he slowed the Topaz, lowered the power window on the passenger side, took a long, deep breath, then let it out. He had practiced for this moment almost incessantly for the past week, but now it was actually happening and much sooner than he had expected. Feeling the moisture from his palms on the steering wheel, he pulled to the curb and stopped a few feet in front of Megan. Would his voice crack, his words tumble over each other? He leaned toward the open window.

"Hi, Megan." Two short words, the voice okay so far. She was, after all, the same age as his students.

Looking into the Topaz, she seemed puzzled and surprised. Her dark eyes were pert and intelligent but hazed a bit, perhaps by the pot. She was clearly curious about this dark-haired, well-dressed man calling her by name.

"What?" she said.

"Hi, Meg, I'm Tony Molina. Your mom sent me to look for you."

The eyes focused and cased him warily. "Why? Who are you?"

"Tony Molina. I work for your father. Your mom couldn't find you, and she had to go home. She asked me to look for you, bring you back to the house."

Hesitating, she stared at him for a moment and then asked, "How do you know me?"

"I work for your father." John felt like he had just started breathing again after several seconds, reassured that so far she's asked only the expected stuff. "I've been out to the house a couple times and saw you, but you probably didn't notice me."

The girl still hesitated. "How did you find me?"

Another one he was prepared for. "Just got lucky. Actually your mom mentioned you knew somebody in this neighborhood."

The girl's face clouded, the eyes narrowing. This was it. She was going to ask something he couldn't answer.

Instead, she blurted, "Oh, god, am I in trouble? Was my mother pissed?"

John even tried a wink. "A little, but we can get you home right away, and we'll think of some story to tell her."

He wasn't sure the wink came off, and Megan seemed frozen, not moving for so long that he actually thought about reaching under the seat for the gun. Finally, she moved to lift the handle and opened the passenger door. She started to get in, then stopped. Leaning down and looked squarely at him, again with eyes more focused. "Where's Robert?"

His mouth went dry and he felt his own eyes flicker for a second at the car's beige cloth ceiling. It was the first question he wasn't prepared for. The practiced voice in his head said play for time. "Robert?"

"He always picked me up," she explained helpfully.

"Oh, Bobby, yeah, he had to go to the airport to pick up your grandfather. He's coming in from Phoenix."

Megan got in and closed the door. "Grandpa Mike's coming? How come nobody told me?"

"Nobody knew until this morning. He wanted it to be a surprise."

"Sounds like Grandpa Mike." She smiled as he glanced at her, and he smiled also as he raised the window on the passenger side and with another push of a button snapped shut the locks on all four doors. Putting the car in gear, he moved away from the curb and used a driveway to turn around, then headed back toward Lake Shore.

The girl turned in the seat to look at him and sounded leery again. "Why do you call him Bobby? Everybody always calls him Robert."

"I know. That's why I call him Bobby. Tease him a little."

"Yeah, I tease him too." She leaned back in the seat against the door. "I call him my favorite child molester."

John managed a chuckle that felt strained. "That's pretty good. I bet he loves that."

"Yeah, he takes it all right."

There was no one on this street, car or pedestrian, so he slowed the Topaz and stopped at the curb well before they reach Lake Shore.

"By the way," he said casually, "I forgot to show you something."

He reached under the seat, pulled out the .22 and pointed it at her low on the seat. He tried for cold and deadly serious, but watching her smile sink and disintegrate made him bite his lower lip. "Now this is the real thing," he said, trying the line he'd so often rehearsed. "And it'll make you very sorry if you don't do exactly as you're told."

Serious fear rimmed those big brown eyes now along with a hint of tears. "Who are you?" Her voice was thin and constricted. "What do you want?"

John managed to keep his voice even. "Right now, I want you to lay down on this seat. Put your head down right here." He pointed to a spot on the seat next to him, and when she looked at it but did not move, he screamed at her: "Do it now!"

Startled, she flinched and then looked terrified. She quickly followed his command, pressing her cheek against his mother's plastic seat cover and staring at him from the corner of one eye.

John reached into the backseat to pick up the pink blanket from his mother's closet. "Good." His voice was quiet again. "Now if you do as you're told, you'll be fine. Nothing bad will happen to you."

Stuffing the gun between his thighs and unfolding the blanket, he spread it over her. "I'm going to cover you with this, and I don't want you to move or utter a sound. If you do, you'll be very sorry. Understand?"

From under the blanket Megan's small, frightened voice said, "Yes."

John moved the Topaz away from the curb and was off again, the wheel in his right hand, the .22 in his left. At the end of the residential street he stopped, then turned onto Lake Shore and proceeded at exactly the speed limit in a flow of light traffic. The girl did not move. John did not speak.

After a few minutes he turned off Lake Shore and traveled away from the lake. Approaching the signal light at Grosse Pointe Boulevard, he watched it turn amber and then red and brought the car to a halt. He looked around as he waited, trying to appear nonchalant, but in his rear view mirror he spotted a Grosse Pointe Police patrol car coming up from behind. An electric jolt climbed his spine. They had already found him. Some neighbor had watched the whole thing and called 911.

The patrol car stopped next to him on the right. For a moment he was frozen, short of breath, stomach churning. Then he remembered the gun and quickly lowered it out of sight next to the driver's side door, just as the cop turned to look at him. The officer nodded, but John, still rigid with fear, turned and stared straight ahead. Could the cop see the blanket covering the girl? And what would happen if there was even the slightest movement under it? When the light finally turned green, he didn't breathe, or move the Topaz, until the cop sent the patrol car forward.

Fifteen minutes later John drove slowly up a residential street in his mother's subdivision and turned carefully into her driveway. Rolling into the backyard he pushed the opener button, and the garage door went up. Cautiously he moved the Topaz in next to his old black Ford, then pushed the button again and watched the door descend.

Chapter 42

That feeling of fate and inevitability was with him again as he drove this rural road past isolated homes and abandoned farms. Carefully observing the posted limits, he almost felt the Ford was driving itself, or maybe he and the car had been picked up and carried by forces that have worked out all the details well in advance.

This thought plus a glance at his watch moved him to snap on the radio in time for local news on the hour. Nothing about a kidnapping or a missing girl. But then it was hardly an hour since he had picked up Megan. Nearing the gate to the cheese factory property, he slowed the Ford and watched carefully for the turnoff. When it came, he moved off the road, stopped in front of the gate and got out to unlock and open it. He had all his keys, each memorized now, on a ring and retractable wire device on his belt.

With the gate open he drove through, then stopped to close and lock it behind before moving up the overgrown dirt road, weeds and bushes brushing both sides of the car. He parked close to the building in a spot where he knew the Ford could not be seen from the highway. At the office door, its window boarded now, he unlocked and opened it, then moved back to the car, unlocked and lifted the trunk lid.

Megan, blindfolded, hands tied behind her back with clothesline, looked pathetic on the pillow and blanket he had placed in the trunk to make the ride a little more comfortable. Reminding himself to strip sympathy from his feelings, he asked sternly, "You okay?"

Megan pursed her lips but said nothing.

"Well, we're here."

"Where?"

"You'll see." He took her arm and moved her to her knees, saying, "I'll help you out." Then with considerable effort he got her out of the trunk. Once inside the factory office, he closed and locked the door with a new padlock and moved Megan to a chair in front of the

118

nearest desk.

"Okay, relax," he said. "I'll take this off."

He removed the blindfold, and Megan, blinking, looked around the office. As she did, he did the same, satisfied that in cleaning it up, boarding its windows and putting heavy new padlocks on all the doors, he had also stripped the room of all identifying signs.

"Now if you don't cause trouble, I'll untie your hands in a few minutes."

To his surprise and dismay the girl began to cry. Between sobs and sounding deeply frightened, she said, "What are you gonna do to me?"

"Don't cry." His words were quick and harsh. "I'm not going to do anything to you. You'll be perfectly safe here. No one's going to touch you."

She continued weeping. "Yes, you are. I can tell."

"No, I'm not going to touch you." He spoke with heat and resentment. "I'm not some pervert who likes to feel up little girls. I'm just going to keep you here, safe and sound, until I've accomplished what I need to do."

Through her tears Megan screamed at him: "Then what do you need to do?"

"Keep your voice down!" he said sharply. "There's nobody who can hear you, but it'll be much more pleasant if we don't scream at each other. Right now we need to get a little message to your father. Let him know you're okay, and tell him how to get you back safe and sound."

Pulling open a desk drawer, he removed a small Panasonic tape recorder and placed it in front of her on the desk. Then, also from the drawer, he took a three-by-five card with a few lines typed on it and placed that too in front of her.

"What do you want, a ransom?" Her sobs were stopping.

"Kind of. Now read those lines over, and when I turn the recorder on, I want you to say them out loud, right into the microphone here on the recorder. Understand?"

Sullen now, the girl looked at the card. "Yeah."

"Good. This is the best way to help yourself and your family. Ready?"

"Wait! Just a second." She read the lines over, mouthing the words to herself. "Okay."

He pushed the record button on the Panasonic and nodded to her.

"Daddy, this is Megan." Her voice was a self-conscious deadpan. "I'm all right. He's treating me well. But please do what he says to get me back, because he is desperate. I love you and Mom. Bye."

He stopped the recorder. "Good. That was real good. Now com'on over here, and I'll show you where you'll stay when I have to go out."

Holding her by the arm again, he led her from the desk to the bathroom door. With a Swiss Army knife from his pocket he cut the clothesline on her wrists. In the process he notices a gold ring with a small sapphire on the ring finger of her right hand.

"What's this?" he asked, holding up her hand.

"A ring, Brain Man."

"I mean who gave it to you?"

She hesitated but said finally, "My father."

Taking her small, thin hand firmly in his, he slipped the ring off her finger without much trouble. "Very pretty. Let's send it to him along with the message so he knows it's really you."

Opening the bathroom door he moved her into the small room. In it he had placed a cot and a number of other items, including books, magazines, candy and potato chips. From the doorway he said, "There's stuff in here to entertain yourself and to snack on if you're hungry. I'll be back in time to give you some dinner. But right now I've got some errands to do."

With the girl standing inside staring at him, he closed the bathroom door and slipped another new padlock into place.

"Please don't leave me in here." She suddenly sounded like she was six.

"Don't worry, I'll be back. And as I said, don't bother screaming. There's nobody within two miles of this place."

Moving quickly now, he crossed the room, grabbed the Panasonic and left the office. In the bathroom Megan waited until it was quiet, then tried the doorknob. Then she slammed herself against the door. It did not budge, and she sat on the cot in tears.

Chapter 43

In the reception area of a spacious, well-appointed office suite of contemporary design, the phone murmured musically. Under a large Ficus that reached to the ceiling, a petite, gum-chewing brunette pushed a button on the phone. "Monelli Enterprises."

She paused, chewing sedately. "Who's calling, please?"

Pausing again, she stopped chewing. "Just one moment, please."

Sitting behind a handsome black desk with stainless steel fixtures, in a large, posh office done in tones of gray, the man they called The Bank held the receiver to his ear. "This is Steven Monelli."

Still in his suit, his tie loosened, his skin oily and his hair wind-blown, John stood in a phone booth, the third he'd tried before finding a phone that worked. He used the disguised voice he had so often rehearsed lately, a drawl that could pass, he hoped, for either black or southern white. "Mr. Monelli, I've kidnapped Megan. If you ever want to see her again, do exactly as you're told."

Glancing at the office door, he asked, "Who the fuck is this?"

In the phone booth John made a face and responded in his drawl. "This is the guy who just kidnapped your daughter, asshole. I prefer not to tell you my name. Now just listen."

He waited, nodded and continued: "Okay. So listen carefully. This is what you need to do. Go to the main bus terminal downtown. And in the men's room, in the stall furthest from the door, you'll find an audio cassette hidden behind the toilet. Play it, do exactly as you're told, and I'll be back in touch. Is that clear?"

After a pause: "Good. By the way, don't call the police, and come alone. You certainly won't want anyone to know what's on that cassette. Bye, asshole."

At his desk Monelli spoke sharply again into the phone. "Wait a goddamn minute!" He listened for a second or two, then put the receiver down feeling stunned and stared into space.

Seconds later he grabbed the phone and punched in a number.

Chapter 44

Deeply vexed, Catherine entered the master bedroom just as the phone on the nightstand began to ring. She moved quickly to pick it up. "Hello?"

On the other end her husband sounded angry. She said, "Steven, I was just going to call you. I can't find Megan."

She sat heavily on the bed.

"I mean I can't find her! We were at the club, and she was with her friends as usual at the pool. I was on the boat sunning and talking with Mary and Florence, and when it was time to leave, I couldn't find her. She was just nowhere. I talked with two of her friends, and they didn't see her leave. I talked with the gate guard, he had just come on duty and the other guy had already gone home."

Catherine paused, nodding.

"Yes, I called him at home. There was no answer. I thought maybe she got a ride home, but there's no sign of her here. Steven, I'm frantic."

Monelli was up and pacing now in front of his big desk. "All right, just calm down. I want you to stay there in case she calls or comes home."

He stopped pacing, closed his eyes and shook his head. "No, don't call the police, whatever you do. I'll be there shortly, and we'll decide then what to do. The main thing is just stay calm."

Slamming down the phone, he pushed a button on his intercom. "Cindy, take the rest of the day off. And have Robert bring the car around. I'll drive it myself. "

Moving around the desk, he opened a drawer, picked up a chrome automatic and made sure it was loaded. Going under his suit coat he stuck it in the waistband of his slacks.

Chapter 45

Robert had the Cadillac waiting at the side entrance of this cinnamon-colored, glass-walled office building in suburban Sterling Heights. Monelli walked briskly out of the building and past Robert without a glance. "Be in my office in an hour."

On I-94 moving at 70 toward downtown, Monelli picked up the car phone and pressed in a number. "Albert, I need to see you and Marco in my office in one hour." He weaved past a woman doing only the limit in the left lane. "I don't know yet. But I want you to call every one of our people and have them ready to go."

Congress, the street in front of the bus terminal downtown, was busy, no curbside parking space available. He drew up near the main entrance, double-parked and hurried inside.

Sitting in the midst of a number of travelers, John peered over the top of a Free Press in time to watch Monelli walk quickly into the station, stop to look around, then head for the Rest Rooms sign. Without a glance in another direction, he quickly pushed through the door marked "Men."

Inside a guy with long greasy black hair was washing his hands meticulously at a sink. There was no one else in sight. Monelli moved for the stalls and found only one door closed, naturally the one to the stall he wanted. Moving to a sink, he washed his hands as the greasy guy dried his with paper toweling, once again taking great care, using several sheets of paper. Finally he left.

Monelli glanced back to the stall with the door closed. He grabbed some toweling and, while using it, leaned low enough to note two feet in battered old gym shoes below the closed stall door. He waited a few more seconds, then walked to the stall door and knocked with force.

"Hey, pal, you gonna be much longer?"

There was no answer. After a few seconds he heard something that sounded like glass bounce on the tile floor. A hypodermic syringe rolled out from under the stall door. He kicked it across the room and moved quickly into the adjacent stall, pulling the automatic and stepping up on the toilet seat. Looking over the top of the wall, he saw a scrawny white guy in his thirties with stringy brown hair nodding on the toilet. His frayed jeans were in place, but his belt was wrapped tightly around his thin upper arm.

Shoving the automatic over the stall wall at the fellow's head, Monelli spoke forcefully, his words bouncing off the tile. "Okay, pal, I want you outta there. Open up!"

The guy looked up slowly, his bloodshot eyes blankly unconcerned.

"Move your junky ass outta there," he barked, "or I'll blow your fuckin' head off. Move!"

The man continued to gaze up with dull, red eyes but finally leaned forward and, with considerable effort, unlatched the door.

Quickly into the stall, Monelli grabbed the fellow's thin arm and yanked him off the john. Jamming the automatic's barrel into the guy's ribs, he again growled, "Move!" and ripped him out of the stall, dragged him across the room and shoved him under a sink.

Back in the stall, he closed the door, then reached behind the toilet. It took a few seconds of groping to locate the audio cassette and pull it away from the adhesive tape on the back of the toilet. Staring at the cassette, he felt his heart pound with rage and fear. Taped to its red label was the sapphire ring he gave Megan for her last birthday. Shoving the cassette and the ring into his coat pocket, he headed out of the men's room.

Monelli was half-running as he moved past several people sitting in the waiting area of the terminal. John stared boldly now with the newspaper in his lap.

At the doubled-parked Cadillac, Monelli grabbed a ticket off the windshield and dropped it in the street. Sliding behind the wheel, he moved the big sedan away quickly. On the I-94 entrance ramp he took the cassette from his pocket, removed the ring and slipped the cassette into a tape player on the dashboard. Looking closely at the ring for a few seconds, he placed it in the breast pocket of his white dress shirt, as John's disguised voice began to come from the tape player.

"Listen to this carefully, because these are the conditions for your daughter's safe return.

"Number 1: You will write out in longhand a detailed confession outlining your own involvement in the importation and sale of illicit narcotics.

"Number 2: You will also name all of your major associates, both in your importation of drugs, including your suppliers in Sicily and elsewhere, and in your distribution chain locally.

"Number 3: You will then sign this confession and bring it along with a kilo of high-grade cocaine to the local office of the Federal Drug Enforcement Administration. There you will ask for and accept the stiffest punishment permitted under the law governing your crimes. And you will supply your full cooperation in the agency's prosecution of your major associates.

"Number 4: Before turning yourself into the authorities, however, you will arrange to appear live this Friday evening with Frank DeFauw on the Channel 5 five o'clock news. On TV you will describe your own role in making narcotics a fucking plague on this city. You will also display your kilo of cocaine and announce that you will immediately turn yourself in to Drug Enforcement agents. All of this you will do precisely as I've outlined here, and you'll make absolutely certain that none of these demands ever reaches the public, or you will never see your daughter alive again.

"Not until you've been appropriately sentenced and until it's clear that you are cooperating fully in the prosecution of your associates will your daughter be released. Now in closing a few words from your daughter."

After a few seconds he heard his daughter's stiff, careful, child's voice. "Daddy, this is Megan. I'm all right. He's treating me well. But please do what he says to get me back, because he's desperate. I love you and Mom. Bye."

The tape continued with only a quiet hiss. His whole body was tense, his hands gripping the steering wheel, his face feeling flushed as the full grim import of the totally unexpected message sank in. Finally, he reached to push the rewind button on the dash. Just then he glimpsed a car cutting in front of him on the freeway, and he slammed on his breaks. The Cadillac swerved badly before he could get it back under control. Shaken, he decelerated and again heard Megan's voice: "...is treating me well. But please do what he says to get me back, because he's desperate. I love you and Mom. Bye."

Chapter 46

The large digital clock over Cindy's desk showed 4:27 when he burst into the deserted reception area. Crossing quickly to the open door of his office, he found Robert, Marco and Albert lounging there on the couch and a chair facing the desk. They promptly straightened up as he entered with hardly glance at them, moved directly to his desk and picked up the phone to check for messages. There were none.

Finally, sitting down, he looked up and stared at them. With these three he was not looking for his brightest counsel. He could have called the two Tonys, senior and junior, for that, his father and son attorneys. He definitely didn't want his smartest people involved in this. At least not yet.

"What's up, boss?" said Marco in that high-pitched voice so weird for a tough-looking fat man. Still the only staff member who can't remember to call him sir, but there was an animal cunning about the guy that made him valuable.

Monelli eyed him squarely and said, "My daughter's been kidnapped."

The younger, well-muscled Albert, who never looked comfortable in the required suit and tie, stirred in the chair. "Megan, sir?"

And Robert sounded stunned. "She's been kidnapped?"

Marco piped, "Boss, sir, you sure she's been kidnapped? You know, kids these days..."

Monelli slammed a palm on the desk. "Marco, fuck your insights on the younger generation. Just shut up and listen."

The guy looked at his large, pudgy hands. "Sorry, sir."

"She was kidnapped this afternoon apparently from someplace in or around the Bayview Yacht Club. She was there with her mother and went off with some friends. Usually, when she does that they stick around the pool, but when her mother was ready to leave, she was gone."

"Any witnesses?" asked Robert.

"I have no idea. This just happened. So that's what I want you two, Marco and Albert to check on. Take your people and canvas that neighborhood around the club, all those residential streets that end at Lake Shore Drive. See if anybody saw anything."

Marco: "The cops know about this?"

"No, and they're not going to. Understood?

Albert nodded. "Yes, sir."

"You know what she looks like." Monelli turned a gold frame on the corner of the desk toward them. Three different candids of Megan shot by the pro he hired last month to come to the house. "Dark hair, slim, very pretty. She's twelve, going on thirteen."

Albert picked up the frame and looked at the photos more closely. "Can we take the pictures along, though? It might help."

Monelli frowned. "Yeah, I guess so."

Marco: "How about what she was wearing?"

"Not sure. I'll check with her mother."

Albert got up from the chair. "So we'll get right on it, sir."

Along with Robert, Marco didn't move. "What about her friends and people at the club? Somebody musta seen something."

"I'll check the club and her friends myself." Monelli paused. Driving back here, he had thought only briefly about just how much he could tell these three. "The thing is, we all gotta be very careful. Discreet. Don't mention any names. I mean no names, not mine, not Megan's. And don't say anything about a kidnapping. One of the kidnapper's demands is that none of this gets into the papers or on TV, or else Megan's dead. So be smart and be careful."

Marco shifted his bulk on the couch. "You heard from this guy?"

"Yeah, he called a while ago."

Marco waited, then finally asked, "So what does he want?"

Ready for this, Monelli answered quickly. "He wants one mil in cash and a kilo of uncut coke."

Marco's small dark eyes widened. He whistled.

"By when? Albert was back in the chair.

"Two days."

Robert asked, "By Friday?"

"Yeah, Friday night."

A shrug from Marco's sloping shoulders. "Well, if you gotta pay, the snow won't be no problem. We got a load comin' tomorrow night."

Monelli nodded. "Put a key aside just in case."

"What kinda asshole wants coke along with a million," asked Albert.

"Some jive-ass junky asshole," said Marco. "You talked to him, boss, he sound like a shine?"

"Maybe. I'm not sure. He sounded like maybe it was a put-on voice."

Albert leaned back in the chair, shaking his head. "This is the lowest kinda scum, messin' with kids."

"Look," said Monelli, "we can't afford to make any assumptions about who it might be. Anybody's a possibility. That's why I want you, Marco, and Robert, to kinda check with the people you know with Carolla and Gigante. See about any kidnap talk, or wanting in on our business or anything that sounds suspicious like that."

Robert nodded, but Marco shook his big head with impatience. "Okay, right, but what about the niggers? This sounds like some nigger thing to me. They're always fuckin' with each other, and them assholes don't give a shit about nothin'. Kids, nobody."

Monelli thought for a moment. "I'll get somebody else to look into that. So anyway, get on it. And keep me posted, like constantly. I'll be home shortly."

Robert and Marco got to their feet. The fat man said, "Okay, boss, hang in there."

Albert was up also, holding Megan's photos in the gold frame. "Don't worry, everybody'll work their ass off on this. We'll find Megan and then hang that fuck by the balls."

"Just remember," said Monelli, and they paused going out the door. "No names and stay quiet about this."

"You got it, boss," said Marco as they left.

Once they were gone, Monelli leaned back in his chair, closed his eyes and breathed deeply. After a few seconds he opened them, gazed at the corner of the desk where the gold frame had been and tried to visualize the pictures of Megan in her three different poses. Leaning forward he covered his face with his hands. After a while he picked up the phone and pushed a speed dial button.

He waited briefly. "Pa, how you doin'?"

He looked at his watch. 4:44. "We're fine. How's Mom?"

He moved a pad of engraved notepaper closer to him and picked up a pen. "Good, good. Ah, listen, Pa, I got a situation here I can't really talk about on the phone. But I need your advice and good counsel."

He drew a box on the note pad. "Well, it's about Megan." Inside the box he put a circle. "Yeah, but, you know, I can't talk about it here. There any chance, you could fly up tonight?"

He outlined a heart inside the circle.

"That would be great."

Monelli looked at his watch again. "Yeah, the one gets here at 9. I'll have Robert there to pick you up."

Around the box, circle and heart he drew another circle. "All right, good. Thanks, Pa. I'll see you then. Yeah, bye."

Putting the receiver down, Monelli gazed at the note pad. But within a few seconds the phone murmured, and he grabbed the receiver again quickly.

"Monelli."

Chapter 47

At a gas station pay phone he once again used his drawl.

"Mr. Monelli, I assume by now you've listened to the tape and understand the demands. Is that true?"

Monelli worked his mouth and then said, "Yeah, it's true. What I don't understand is how you think you can possibly get away with this kind of shit. We'll find you, and you'll wish you'd never been born."

"With your daughter in my custody, Mr. Monelli, your threats seem foolish."

"You even touch my daughter..."

John cut him off. "I'll do a lot more than touch her if you don't do exactly as you're told. I'd suggest you call Channel 5 News and confirm the appearance I just arranged for you with Frank DeFauw on Friday night. They jumped at the chance, and I'll be watching. See you then."

He hung up and walked to the Ford.

"Wait a goddamn minute!" screamed Monelli. He listened for a few moments, then threw the receiver at the phone and knocked it off the desk.

Chapter 48

Still dressed for the boat—white canvas shoes, a short yellow skirt and a matching sleeveless top—Catherine felt slightly dazed as she wandered out of her elaborately decorated master bedroom suite. All these beautiful things, assembled with such thoughtful care, suddenly meant nothing. From the long upstairs hall she entered Megan's darkened bedroom and snapped on the carousel chandelier they had found at FAO Schwarz. An affluent 12-year-old's fantasy, with a canopied four-posted bed, large stuffed animals, posters of rock and movie stars and lots of electronic equipment, CDs and tapes. Moving to a desk holding a large Sony tape player/recorder with two cassette doors, she pushed a button and listened to a few seconds of Dire Straits doing "Money for Nothing." She turned it off and left the room.

Descending a circular staircase to a large front hall, she moved into her cream-carpeted living room, peered out a front window both up and down the street, then left. She walked to her husband's birch-paneled den and went for the phone on his large desk. Picking up the receiver, she dialed 911.

"Yes, I want to report a missing child."

Feeling weak in the knees, she sat at the desk. "My name or her name?"

She looked up to find her husband entering the room, carrying an attache case, just as she said, "My name is..."

Monelli spoke sharply: "Catherine, who are you calling?"

Stopped in mid-sentence, she lowered the receiver and put her hand over it. "Steven, where have you been? I'm calling the police. I couldn't wait any longer."

He moved quickly toward her, his face full of menace. "I told you not to call the police."

"But I couldn't reach you, and I thought..."

Leaning across the desk, he grabbed the receiver from her and rammed it down on the phone. "Just let me do the thinking!"

Shaken by his rage and contempt, she got to her feet feeling weak. "But I finally reached the gate guard at home, and he said he remembers Megan walking out of the club just after noon. And then I talked with some of her friends again, and I got one of them to admit that Megan was at Danny Welland's house for about an hour this afternoon. She left by herself at about one, and nobody's seen her since."

"Where's Danny Welland's house?"

"On Chalet, about two blocks from the club. Steven, I tried to reach you, but first your line was busy and then no answer. I tried calling you in the car, and there was no answer there either." She started to weep, her tears only making her more frightened. "I didn't know what to do. I just know something awful's happened to Meggie."

Monelli moved around his desk, pulled his wife into his arms and held her as she sobbed. He said softly, "Don't worry about Megan. She's all right. I've talked with her."

She leaned back to stare incredulously at her husband. "You talked to her?"

"Well, I heard her voice, and she sounded okay."

"What do you mean you heard her voice? Where is she?"

"I don't know where she is. She's been kidnapped."

Catherine screamed, "Oh, my god! Oh, my god!!"

Monelli grabbed her roughly by the shoulders. "Catherine, hold onto yourself! We don't need your hysterics."

Still crying, she screamed again. "But tell me something! What's happened to her? What's happened to our baby?"

"I told you, she's been kidnapped. They called me this afternoon demanding a ransom, and they let her say a few words."

Regaining some control, she freed herself from his arms and lowered her voice. "What did she say? How did she sound?"

"She said she was okay and that she loved us. She sounded scared but like she was holding up all right."

"But who's *they* and what do they want? What kind of ransom?"

Monelli looked steadily into his wife's glassy, bloodshot eyes. "They want a million dollars cash by Friday night."

Catherine shrieked, "A million! Can you do that? How can you do that? By Friday?"

132

"I'm sure I can. I've already started putting it together. But in the meantime I've got all my people working on this. And I've got a feeling we're gonna turn something up."

"But, Steven, we need to call the police. They're the experts at this kind of thing."

Moving in again, he held his wife by the shoulders and spoke with quiet force. "The police are not our friends. Don't you understand? After all these years? The police won't help us. Besides, the kidnapper told me, if any of this is made public, we'll never see Megan again."

She buried her face in her husband's chest. "Oh, my God. Meggie!"

Chapter 49

In his den two hours later, Monelli, in a black jogging suit, sat at his desk and searched the inscrutable face of Charlie Watts. Dressed casually, white polo shirt and tan slacks, his fit, muscular body filled the chair next to the desk.

"One million dollars by five o'clock Friday afternoon," said Monelli.

Charlie said quietly, "Not a problem, I presume."

"Correct. But obviously I'd rather not. That's why you're here."

"But why me? You've got lots of, shall we say, skilled people."

Monelli smiled faintly. "I told you, I was impressed with you, Charlie. Besides, I have a feeling the key to this thing may be in the black community. As I'm sure you know, there's always some war going on between factions, and it wouldn't be the first time that one or the other may want to blame my people for something. I want you to look into that possibility. Basically, I need your knowledge and contacts."

"And how much are you willing to pay for 'em?"

"How about ten grand for the next two days? Five now and five later."

Charlie didn't hesitate. "How about ten now and ten times that if I find her by five Friday?"

Monelli stared at Charlie. Finally he said, "All right, you got a deal. But remember, keep it quiet. Don't let anyone know you're working for me, or what your assignment is."

"Okay. You get me the cash, I'll get started."

Monelli nodded, rose and moved around the desk. "It'll take me a few minutes to put the money together, so come out here, and I'll get you a photo of Megan."

Charlie walked out of the den with his new client. In the front hall they came upon Catherine in a long white dressing gown as she moved down the staircase. She looked curiously at Charlie, then glanced expectantly at her husband.

"Catherine, this is Charles Watts. He's going to help us with Megan. Charles, my wife Catherine."

Charlie took the hand she offered. "Hello. I'm very sorry about your daughter."

Catherine looked at him with interest. "You're going to help us find Megan?"

"I'm gonna try."

"Charles needs a photo of Megan," said Monelli. "And maybe tell him what she was wearing. I've got some business to take care of for a couple of minutes, so I'll let you handle that. Charles, I'll be right back."

The black man nodded, and Monelli walked back into the den, closing the door behind. Sitting at the desk, he reached for a small carved figure displayed on a wall shelf to his right, along with framed photos of his mother and father. The figure was a rhinoceros dressed in a business suit and carrying an attache case. He twisted the rhino's head counter-clockwise, and the attaché case popped open revealing a small button. When he pushed the button he heard a quiet snap inside the desk that told him the lock had been released. He then reached down and pulled open a large drawer on the right side, revealing a good-sized metal box. When he lifted the lid, the red-labeled cassette sat on top of several rubber-banded bundles of cash. He moved the cassette aside and extracted one of the bundles.

In the front hall Charlie was looking closely at a small photo of Megan. "A very pretty little girl."

Catherine cocked her head at him. "Are you a private detective or something?"

"That's right."

After an awkward pause she asked, "What did my husband tell you about the ransom?"

He tucked the photo into his wallet. "A million by Friday afternoon."

She nodded. "Do you have a card?"

"Yeah, right here." He opened his wallet again, slipped out a card and handed it to her. "I've got a phone in my car, so you can reach me just about anytime."

The door to the den opened, and Monelli emerged carrying a fat white envelope. "Okay, Charles, let's get you started."

Chapter 50

At 9:20 pm, carrying a small, black Sampsonite, Robert led a deeply tanned, white-haired man in a black golf shirt and slacks past a sparse crowd of travelers moving through an exit to the pick-up area at Detroit Metro. At the Cadillac waiting curbside, Robert slipped the bag in the trunk while the older man climbed into the backseat and lit up a large Cuban.

As Robert drove quickly through light airport traffic to I-94, in the backseat Mike Monelli took a long drag and exhaled out a cracked window at the night sky. "So, what else do you know about this thing with my granddaughter?"

"Nothin' much, sir. But that ransom deal's kinda strange. I mean a mill plus a key, pretty weird."

"Tells me it's probably the shines. Fuckin' animals."

"Yeah, maybe so."

"Cause they don't like us takin' care of business."

"Yeah, well, you know the shines."

"Yeah, I know the fuckin' shines."

Chapter 51

The neighborhood looked like it was bombed from the air several years ago—a few abandoned Victorians still standing, the rubble of others piled nearby, but mostly wide-open fields with six-foot-tall weeds flourishing.

On one corner a streetlight illuminated three black teens dancing mock-karate moves on each other, trying to appear as if they were simply hanging out. On the opposite corner, under another streetlamp that also improbably produced light, several older black men were in fact hanging out, sitting on crates and broken chairs, sharing their philosophy of life and passing a bottle in a brown paper bag.

At the edge of this group Charlie was talking to a small, very black man in a wide-brimmed white straw hat. After awhile they bumped fists, and Charlie waved to the others.

Some of them nodded or waved back as he moved to the Nova with the dented roof.

Chapter 52

At the back entrance off the kitchen, Monelli embraced his father. "Pa, thanks so much for coming."

Reeking of his Cuban, old Mike moved on to hug Catherine in her white dressing gown. "Something like this happening, I'm not gonna come?"

Through tears, she said, "Oh, Dad, it's so good to have you here."

He held his daughter-in-law at arms length. "Catherine, I know this is terrible for you, but don't you worry for a second. We'll have her back safe and sound in no time. In the meantime, you look more beautiful every time I see you."

She moved to embrace him again. "Oh, Dad, what are we going to do? I'm so frightened for our baby."

The old man held her at arm's length. "Look, don't worry so much. We been through these things before, especially in the old days. Happened all the time. We'll have Meg back here in no time."

"Oh, god, I hope you're right."

Monelli to Robert standing there with the suitcase: "Bring it right up to Pa's room."

"Yes, sir."

Robert left, and Monelli headed for the den. "Com'on, Pa. I know you must be tired, but maybe we could talk for a while."

Father followed son. "No problem."

"So Pa, how you doing? How's the knee?"

"I'm fine, for a retired old bum. The knee I feel in morning when I get up. Otherwise it's okay."

Catherine followed. "Dad, are you hungry? How about something to eat?"

"No, no thanks." The old man stopped briefly. "I never eat this time of night. Maybe you got a little glass of wine?"

"Of course, you go ahead. I'll bring it right in to you."

In the den Monelli sat behind his desk, his father in an armchair close by. "How's she taking it?"

"Catherine? All right, I guess. A little hysterical. God knows, if she really knew what's going on."

"Meaning what?"

"Well, I told her the ransom's a million bucks."

"Yeah, and a key? Robert filled me in."

"I asked him to." He sighed heavily. "But it's a lot more complicated than that."

Old Mike looked hard at his only surviving son. "Complicated?"

Monelli took the red-labeled cassette from a drawer in the desk. "Yeah, it's all right here. But we gotta wait till she goes upstairs."

Robert stuck his head in the doorway. "Anything else you need, sir?"

Monelli looked up, surprised. "Oh, Robert. Forgot you were here. No, see you in the morning."

"Right. Good night." He nodded at both men and left.

Shaking his head silently, Monelli frowned at his father, waiting for Robert to be out of earshot. Finally he heard the backdoor off the kitchen open and close. "I gotta be more careful around here."

Then the tinkling of glass preceded by a few seconds his wife's entrance with three glasses of red wine on a small silver tray. Monelli used those seconds to slip the cassette into a jogging suit pocket.

"Here we are, Dad. Steven, I brought a little for us too. Seemed like a good idea."

She carried the tray to her father-in-law, who took a glass. Up from his chair, Monelli moved to take the tray from her and place it on the desk. He handed her a glass.

"It's a very good idea, but I want you to take yours upstairs and climb into bed. You must be exhausted, and I have to talk with Pa for awhile."

"But..."

"No, I want you upstairs. I'll be up very shortly."

She glimpsed the old man looking at his son. She knew from the dead-sure look of her husband's dark brown eyes that he would not relent. Clearly her only hope was the intercession of her father-in-law. "Steven, I want to hear what Dad has to say about all this."

When no word came from his father, Monelli took her arm and moved her toward the door. "We'll talk again in the morning."

She looked back at her father-in-law pleadingly. "But, Dad..."

The old man did not turn to her. "Go ahead, Catherine. Steven and I need to talk."

With his hand firmly gripping her arm, Monelli ushered her through the door from the den to the foot of the stairs. "All right, get some rest now. You'll need it."

Her eyes moist again, she spoke softly. "Steven, she's my daughter too."

His eyes turned even harder. "Catherine, "Upstairs!"

He watched as she climbed the staircase. When she neared the top, he walked back into the den and closed the door.

As he crossed the room, his father asked, "She knows nothing about the business?"

Monelli took the cassette from his pocket and moves to the tape deck in a cabinet behind his desk. "Nothing. I've always taken your advice about that."

"And she hasn't heard this tape."

Opening the tape deck door, he slipped in the cassette. "Christ, no."

He pushed the play button, and the guy's drawl came from two large speakers, one on each side of the room:

"Listen to this carefully, because these are the conditions for your daughter's safe return..."

Chapter 53

There were several suggestions from issues of Architectural Digest in the large master bedroom. How much pleasure she had taken in re-decorating this house with almost no concern for budget. How wonderful her life had seemed in those days. How awful it seemed now.

How could she have married someone like Steven and joined her life to a family with a reputation like the Monellis'?

When her own father, a steel plant worker, had died of lung cancer, she had been younger than Megan. Along with her embittered mother, who had worked two jobs, as a waitress and a grocery checker, to support her family of three, Catherine had always blamed the plant's working conditions for his cancer. She could certainly understand how a father and his family might be victimized by society, and maybe that was why she had so readily accepted Steven's defense of his family's reputation.

When she thought about it now, though, the comparison seemed absurd.

Yes, maybe her marriage to Steven had more to do with the fact that her family would never have to worry about money again, with a pleasant little home for her mother and a job for her brother. Yes, Steven had been bright and attractive, but she should have known that a man who had always treated her as a fragile princess or an incompetent girl would inevitably dominate and cheat on her.

She had long suspected he was sleeping with other women, but as with just about everything else in her life as a Monelli, she had managed to avoid seeing, or even thinking about, something so unpleasant. Was she now about to pay for it all with the loss of her only child, truly the light of her life?

The thought was too awful to hold in the mind as she sat on the edge of the king-sized bed and wept.

Chapter 54

In the den Monelli was at the tape deck again, this time pushing the re-wind button. "So obviously you're the only one, Pa, besides me, who's gonna hear this. For everybody else the ransom is a million and a key."

The old man somehow looked older than when he had walked in tonight.

"Yeah. Sure."

"I mean, if a word about this gets out to anybody inside our business, Pa, I'm a dead man."

His father shifted in his chair and blew smoke from the Cuban at the ceiling. "Yeah, but look, the thing to remember is what I said before. There ain't nothin' new about this. In the old days, with the Black Hand, there used to be lots of kidnappings. One bunch would grab a kid belonged to somebody they was tryin' to squeeze and hold 'em till they got what they wanted. Or till they got tired of movin' 'em around from place to place in a flour sack or whatever. I remember one day I was four or five, they brought a kid like that to our house, and my mother took better care of that kid than she did of me that week. Then they let him go. The kids never got hurt."

"Pa, that was the old days. Things have changed."

"Yeah, but you want my guess, you got the same thing here. From what I hear, Gigante and Carolla ain't doin' great business these days, and they want what you got with that pipeline from them Cubans. The chance they would harm that child is next to none. They do, whatta they got? Nothin'. Nothin' but a war from you when we find out who it is. And kidnappin's is always hard to keep quiet. Always somebody knows somethin'."

"So what are you saying? What would you do?"

The old man leans forward in the chair. "Stall 'em off. Tell 'em you can't get that much coke, or DeFauw don't want you on his show this week, anything. Give it some time, and they'll get tired of this

142

game."

Leaning back, Monelli put his hands behind his head. "I don't know. It just makes no sense for Gigante or Carolla to pull something like this."

"Then maybe it's some small timer trying' to get started, tryin' to make his balls. It's the same thing."

"I'll tell you, I'm beginning to think it's somebody black. That makes more sense."

The old man shook his head. "Coloreds don't have the balls to do something like this."

"Some of 'em do. Some of 'em are crazy. And in this city, with the mayor and the cops and the schools and every other goddamn thing just about all black, they think they own the fuckin' place. It's not like other towns where they still know their place. Here you got all these punk kids drivin' around in Mercedes and flashin' all this green, and they want to be runnin' everything. Anyway I hired a black guy tonight, a private dick, very resourceful type guy. At least I'll have somebody lookin' at that possibility."

The old man showed his son a tired frown. "Let me listen to that tape again. Turn it up a little this time."

Chapter 55

At midnight, Floods, a glitzy art deco downtown club, was jammed with businessmen and high rollers, players and posers, most of them black, most paired off with a remarkable collection of attractive and provocatively dressed women of all colors. Some were dancing, breaking seemingly ever more elaborate moves, as if there would be prizes awarded later. Others sat, at the bar, at tables and in booths, some conversing in subdued tones, others laughing and talking loud enough to be heard over the very hot quintet playing on a raised platform in the middle of the room.

In a booth Charlie Watts leaned at a fat man dressed entirely in white, his massive arms around two young women, one blond and one coal black with a shaved head. The fat man was slowly shaking his head.

Chapter 56

Still sitting on the edge of the bed, Catherine used a tissue to dry her eyes. Getting to her feet, she walked out of the bedroom, through the hall past Megan's darkened room and down the staircase, all with the same deliberate pace. On the first floor she crossed the front hall to the den's closed door. But there she was stopped by a strange voice coming from inside. Her ear close to the door, she could hear clearly most of the words in a young man's drawl:

"...you will immediately turn yourself in to Drug Enforcement agents. All of this you will do precisely as I've outlined here, and you'll make absolutely certain none of these demands ever reaches the public, or you will never see your daughter alive again. Not until you've been appropriately sentenced, and until it's clear that you are cooperating fully in the prosecution of your associates, will your daughter be released. Now in closing, a few words from your daughter..."

And now she felt her heart pound even harder.

"Daddy, this is Megan. I'm all right. He's treating me well. But please do what he says to get me back, because he's desperate. I love you and Mom. Bye."

She listened for a few more seconds, but with the sound of buttons being pushed on the tape deck, she opened the door.

A red-labeled cassette in his hand, her husband was turning from the tape deck, surprise and anger covering his dark face. "What are you doing in here? I told you to go to bed."

With a fierce resolve, she stopped in the middle of the room next to the armchair where her father-in-law was blowing smoke at the ceiling. "Well, for some reason I couldn't sleep. And so I come down here, and there's my kidnapped baby on that tape. The one you wouldn't let me hear."

Something told her not to mention the rest of what she'd heard through the door, as he put down the cassette and moved with a kind of menace around the desk. "Look, there's nothing you can do about any of this. And I want you and your hysteria out of here. I'll handle this."

"You'll handle it?" she screamed. "Goddamn it, Steven, she's my daughter! She came from this body. I want to hear all of what's on that tape!"

They were close now, and he ducked his face only inches from hers.

"You're talking nonsense. Now get out of here before you get hurt."

Without giving ground, she turned to her father-in-law. "Before I get hurt! That's some boy you got there, Dad. How can you sit there and say nothing when he threatens me like that? You're as evil as everybody says you are. You're both scum!"

Her husband slapped her hard across the face, then shoved her and followed as she reeled back toward the doorway. "You ever talk to either of us like that again, and I'll kill you. Now get out, and don't come back."

She was stunned for a moment, pain and then numbness spreading across her left eye. He had never struck her before. But now he was close enough to land another blow, and she backed away, glaring at him between her hands, raised in front of her face, with fear and rage.

Turning to leave, she glimpsed his father staring stoically into a corner.

Chapter 57

With the door and both office windows boarded up, there were no lights visible at the old Giordano cheese plant as it sat silent in the summer darkness. The black Ford was parked close to the building.

Inside the office he lounged on the couch with a single light on, a floor lamp glowing over his shoulder as he jotted in the red spiral notebook a list of things to do. They included: "Groceries — for Megan: hot dogs, buns, mustard, bologna, white bread, ketchup, potato chips, root beer." Finally stretching out on the couch, he put the notebook and pen on the floor, reached back to snap off the floor lamp and stared at the dark.

Behind the padlocked bathroom door a Donald Duck nightlight glowed softly in a corner. On the cot Megan curled herself in a tight ball, her eyes wide open.

Chapter 58

Tense with anxiety and impatience, she lay on her daughter's bed waiting for those three electronic digits to line up on Megan's Sony clock radio. The three and two zeros aligned would be her moment of release, her permit to join the battle, to fight back with all the strength and cunning she could muster.

Her husband and his father had come up to bed just before two, Steven to their bedroom and the old man to what they called the guest suite, but which really belonged to her father-in-law, the closet filled with his clothes, his personal belongings on the shelves and in the drawers. Still in her dressing gown on the narrow bed, she had faced away from the door, knowing her husband would soon leave their bedroom to check on her before trying to sleep.

A few minutes later, hearing his step in the hall and the door to this room opening, she had felt her body go rigid with fear, no longer certain of what this man might do. Her breath held tightly, even though he'd surely be more easily reassured by deep, even breathing, she had fought off terrifying images of a knife in his hand and her gown soaked with blood.

The door had finally closed, followed by the sound of his walk back to their room, and she had breathed again.

Now the wait for three, zero, zero. Ever since her banishment, with eyes wide open and tears long since dry, she had thought meticulously about every step, every move she would make. Steven usually had no trouble sleeping and, once in bed, was not likely to rise again until the morning. His father was much more likely to prowl during the night, his sleep disturbed by the aches and pains of age, or by who knew what qualms of conscience or horrific memories. But the guest room was at the opposite end of the hall, and despite constant vigilance she had heard not a solitary sound. With any luck, even if he were awake, she could negotiate the staircase without alerting the old man.

Three, zero, zero. She was up from the bed quickly, her senses keen, to leave the room. Every move—closing the door, turning the handle so there was no click, walking with bare feet in the carpeted, low-lit hallway—no matter how normally inconsequential, she executed with special care.

On the darkened staircase, she reminded herself to move slowly down the outside curve where the steps were wider and, she knew, the small creaks were less frequent. Even so, those tiny noises reverberated in her brain. She could only hope they were much louder there, than in the silence of this big house. She ignored the urge to move faster, to get the descent over sooner.

When she reached the bottom, she turned, half expecting to find Steven or her father-in-law at the railing above, pointing a gun at her. There was no one. She moved quickly toward the soft light coming from the den. It was unlike Steven to leave a light on. Maybe she'd missed something, dozed for a minute while he had returned downstairs. Maybe he was sitting there behind his desk, waiting for her. She moved forward, nonetheless, and peered into the room. It was empty.

Closing the door behind her, she moved to the tape deck in the cabinet behind the desk. Pushing the eject button, she found no cassette in the machine. She tried the large tape container with four drawers on a self nearby and searched them carefully. Having checked every tape, she gazed around the room, then sat at the desk and began trying drawers.

Slowly, carefully, she pulled each one open, examined its contents, then pushed it closed. Finally, she tried the large drawer on the lower right and, as she expected from past experience, could not open it. She tried again more vigorously. Obviously it was locked, but with no keyhole and no apparent way to open it.

Leaning down in the chair to check the desk's underside, she looked for a lever, a button, something that looked like it shouldn't be there. Nothing. Perhaps the sides. No. And finally every square inch of the top, moving everything—a calendar, his penholder, the blotter. Again nothing. Leaning back in the chair, she very slowly surveyed the room. She had prepared herself to be stymied this way, puzzled and frustrated. She had expected it. So now she gave herself a silent exhortation: Stay calm, let your imagination roam, put yourself inside Steven's head, be absolutely determined.

Despite the little speech, nothing in this room suggested itself for further scrutiny. The knife-edge of panic began to press against her.

Then for some reason, on the shelf to her right, perhaps because to her eye it seemed slightly out of place, too close to the edge and too far from the photos of Steven's parents, she found her gaze resting on the carved rhino in the business suit and carrying an attaché case.

Steven had decorated and furnished this room himself, and in fact she had never spent much time in it. Once, a year ago he had been out of town with, she was quite certain, female entertainment, and she had rummaged through this desk, not really sure what to look for and perhaps not really wanting to find it. That lower right hand drawer had been locked then as well.

She had never really taken a good look at the rhino, and, curious now, she reached up to lift it off the shelf. In her hand it was heavier than she expected.

Looking closely at the dark carved wood, she focused on the rhino's head with its large horned snout. Was this how Steven saw himself? A tough, rugged beast in the civilized armor of corporate America? As she stared at the head, she finally noticed a very fine line around its thick neck. Did that mean the head moved? She tried twisting it clockwise. It didn't budge. Then without thinking, as she was about to place it back on the shelf, she twisted it back.

The head moved smoothly and easily, and her eyes widened as the attaché case popped open. Glancing up at the den's closed door, then down at the open case and its small button ready to be pressed, she waited for a few seconds for her husband to barge into the room. When that did not happen, she put a finger on the button and pushed firmly.

A soft thud came from inside the desk. Could this be? Could she trust her hearing? Carefully pressing the button again, this time she heard a snap. One more press of the button and it was the thud again. Her heart beating fast, she reached down and tried the large lower right hand drawer.

It slid out easily. And there, tucked in next to a metal cash box, was the red-labeled cassette she had seen in her husband's hand just hours ago. On the label she read in somebody's handwriting, "Listen Carefully."

Short of breath, she reached in, took the cassette and pushed the drawer closed. Should she check the cashbox? No, she can do that later. She pushed the button, heard the snap and, closing the tiny attaché case, put the rhino back on the shelf.

With the cassette in a pocket in her gown, she left for the trip back to Megan's room.

Upstairs, behind her daughter's closed door, she opened both tape compartments of the Sony player/recorder, placed the red-labeled cassette in one and a new white-labeled cassette in the other. Knowing she will not breathe normally again until the red-labeled tape was back in her husband's desk, she pushed both the play and record buttons with the sound set so low it was barely audible.

"Listen to this carefully, because these are the conditions for your daughter's safe return..."

Chapter 59

At 8:35 Thursday morning Anna was working at the sink as Catherine, with maybe two hours sleep, walked into the kitchen and looked out a window toward the backyard.

"Anna, have Mr. Monelli and his father left yet?"

"*Si, Signora*, a little time ago."

Catherine turned from the window. "Just leave the sink for now. There's a lot of ironing to do in the basement."

"*Si, signora.*"

Not that she really had to worry about Anna. But now that she had finally decided what she needed to do, after hours of nervous, dry-mouthed wrestling with it, she wanted no one anywhere near her when she made the call.

Chapter 60

In the Nova, as he drove up Woodward toward Tex's Unisex Barber Shop on another of the city's failing commercial strips, the phone did its musical flutter.

"Charlie Watts."

He listened for a while and slowed the Nova as the signal light ahead turned amber. "All right. I'll meet you in front of the fountain in a half-hour."

As Charlie brought the car to a stop, he watched a woman on the corner hit an old man in the head with her purse and then kick him in the ankle. "Okay, see you then."

Chapter 61

On this quiet back highway, he'd seen maybe 10 other cars and small trucks over the past two days. And it was empty again as he neared the cheese factory and listened to the news on the Ford's static-laced radio. Again no mention of a missing girl or a kidnapping. He slowed as he approached the turn off, then swung in and stopped in front of the gate. Out of the car he walked up to unlock and push it open. As he turned back to the Ford, he spotted a police car coming from the opposite direction on the road's weathered gray pavement.

"Jesus Christ," he whispered with fear in his throat. Then he quickly told himself to look busy and act like he belonged here. If he didn't even look at the car, and the cop would just pass right on by. But within a few seconds his stomach sank as the car — actually it was a Macomb County Sheriff's cruiser — slowed and turned in to park behind the Ford. The deputy climbed out of the cruiser and walked over.

"Morning." He was tall, middle-aged, with an amiable face, but he wasn't smiling.

His stomach churning, John tried to look and sound friendly. "Hi, how you doin'?"

"Okay. This your property?"

"Yeah, it is. Well, it's my mother's really."

The cop tipped his hat back a bit and cocked his head. "I haven't seen you out here before. Haven't seen anybody out here. And I been coverin' this area almost ten years."

"Yeah, well, we haven't done anything with it for a long time. Maybe twelve or fourteen years."

The deputy nodded. "What is it back there? Can't really tell from the road."

John turned to look at the building, hardly visible through the brush and trees. "Just a big old empty building. At one time it was a cheese factory. Back when my father used to run it. But he died, and we just never did anything with it."

"A cheese factory. You starting it up again?" The guy sounded interested, as if he liked the idea.

"No, I'm a teacher. I've been coming out here lately to clean it up a little. Thinking maybe we could sell it or something."

The deputy smiled for the first time. "Yeah, well, it would make a great hide-out for somebody up to no good. You know, hidden away back there."

John laughed nervously. "Yeah, I guess so. Never thought of that."

The deputy tugged his hat down and turned back to the cruiser. "Well, there's a cop for you. Always suspicious. Anyway, have a good day. Maybe I'll see you around."

"Yeah, you too. Thanks." He watched as the deputy backed the cruiser on the shoulder and drove off.

Feeling damp all over, he got into the Ford and rolled through the open gate.

Chapter 62

On Belle Isle in the middle of the Detroit River, the large, discolored white marble fountain flowed erratically, some parts of it working fine, others not at all, while a few small children, watched by their mothers, waded in dirty, ankle-deep water. On one park bench a man was on his back with a newspaper over his head, and on another a pair of female lovers were necking. On a third sat Charlie. When he saw the woman with a purse on a strap over her shoulder striding briskly toward him, he got to his feet.

She offered no greeting. "Have you been followed today?"

"I made sure I wasn't."

As they both sat on the bench, she asked, "Have I? I mean, is anyone watching us?"

Charlie looked around casually. "Not that I can tell."

"What about that man under the paper?"

"He was here before I got here. What's this all about?"

The woman dug in her purse. "The ransom demands are not what my husband told you. I want you to know what they are, so you can have the best possible chance to find my daughter. That's all I care about. I want her home safe with me."

Charlie looked into her purse as she groped in it. "So what are the real demands?"

After another moment of searching, she found the white-labeled cassette, palmed it and placed her hand on the bench between them. "It's all on this cassette. It's a copy of the one the kidnapper gave my husband."

Charlie put his hand over hers, feeling it tremble before she moved it away. He slipped the cassette into the pocket of his slacks. "What else can you tell me?"

"Nothing." Catherine got up. "I don't know why I trust you. I guess because there's no one else I can turn to."

With Charlie also on his feet now, she gazed at him intensely with

156

moist blue eyes. "Please find my daughter."

"I'll do what I can." He looked more closely at the area around one of those eyes. There was a lot of make up he had not noticed last night. "Are you all right?"

She stared at him for a second. "Yes, why?"

"Looks like maybe somebody hit you."

"He did, but it was worth it. I got that tape."

He nodded and watched as she turned and walked away. His gaze followed her until she got into the gray BMW and drove off. Then he did a slow, careful sweep of the area as he moved back to the Nova.

Chapter 63

In the bathroom that was her jail she sat on the cot and listened as a car door slammed. She heard footsteps leading to the office door, the sounds of the door being unlocked and opened, then closed and locked again from the inside. She listened as a paper bag was placed somewhere, then more footsteps in the office to the bathroom door, and the door being unlocked and opened. Still sitting on the cot, she glared at him standing in the doorway.

"Hi," he said. "Com'on out. I got you the things you said you like to eat."

He stepped back to encourage her to leave her cell, but she didn't move.

"Hey, if it isn't the Jerk-off Creep."

He shook his head glumly. "So instead of reading one of the books I gave you, you spend your time coming up with stupid names."

And then he noticed those half-dozen books she had kicked all over the floor. And the one she had guessed was his personal favorite, *The Catcher in the Rye*, with all the dumb notes written in the margins, was more or less destroyed, pages ripped off the spine and some of them now in small pieces.

He looked very unhappy. "Now why would you do something like that?"

"Oh, and why would you just barge in on me like this?" She finally got up and walked out past him. "I could have been on the john with my pants down or something."

He put the books back in a stack and started picking up the ripped apart pages. Finally, he gave it up. "Well, I'm sorry, but I guess you're gonna have to put up with things like that."

"Yeah, well, at least you could knock. That's what any *normal* person would do."

"Okay, from now on I'll knock."

She flounced down on the couch. "Maybe you *want* to catch me

158

with my pants down."

"Don't be ridiculous." He looked at her closely, as if wondering if she was serious.

"Yeah, well, some guys like to do things to little girls. Is that what you like? Is that why you've got me here?"

He looked very annoyed. "No, it's not why I've got you here. But anyway, you're hardly such an innocent little girl. I've seen you drinking and smoking and necking."

She tossed her head back. "God, you're disgusting! Spying on people is like totally disgusting."

"There are a lot more disgusting things. By the way, at the store I was thinking, have you started getting your period yet?"

She stared at him, then ducked her head and stared again, like she couldn't believe he would ask such a thing. It made her want to double down. "Of course. Why? You wanna knock me up?"

He said nothing for a second, and she knew this was making him very uncomfortable. "Yeah, maybe that's your thing, knocking up little 12-year-olds."

"Would you stop talking like that. I only asked because I thought maybe I should get you something to take care of that, in case, like Tampax or something."

"Hey, you don't have to worry. I had the curse last week. In fact if you do want to knock me up, this would be a good time."

"I told you to stop talking like that." Now he seemed embarrassed and angry. He moved to the large grocery bag sitting on the desk. "Are you hungry? I got you some of the things you said you like."

She watched him remove items from the bag and place them on the desk. "Like what?"

"Like hot dogs, bologna and white bread and ketchup, potato chips, root beer."

She made a face. "I hate that stuff! I'd rather eat dog food."

"Then why did you lie to me and say you liked it?"

"Oh, it's Mr. Morality! The question is, why did you kidnap me? And why am I suppose to like it enough to eat your stupid food while you're trying to rip off my parents? Or whatever you're trying to do."

He stopped and stared at her. "Look, I know it's not your fault that your father's destroying the lives of thousands of young people in this city. But this is just the way it is right now."

She stared back boldly for a few seconds then looked away. "You are sick," she said slowly. "You are really sick."

Chapter 64

Susan slouched low in one of the chairs in front of the scarred metal desk. Charlie's demeanor behind it was similar, as if both were trying to slide under a thick gray cloud of frustration filling his office. She found herself staring at the framed photo behind his head, the one showing him and his partner with all the dope, the case that ended up causing him so much grief. Why would he have that picture up, a constant reminder of something good in his life that went so bad? She had never really thought about that before. A conversation for another day.

"Baby, I'm sorry, I've really got to get back to the office. I had only paperwork for the first couple hours, so I told them I had car trouble. But in 20 minutes I'm meeting with two families that desperately need help."

He straightened up and leaned forward toward the tape recorder on his desk. "I know, and you're great for coming by. But let's listen one more time."

Susan sat up in her chair as well. "Charles, you've been playing that tape for the past hour. Same thing, over and over. You're not gonna find the guy just sitting here playing that tape."

"Well, baby, I've hit a goddamn dead end. For once, I got a major league case, and it's like the fucking needle in the fucking haystack."

"I wish I could help you," she said. "I wish I could think of what it is about this guy's voice or what he's saying that sounds familiar. But I just keep drawing blanks."

"You think he's black?" he asked for about the third time.

She shook her head. "I told you, I don't know. It sounds more to me like some white guy trying to make his voice sound black."

"Yeah, you said."

Susan leaned forward and pointed to the recorder. "Okay, play it one more time. Just the last part of it. From where he talks about going on the TV news with DeFauw. Something in that part rings a

161

bell."

He pushed the rewind button, watched the counter, stopped the machine and pushed play. They listened again to the tape.

"...live this Friday evening with Frank DeFauw on the Channel 5 News at 5. On TV you will describe your own role in making narcotics a fucking plague on this city. You will also display your kilo of cocaine and announce that you will immediately turn yourself in to Drug Enforcement agents. All of this..."

She waved in disgust, giving up, and he turned off the recorder. "There is just something about that voice that sounds familiar. Or there's something else in that part, but I'll be damned if I can think what it is."

"Well, if it comes to you, call me."

"Obviously."

"Meantime, maybe I should market this little tape."

"What do you mean market?"

"I mean if this lands in the wrong hands, Monelli's a dead man. No ifs, ands or buts."

"Yeah, so?"

"So some of his people would probably pay big time to know what's on this cassette. Or maybe I can get Monelli himself to shell out more, if I tell him I got the tape or let him know I know what's on it."

"Charlie, you do either one, and *you're* the dead man."

He cocked his head. "Maybe."

"Guaranteed. Besides, then what happens to the little girl?"

"Probably nothin' good."

"Right, so he's paying you good money to look for his daughter. And big money to find her. So do it and cash in."

He nodded first, then shook his head. "Easier said than done, as someone once said."

She said, "Really, I'm torn. Of course I want you to find the girl, but I'd also like to see her father burn."

"Yeah, well, even if he does and goes down with his whole crew, it won't make one damn bit of difference. There's guys already lined up to take their place."

She got to her feet. "I know, I know. There's no hope. There's nothing we can do. It's too big. The city's a lost cause, and so are it's kids. But I'll tell you one thing. Awful as this is for the little girl, this

162

guy's pretty damn inventive. I mean, the real question is, what kind of person would even dream up something like this, let alone actually try to do it."

"Someone like you."

"Someone like me? That's crazy, Charlie. I would never do anything like this. And I could never dream it up."

"No, I mean, someone like you, who really, deeply cares about all this, the narcotics shit, what it's doing to kids. How it's destroying the city. You think about it, the guy's riskin' his life, and he's gettin' nothing for his trouble but grief. Got to be somebody who's desperate about it. And cares big time."

She looked at the big, heavily muscled black man rising from behind his desk. "That's good, Charlie. Really good."

"Yeah, that and a buck twenty buys me a Starbucks."

A glance at her watch. "I gotta go. I'll call if I think of anything. In the meantime, drive carefully. These mob scumbags are vicious."

Chapter 65

"Charlie, it's me." A pay phone receiver in hand, she stood at the edge of a small park with burned-out grass and a broken swing set. Her Rabbit, still running, was at the curb a few feet away. "Something you said got me thinking."

Holding the phone to his ear with his shoulder, he turned into the drive-up lane of a Burger King and rolled down his window. "Something I said?"

"Yeah, remember you were saying it's got to be someone who cares and who's desperate? Well, that started me thinking about Lissa Martin's funeral. You know, the little girl who was killed by the kid at the dope house a couple months ago."

"Yeah, I remember."

A tinny voice came from the Burger King order box: "May I take your order please?"

He said, "Two Whoppers with cheese and a large diet coke."

Susan rolled her eyes. "Charlie, why do you bother ordering a *diet* Coke with two Whoppers?"

"Because that's what I want. So are you saying you remembered something about what sounded familiar?"

"Yeah, remember the guy I mentioned I met at that funeral?"

"No."

"You know, when I told you there were only three white people there, that news guy DeFauw, this strange blond and this young guy I talked to briefly who turned out to be Lissa's teacher?"

"Yeah, I guess so. What about him?"

"Well, remember, I thought he really seemed to care about what was happening to his kids?"

"Baby, I don't really know if I remember. Cut to the chase."

"Well, anyway, the kidnapper on the tape used the same line this guy did at the funeral. He said something about narcotics being 'a fucking plague on this city.' That was the line I remembered: '...a

164

fucking plague on this city.'"

Charlie shook his head as he moved up to the second window. "That's it? That one line? That's pretty flimsy, baby."

"Well, I don't know, there's that and now I'm more and more thinkin' it's his voice, even though he was changing it. Anyway, what else do you have to go on? It wouldn't take much to go over to the Lincoln Middle School and find out who Lissa's home-room teacher was."

"I suppose."

"Hope it helps."

Chapter 66

With only a few summer school classes in session, the principal's office at Lincoln was quiet this Thursday afternoon. Sara Whitaker was alone in the outer office typing as Charlie walked in and stopped in front of the counter.

She looked up from the typewriter. "Can I help you?"

Charlie gave her a warm smile. "Oh, I hope so. I'm Charles Watts, and I've been asked by a family in the neighborhood to see if I can find a young man they would very much like to meet again."

"What's his name?"

"That's just it. They don't know his name. All they know is that he taught the eighth grade here this past year. And that he was the home-room teacher for that little girl who was shot doing her paper route a couple months ago."

The secretary got up from her chair and moved to the counter, obviously more cautious now. "So what are you, a private detective or something?"

"Yeah." He offered another smile, "A private investigator. See, a while back, this young man did a small kindness for this family. And recently they hit the lottery. Two point four million dollars."

"Really?" She smiled for the first time.

"Yeah, and now the family would like to repay that kindness with a little something for the young man. But they don't know who he is."

Sara smiled again, reassured. "Well, that's really nice. You know, some of those people who win the lottery seem real selfish and awful."

"Right, I know what you mean. So I was hoping you could help me with the young man's name and perhaps his address."

She reached back to a desk behind her, picked up a printed newsletter and placed it on the counter in front of him. "I can do even better than that. Here's a picture of him. His name is John

Giordano. He was laid off this last term, but I'm sure we still have an address for him."

Moving to a filing cabinet, she opened a drawer and began to search. "When you see him, please tell him Sara Whitaker says hello."

"I sure will." He picked up the newsletter and studied a head-and-shoulders photo of a young fellow with dark features. The heading was: John Giordano: Teacher of the Year. "Any chance I could keep this?"

"Oh, sure. Here it is, 1244 Mt. Morris, apartment 1B." She wrote the name and address on a slip of paper, moved back to the counter and gave it to him. "That's not very far from here. Of course, he may have moved since then."

"Well, thanks very much. You've been a big help."

He started for the door, but Sara spoke again, almost as if she were talking to herself. "The only place I ever heard about him going to or hanging out in was this bar — and this was really strange — this neighborhood, like, topless place. I mean he didn't seem like the kind of guy who would get off on some topless joint."

"Yeah, well, you never know about guys. You remember the name?"

"Of the bar? Somebody told me once they saw him there. The Paradise or something like that, I think. It's in the neighborhood, anyway."

He headed out the door. "Well, thanks again."

Chapter 67

Gazing back at the sidewalk above him, he knocked on the outside door of the basement apartment. Then he knocked again, louder, this time staring at the Free Press rolled in a rubber band and waiting on the doorstep. Still no response. Moving to a window a few feet away, he leaned close to the glass and peered in at a point where the curtains didn't quite meet. The place was dark, and it looked like no one was home.

Glancing up at the sidewalk again, he moved back to the door and drew out of his pants pocket a small metal tool. After inserting its two thin prongs into the keyhole of the door lock and maneuvering them for several seconds, he opened the door.

Heading cautiously into the small, dingy apartment, he moved his gaze from side to side, his eyes adjusting to the low light. This one room combined kitchen, living room and bedroom. Walking to the open bathroom door, he glanced in and on the sink noted a toothbrush in a plastic cup. He felt the bristles and found them dry.

He spent several minutes looking through a big old bookcase next to sad-looking armchair. Many of the titles sounded familiar, but he himself wasn't much of a reader, and he didn't even know what the hell he was looking for. Rifling through a number of books, what did he think he would find? A scrap of paper with an address that would lead him right to the girl?

He moved back to the kitchenette and there spotted a magazine stuffed in a wastebasket. He pulled it out and found the cover had been ripped off. The bottom of a page said it was the May issue of Metropolitan. Thumbing through, he found several pages, perhaps a whole article, had been cut out. Tossing the magazine back in the wastebasket, he moved for the door.

Outside, after he had relocked it, he thought again about the magazine and decided he should have checked the table of contents to find out what had been cut out. Instead, he had been an impatient fool and moved too fast. On this job, of all jobs, he needed to be smarter, more efficient.

Still, rather than risk entering again, he knew he could check the May issue at the library.

Chapter 68

The mid-afternoon ne'er-do-wells were scattered thinly in the Oldies Paradise. The Pointer Sisters sang Neutron Dance as Doris did her buxom best to keep up with the high-energy number, her big tits bouncing all over the place. Half-way back in the bar Charlie sat at a table having a drink with a dancer named Sally.

"So maybe I know him," she said. "And maybe he comes in here a lot. So what?"

He tried his quiet, mysterious grin, the one that almost always worked on women. "I told you, I'm looking for him, and he's going to be real pleased with the information I have."

She cocked her head one way and then the other. "Are you a cop? I bet you're a cop. I can smell a cop a mile away."

"You've got a great nose, Sally. I used to be a cop. Now I'm a private investigator."

"A private dick." The woman nodded with a self-satisfied smirk. "Well, I hate cops, and private dicks are right up there with 'em on my shit list."

"Honey, let's not let our personal prejudices get in the way here. I've been hired by a family for whom John once did a small kindness. Now it so happened that fortune smiled on the family recently, and they hit the Lotto for two point four million dollars."

"And now they want to repay Johnny G for his small kindness."

"How'd you guess?"

"The whole thing sounds like a crock to me." She downed the last of her drink.

"So I see you've been to charm school, Sally."

"Yeah, right here in the bar, pal. Amazing what you can learn in a place like this."

While they continued to fence, petite Tina walked through the front door in a sleeveless t-shirt and shorts and moved to a spot at the bar close enough to Sally and Charlie to hear much of their conversation.

"So that's what you call him, Johnny G?" Charlie tried his grin again.

"Yeah, he's kind of a mascot for the girls in here."

"So tell me this. Did you ever hear him talk about a guy named Steven Monelli?"

She smirked again. "You tellin' me Monelli was the family he did the kindness for?"

"Well..." said Charlie, and then Tina suddenly moved forward to interrupt.

"Sally, where's Al? I need to talk to Al."

Sally seemed surprised. "Tina, what are you doing here? Al's in the back, but he ain't gonna talk to you."

Tina looked terrible—eyes watery, hair stringy, complexion a sickly pale. Her clothes were soiled and wrinkled, and there was a desperate quality to her voice and movements. Wheeling away from Sally, she headed for the back as Al, the bar manager, a huge, muscular man with extremely hairy arms, emerged from an office.

Tina rushed at him. "Al, you gotta give me my job back!"

Al held her at arm's length. "I told you not to come back here, Tina."

"But I'm popular here. Ask these guys. They all want to see me dance." Everyone in the bar had turned to watch this scene. Even Doris on stage had slowed down.

"Nobody wants to see you do nothin', Tina. Now get outta here."

"Please, Al, you gotta give me another chance!"

"I don't gotta do nothin'." Al simply picked Tina up and tucked her under one big arm. She kicked and screamed to no avail as he carried her out the front door, where he put her down and shoved her away.

"Stay outta here, Tina. Next time I'll call the cops, and we'll talk about those tracks on your arms."

Al closed the door and walked back through the bar, smiling and trading gibes with some of the regulars. Up on stage Doris started a much less frantic performance to Stevie Wonder's "I Just Called to Say I Love You." And Sally and Charlie were talking again.

"She's a mess. We all told her she couldn't handle that stuff."

"Smack?"

"Yeah."

Charlie tried again. "So did Johnny G ever mention Monelli?"

"Look, I ain't tellin' you nothin' about Johnny G. So go do your dog-shit job someplace else."

"But Sal, I thought we were just about to fall in love here."

"Fuck off, pal."

Charlie got to his feet with one last grin. "Have a nice day."

As he left, Doris called from the stage. "Hey, baby, where you goin'?"

He waved and said, "I'll be back."

Something told him he needed to talk with Tina. And at the back of the parking lot next to the bar, he found her trying, without much success, to kick in the fender of a black Eldorado. The Nova was parked nearby, and as he walked to it, he stopped to watch.

"Hey, Tina, whose car?"

She paused her attack. "Big Al's. What's it to you?"

Charlie grinned in a disinterested way. "He finds you out here, there's gonna be little pieces of Tina scattered all over the lot."

"Hey, aren't you the one wanted to know about Johnny G?"

"Yeah, you know him?"

"Sure, I know him." Tina moved unsteadily toward Charlie. "You were askin' about him and Monelli."

"Yeah."

"How much is it worth to you?" She was standing close to him now. Her eyes were glassy and red-veined.

"Depends on what you got. How much will it take to get you fixed?"

She stood there, as if calculating. "Maybe two hundred?"

Charlie took a wad from his pocket, peeled off two 50s and gave them to her. "Here's half. You got anything at all, I'll give you the rest."

Tina tucked the bills in her shorts and said quickly, "He's very interested in Monelli."

"Meaning what?"

"Meaning I gave him that magazine — what's it called? Metro-City, or somethin' — with Monelli's picture on the cover. And he said Monelli was his favorite topic."

"How long ago was this?"

"I don't know, maybe a couple weeks. After that, he said he read it, and we talked some."

"What'd he say?"

"He said Monelli was killin' a whole generation of kids, and somebody should do him. I said he was crazy."

Chapter 69

John placed two McDonald's bags and two Cokes on the desk and moved back to the outside door to snap the padlock in place. Then he walked across the office to the bathroom door, opened its lock and knocked.

"If you're hungry, come on out and get yourself a cheeseburger and fries."

Moving back to the bags, he reached into one for a Big Mac and sat at the desk. After a few seconds the door to the bathroom opened, and Megan walked into the office.

"How you doin'?" He tried for natural and friendly. "You gotta be hungry. You've hardly eaten since you've been here."

The girl moved to the bags and took a cheeseburger, fries and a Coke. "I don't know how you can eat this shit."

"Hey, it's un-American not to like McDonald's."

"Where's that ketchup you bought?"

John gestured toward an old, half-sized refrigerator in the corner. "In there."

She put the food back in the bag, then carried it and the Coke to the small fridge. There she removed the ketchup bottle and headed back to the bathroom.

"The only way I can eat this stuff," she said, holding the bottle upside down over the bag. "And if I don't have to look at you," she added, closing the door behind her

"Suit yourself."

Chapter 70

In the gloom enveloping his personal suite at the Eastbrook Manor Motel, Monelli sat with his father, Robert and Marco, listening to Albert report, glancing at scribbles on a 3 by 5 card. The 40-inch projection Mitsubishi offered pictures but no sound from the Thursday Night Movie, "Kramer vs. Kramer."

"So we got a neighbor seen her get inside that red Mercury, a Topaz, he thought. But after that she absolutely fuckin' disappears."

"And the plates was stolen?" asked the older Monelli.

"Reported stolen the same day," said Albert. "Whoever did it planned pretty careful."

Monelli slouched in an armchair, placed his hands together in front of his face as if he were praying. "What I don't understand is if he didn't just grab her or anything, why she just got in the car. Why would she do that? She knows better than that."

"Kids don't always do what they should," said Marco.

Robert added, "Maybe he pulled a gun on her."

Monelli shook his head. "Even if he did, she would know better. We talked about it. She knew her best bet was always to run, even if somebody had a gun in a situation like that."

Old Cigar Mike blew a cloud of smoke. "Look, it don't matter how they got her in the car. The fact is they did. So, Marco, what about Gigante's people? You didn't hear nothin' from them?"

"Not a fuckin' thing. Not one fuckin' word like they was involved."

Robert nodded. "Same for my guy with Carolla's crew."

Marco waved at the TV screen where Frank DeFauw was doing a pitch without sound. "There's that fuckin' DeFauw says you're gonna be on his show tomorrow night."

Monelli picked up the remote and raised the volume.

"Steven Monelli. Is he the model citizen some say he is? Or is he one of Metro Detroit's top crime lords? Watch our exclusive, no-holds-barred live conversation and decide for yourself. That's Steven Monelli 'Up-Front' tomorrow on the Channel 5 News at five."

He zapped the sound.

"'Top crime lord,'" growled Marco. "Fucker should be stuffed in a freezer."

"I thought this guy don't want publicity," said Albert.

"He doesn't," said Monelli quickly. "I'm supposed to be on that show to say a certain word, like a code word, that says everything's set and he can pick up the cash."

"And this." Marco reached into a jacket pocket to pull out a good-sized zip lock bag filled with white powder.

"Right," said Monelli. "You better give that to me. You're sure it's good?"

Marco handed over the bag. "Best we got."

"Okay. But make sure you keep digging. Everybody we got should be on this. We got less than 24 hours now."

Robert and Albert were on their feet saying, "Yes, sir," and "We'll do it."

Marco also stood. "What about the shine? You hear anything from him?"

"Not yet."

"I still think it's niggers," said Marco. "Even if that neighbor says he saw a white guy in the car. Some of them shines look whiter than you or me."

"Keep pluggin', fellas," said Monelli. "Right up to the deadline."

"You got it," said Marco.

Albert waved. "See you later, Mr. Monelli."

The old man nodded grimly as the three left the suite.

Chapter 71

The two Monellis sat without speaking for long time, staring into space without a glance at the big TV where Dustin Hoffman looked very unhappy with Meryl Streep.

The old man finally broke the silence. "You still ain't talkin' to the two Tonys?"

His son shook his head. "No, Pa, they're gonna ask too damn many questions. These three are soldiers. They'll do what I tell them but not ask why this, why that."

"So you decided you gonna go through with this?"

The son grimaced. "Nothing turns up in the next 24 hours, well, actually, less now, what else am I gonna do?"

"I told you, wait it out. Call their bluff. They ain't gonna do nothin' to the little girl. If they *do,* they got nothin' on you any more. And they got nothin' but the worst trouble they ever seen, and they know that better'n anybody."

"Pa, that's a chance I cannot take. I can't risk them hurting Megan."

His father frowned his disapproval. "Goddamn coke. I told you I didn't like it when you started with that shit. You deal with our people in the old country, like with the heroin, that's one thing. But you try to do business with them Colombians or whatever they are, and you got nothing but trouble."

"They're Cubans, Pa, anti-Castro Cubans, and they haven't caused me one ounce of trouble since we started. They got the whole U.S. government behind them. You know, these government people don't give a shit about drugs, as long as the money goes to fight Castro. It's the safest thing we ever done. And I remember you saying the same thing back when you thought it was a good idea."

"I said, you don't need this. You got enough goin' without it."

"Look, Pa, there's just too much money in this stuff to pass it up. You can't just turn your back when there's so much changing hands, and it's so damn easy. You pass on it, and pretty soon these black assholes are gonna be taking over everything. You taught me that."

The old man shrugged and shook his head.

"No," said his son, "once I made that connection in Miami, I had to move on it. One hundred Ks every 30 days. Like clockwork. And we don't even have to get it up here. They bring it, in these semi-truck trailers with a false bottom and the trailer's full of used office furniture or some damn thing. Then they unload the stuff, put it in a bin in that storage company right nearby in Sterling Heights and call and tell us where we can find the key as soon as we transfer a mill and half to that off-shore bank they use. Our people supply three different outfits around the city, and we put a cool two and a half mill in our own Cayman bank every four weeks. No way they connect me with any of it, and, like I said, the money's going to fight that commie Castro. It's like winning the lottery every month."

The old man stared hard at his son. "The lottery don't take your little girl away from you."

His son moved awkwardly in his armchair. "And neither do the Cubans. It's absurd to think they had any part in it."

"Well, it's your call. But I see these people, whoever they are, like them scum terrorists that blew up the airport in Rome. You give 'em what they want, it's just askin' for more trouble."

"Pa, that's ridiculous..."

"Besides, you rat on your people like that, and there ain't gonna be nobody safe in your family."

Monelli sat up in his chair and leaned forward. "Look, Pa, I'm not gonna lay it out like I just did for you. I'll give 'em some low level guys, and once I know Megan is safe, we'll spread the word about what happened, and everybody'll understand."

"They ain't gonna understand nothin'. The only thing they gonna understand is you ratted."

Monelli said nothing, wondering why he'd ever asked this senile old man for counsel. On the silent TV the cute little boy got a big hug from Dustin Hoffman.

Chapter 72

The kitchen felt like an oven, the lacy curtains limp and unmoving at the wide-opened window, the darkness outside thick with humidity. In an old Pistons t-shirt and shorts Susan poured herself a glass of diet Coca Cola over ice. A storm had been forecast for later in the night, and the drought that had lasted for three weeks was finally about to end. As she opened the fridge to replace the large plastic bottle, she called to the living room.

"You sure you don't want some Coke?"

"Christ, all that caffeine?"

"How about a beer then?"

"Okay, thanks."

She grabbed a can of Bud and walked back to the living room. There were two windows wide open, but it still felt just like the kitchen. Clad only in jeans, Charlie slouched at one end of the sofa and stared blankly at the silent TV with a picture on screen of the Supreme Court nominee, Ruth Bader Ginsburg. It was the Channel 5 news, but with Frank not on tonight and some other guy doing it, they had watched the first 5 minutes, then hit the mute. She placed the beer next to the tape recorder on the coffee table and sat with him on the sofa.

Charlie snapped open the beer. "How can you drink that stuff and still sleep?"

Susan sipped the Coke. "Good conscience."

"I guess it's good for something."

"That and good sex."

She put her glass down on the coffee table and reached over to unbutton the top of his jeans. "Hey, Charles, how about a little fun?"

Gently but firmly he removed her hand and redid his jeans. "Jesus Christ, here I've got the biggest case of my so-called career, and you're want to fool around."

"What's wrong with that?"

179

"It's distracting."

"You need a little distracting."

With a slug of his beer, he gazed at Susan. With her glasses off, her hair in tight moist ringlets, her nipples showing through her thin t-shirt and her legs long, trim and shapely with her feet up on the coffee table, she looked so fetching he wondered about his own lack of desire.

She traced the muscle in his arm. "You sure you don't want to play?"

Leaning back on the sofa, he stretched. "I think we need some sleep. Even if I get up before dawn, I'll still only have about 12 hours."

"Yeah, but I don't know why you want to find this guy, anyway. I don't want anything to happen to the little girl, but I sure would like to see Monelli go down."

"I know. We've been over this a million times, and I keep telling you it won't matter if he *does* go down. There's always somebody else gonna take his place."

Getting up, she started to walk out, then stopped and turned, fixing Charlie with a riveting glare. "I don't care. I think of what happened to Lissa Martin and what's happening to so many kids in this city. And when you have a chance to do something, anything, to stop it even for just a little while, you've got to do it."

"You're such a good-doer."

"That has nothing to do with it! Think about your own sons. In a year or two they'll both be old enough to be out on some street corner selling that shit! How would you feel about that, Charlie? Think about it."

She turned to leave but glimpsed something on the TV that stopped her. "Charlie, turn up the sound."

He had his head back on the couch, his eyes closed. "What?"

"Turn the sound up on the tube!"

He opened his eyes and grabbed for the remote next to him on the couch. On the screen, a man in his mid-20s with heavy stubble covering his face was speaking in what looked to be a cemetery. Charlie hit the volume up button.

"...mostly black and Hispanic kids. They're worthless, they scare us and we'd be better off without 'em. That's what too many people think, so the powers-that-be simply don't give a..."

180

Susan moved up close to the TV. "That's him! I was right!"

"That's who?"

"That's the young guy I met at the funeral, Giordano. And that's the voice. Listen!"

On the TV the guy continued: "...fund education enough to help them get out of this hellhole they're in. Look, maybe if they really went after the big guys, the importers, the guys who drop tons of this poison on our neighborhoods, maybe if they really started slamming those guys, it could have an impact. But it's a huge business, and the biggest players are just so well protected. And connected."

On screen Mary Scott appeared and said solemnly: "Former public school teacher John Giordano tonight in his own words. It's part of an upcoming Channel 5 news documentary called "Kids and Crack," and hosted by my colleague Frank DeFauw. Watch for it soon on Channel 5. Don?"

"Thanks, Mary. Well, it looks like we're finally going to get some relief from this drought we've been going through..."

Charlie muted the TV again and stared at Susan. Finally he said, "I think you're right."

"Of course I'm right. That's the voice, and he's your guy. I mean you already pretty much knew it, but now it's for sure."

He was frowning and silent.

"What's the matter?"

"Nothin', except there's so little time left, and we still don't have the slightest idea where this guy's hiding and where he's got the girl. And also, what if Monelli was watching tonight and recognized the voice?"

She thought about that for a second. "Well, if he did, you'll be hearing from him very soon."

Chapter 73

In the late evening darkness a crack of thunder bounced off the cement block walls of the cheese factory and announced a heavy summer downpour. As usual there were no interior lights visible from outside the plant.

Inside the office he slept fitfully on the couch in his underwear. And behind the padlocked door in the girl's hot little bathroom cell, the Donald Duck light glowed as she lay curled on the cot.

Rain began drumming on the building, and when another thunderclap split the night's silence, she moved with a start. With her eyes wide open she listened to the rain and thought for a long time. Then curled tighter on the cot, she hugged her pillow and smiled.

Chapter 74

"So how'd you find out where his mother lives?"

In a short lacy nightgown she was propped against a pillow in bed while Charlie slowly removed his jeans.

"From that secretary at the school. Called her up and said I was drawing a blank and asked did she have a next-of-kin or emergency number."

The heavy rain had finally brought relief from the muggy, oppressive heat, and a light breeze at the open window was already making the room more comfortable. He always slept naked, even in the dead of winter, and she loved to watch him strip. It was about the sexiest body she had ever seen, strong and hard and graceful. Yet there was a vulnerability about him that seemed especially poignant when he was naked. It was that combination of apparent opposites that had drawn her to him from the beginning.

A case had brought them together, actually two cases, hers and his. She was working with an ADC mother with four children under seven, and he was tracking down the man who was living unofficially with the family and who owed his ex-wife, Charlie's client, big time child support. Susan had known at the time she was, to some extent, taking Charlie on as a "project," just as with previous men in her life, but somehow his upside had seemed much greater than with the others.

"So his mother wasn't home either?" she asked now.

"Yeah, the neighbors said they were up north, renting a cottage for a couple weeks."

"They have a phone number?"

"Nope. So I let myself into the house through the back door, and made sure no one was there."

"He could be anywhere, up north, any place. When will you tell the Monellis about him?"

"I don't know. I mean even with what we heard tonight, we're

183

still just guessing."

"I'm not guessing, Charlie. That's him."

"Yeah, but when you come right down to it, I really don't have anything solid yet."

"But if you told the Monellis about him, they might have other ways to find him."

Charlie pushed down his shorts and stood naked in front of her. "And then I'd forfeit any chance at enough cheese to keep us comfortable for the next couple of years."

In spite of herself she glanced at his cock, so soft and, yes, vulnerable now compared to the way it got when they made love. With a matter-of-fact sarcasm she said, "You're a helluva team player, Charlie Watts."

"I was never a team player. It always seemed like a dumb thing to be."

"That's because you grew up in a house full of women who absolutely adored you. All those sisters and your mother and your aunt, they all made you lazy."

The affection in her voice made Charlie smile. "Yeah, I can't help that. I am what they made me."

"Well, I hope you don't find the girl until all this comes down on Monelli's head."

The phone rang on the nightstand. Charlie, surprised, sat on the bed. "Here we go. He must have seen it." He let it ring one more time and picked up the receiver. "Yeah?"

The voice on the line spoke softly. "Mr. Watts, this is Catherine Monelli. I was wondering if you had any news."

He glanced at Susan and shook his head, "No, I'm afraid not, Mrs. Monelli. Nothing solid yet, but I'm still working on it, even at this hour. Maybe I'll have something for you tomorrow."

"All right," said the woman. "I'll be waiting for your call. Good night."

"Good night." He hung up the phone and, after a few seconds, slipped under the sheet and released a deep breath. "Jesus."

"That poor woman," said Susan.

"I thought you wanted to see her husband burn."

"I do, but I still feel sorry for her."

"That's the trouble with you professional good-doers. You got so much sympathy it ties you up in knots."

184

"I'm not tied in any knots. I want that little girl safe and sound, but I also want to see her father locked away for the rest of his life. I just hope if you do find her, you think about those two little boys of yours, Charlie."

Chapter 75

Except for Anna, alone in this big house, Catherine reached to snap off the lamp next Megan's bed. In the dark she laid there thinking about the black man she had somehow decided to trust.

All day and all evening, ever since their meeting this morning at the fountain, she had been wondering, torturing herself, really, thinking that she might have done something horribly stupid in giving the tape to this man about whom she knew next to nothing. Even as she had walked away from him, moving to the BMW, the thought had occurred that once he had listened to it's shocking demands, he would take it straight to Steven, betraying her to ingratiate himself. For hours she had half-expected a frightening call from her husband, or his sudden angry appearance at the house.

Beyond his own financial gain, what could possibly motivate this fellow with the card that said private investigator, a guy who looked like he always took care of himself first? He could sell the tape, maybe, to someone who would certainly decide that expediency dictated the elimination of Steven and probably his father as well. How would she feel if that were to happen, if someone took the lives of her husband and father-in-law? Her answer two days ago would have been very different, but now, as long as she got Megan back safely, she wouldn't care what happened to them.

Could that really be true? Did she suddenly no longer care about the man she had married and spent all of her adult life with? She thought about that moment last night when he had struck her in the face and threatened something worse, and she knew the truth.

Why had she not taken that tape to the police? She had actually been on the phone with them when Steven had walked in and grabbed the phone. But if she had managed to give them the tape, Steven would probably know soon enough and come after her with a vengeance.

Most importantly, though, would the police really care about finding Megan? Not until the tape had done its work for them, not until they had given it every chance to force Steven to finally give in to it's demands, admit his guilt and give then what they'd need to prosecute others.

The fact was that she had not been able to think of one other person to whom she could turn. When she had met Charles Watts for the first time last night, there had been something in his eyes, a warmth, or earnestness, perhaps. What about the strange electric shock that had coursed through her at the fountain when his hand covered hers before he took the tape? And on the phone just now, while there had been a hint of evasiveness, of something held back, she had still felt a kind of basic human sympathy or connection.

And that told her now she had probably done the right thing.

Would she end up sleeping tonight? It seemed unlikely.

Chapter 76

He was trying to run the length of a football field under water, and, though breathing was somehow not a problem, his body was aching now with total exhaustion. Still, he could see those three little kids far ahead of him, and he could tell they were in fact drowning. He needed to get to them in time, but it seemed impossible that he would have the strength to do it. And now he felt swamped with fear and despair. Finally a ringing phone woke him.

Reaching a hand to the receiver on the nightstand, he eyed the clock next to it: 4:44 am. "Yeah."

"Charlie, why are you sleeping?"

The voice was Monelli's, but to give himself a few extra seconds, he said, "Who's this?"

"What'd ya mean, who's this? You know damn well who this is. Shake the shit outta your ears and give me a status report."

Status report. Piercing the fog in his head was the thought that if Monelli recognized the teacher's voice on Channel 5 last night, he would not be asking for a status report.

He said, "Nothin' new to report, man. I'm workin' on some things but nothin' I'd feel good enough to talk about yet."

"What'd you mean not good enough to talk about yet. Gimme something, goddamnit."

He moved the receiver away from his ear and quickly twisted his head, trying to lose the dull, fuzzy ache from his dream. He needed to be a lot sharper than he felt right now. "I told ya, I got nothing to talk about yet. I got something, I'll call you."

"Yeah, well, don't fuckin' sleep. You can sleep all fuckin' weekend, the rest of your fuckin' life, for chrissake. Just find me what I need by 5 today and call me."

It crossed Charlie's mind to tell Monelli what he knew about the ransom, but by the time he said, "Okay, you got it," Monelli had hung up.

Chapter 77

With a two-day growth of beard he was stretched out on the couch, waking to a strange noise he could not place. After a while, as it came again and again, it began to sound like low moans, and they were coming from the bathroom. He opened his eyes.

"Megan, what's the matter?"

The moans, yes, they were definitely moans, grew louder and more distinct. He moved to the padlocked door and put his ear to it.

"Megan, is there something wrong?"

Another moan and then another.

"Megan," he said sharply.

"Please help me," she gasped.

He found the right key on the ring attached to his belt and slipped it into the padlock. "Just a second, I'll get this open."

Before he cracked the door a few inches, he told himself to be wary. This girl seemed capable of anything. But when he finally got a glimpse of her, she was rolled up in a tight ball on the cot, her face to the wall.

"Megan, what's wrong?"

She didn't answer and moaned again.

"Please, Megan, I want to help you."

"Sure you do."

"I do, so turn over and let me have a look at you."

She didn't move. "It hurts, and I'm bleeding."

"What hurts? Com'on, turn over."

Slowly she unfolded her legs and rolled to her back on the cot. And now he could see a large red blotch in the crotch of her white shorts. "Please, help me!" The girl's cry was louder this time.

Finally he found his voice: "Christ, what is it? Maybe it's your period."

She moaned and said, "No! I told you, I had my period last week. There's something wrong with me!"

189

He glanced back at the office behind him, as if help might be waiting there. "Well, god, are you sure?"

"What do you mean? Of course, I'm sure!" Her voice was seared with pain. "This isn't that kind of bleeding. Please do something!"

He finally reached in and took her hand. "All right, com'on. We'll get you some help." He helped her slowly up off the cot and out of the bathroom, but the girl appeared weak, to the point of fainting. After a few steps she stopped.

"I don't think I can walk."

"It's okay, we'll go slowly." He grabbed the pink blanket from a chair. "Here, put this around you." He tried wrapping it over her shoulders, but she pushed it away.

"Get that off me, I'm burning up."

Her hand was warm as he helped her walk slowly across the office to the outside door. She leaned against the wall while he dealt with the lock.

Emerging from the office into bright morning sunlight, they moved slowly, step by step, around muddy rain puddles on the ground to the Ford. He helped her into the passenger seat, then moved quickly around to the driver's side. The engine ground for a while before starting, and he let it warm up for a few seconds before putting it in gear. Driving slowly around the front of the plant on the overgrown road that led to the front gate and the highway, he glanced at the girl, slumped in the seat, holding herself tightly and making a face.

"Now look," he said sternly, "I'm going to take you to a hospital, and we'll tell them I'm your brother. But you've got to understand something. I've got a partner in this project. And his instructions are simple. If anything goes wrong with our plan, and I mean anything, he will put an end to your father. Like immediately. You understand?"

He watched her as he approached the gate, and after a second or two she gave him a barely perceptible nod.

"So don't even think of saying anything at the hospital. Unless you don't care what happens to your dad."

At the gate, he brought the Ford to a halt, put it in park and got out. He trotted forward, took care of the lock and swung the gate open wide. But as he turned to head back to the car, he swept his gaze up the highway and could not believe his eyes.

A sheriff's cruiser was bearing down on the far-side lane, maybe 100 yards away.

Chapter 78

With his heart beating wildly, he watched the cruiser brake quickly as it passed him, the same deputy who stopped to chat yesterday behind the wheel and looking straight at him. His stomach twisted in a knot as the cruiser came to a stop on the shoulder, then backed up until it was directly across from him.

The deputy lowered his window and said with a friendly twang, "Back again, eh?"

He managed to say, "Yeah," but he was dying inside.

The deputy's eyes moved to the Ford where the girl was certainly visible in the front seat.

His voice sounding strange, John somehow uttered four more words: "So how goes it?"

The officer looked back at him. "Oh, same old same old."

So frightened he felt almost giddy, he plunged ahead and surprised himself. "Yeah, well, I brought my little sister along this morning. Thought I'd show her what it was like. Kids like that kind of thing."

"Yeah, I guess. Well, have a good one."

A nod and a even a wave seemed almost easy now as the officer started the cruiser forward, accelerating slowly on the sparse gravel shoulder. And then as John moved his gaze back to the Ford, he was stunned to find the girl getting out of the car.

A quick glance back at the road told him the cruiser had moved just far enough forward so the deputy could not see the car door opening or the girl leaving. But now she was running full-tilt for the opening to the highway where she could surely catch the deputy's eye in his rear view mirror.

At first flat-footed, he felt almost rooted to the ground. As the girl raced through the open gate and past him, she was just steps away from the edge of the blacktop where she could flag the deputy. When he finally did move, it was just barely in time to grab her around the waist.

Her scream was piercing, as he lifted her off the ground, her feet flailing to kick his shins. Shoving a hand over her mouth, he muffled most of the next scream, then carried her a few yards into the underbrush next to the gate, where, holding her tight, he dropped them both to the ground. Through a small gap in the bushes he watched the sheriff's cruiser continue to roar off down the highway.

Chapter 79

A few minutes later, holding her firmly by the wrist, he swung her back into the office and sat her down on the couch.

"Now just sit!"

Closing the door to the outside, he locked it again, then turned back to the girl. "So it was instant recovery when you saw that cop."

She said nothing.

He leaned down to look her squarely in the eye. "Look, I don't blame you. If I were in your position, I'd probably do the same thing. But if you try something like that again, you're gonna get hurt. And so will your dad."

She still said nothing, and he moved past her to step inside the bathroom. He came out with a wastebasket filled with toilet paper. Removing most of it, he finally pulled out the plastic ketchup bottle, turned it upside down and squeezed. A sputter delivered the last dribble of red stuff. With no expression on her face, the girl watched as he held up the bottle and nodded.

Putting the paper and the bottle back in the basket, he turned back to her. "What size do you wear?"

She made a face and stared at him before answering. "What size do I wear? What's it to you?"

"Well, just to show there's no hard feelings, I'll go out in a while and get you some new jeans."

She shook her head and looked away. "You are such an ass."

"Well, I bet if I get them, you'll wear them."

She fixed him with the hardest look he'd ever seen from a 12-year-old. "I wouldn't bet on anything if I were you. You're a total loser."

Chapter 80

In a cash register line in the teen girls department of the Sears at Lakeside Mall, he waited behind a woman and a girl about Megan's age and size. He was holding a top, underwear and jeans, but his attention was directed across the aisle to another department where a large bank of TV sets all had the same picture—a head-and-shoulders shot of Frank DeFauw. The sound from one of the sets was just loud enough for him to hear what the man was saying.

"Crime lord or model citizen? Steven 'The Bank' Monelli 'Up-Front' today at five on 5."

John caught the eye of the woman standing in front of him. "You going to watch him tonight?"

"Who?"

He gestured toward the TV sets. "Frank DeFauw."

The woman made a sour face. "Oh, I hate that guy. I think he's a total jerk."

Her daughter shook her head and widened her big brown eyes. "Mom, you watch him all the time!"

"So? I still think he's a jerk."

John said, "Actually I've met him. He's a pretty good guy."

The girl's eyes widened again. "Really? You've met him? I just think he's so sexy!"

Now the mother's eyes widened. "Junie!"

Chapter 81

Jimmy Long was on the same Fort Street corner he'd been working the last time John stopped to say hello. In a banged-up station wagon at the curb, a woman was negotiating with Chink hanging in the passenger-side window. As Jimmy watched the street he recognized the old black Fairmont approaching the intersection. From behind the steering wheel John gazed squarely at him, then looked away.

Jimmy waved and yelled, "Hey, Mr. G, man, how you doin'?"

He slowed the Ford long enough to look back at the boy and shake his head.

Jimmy watched the car drive off. "Hey, Mr. G! Damn! What's the matter with you, man?"

Chink turned away from the station wagon to look at Jimmy. "Who that, man? Why you care 'bout some head."

"That's no head, man. Used to be my teacher."

Driving now on Mt. Morris, John decided his neighborhood looked somehow even more dilapidated and depressing in the two days since he'd been home. When his building loomed on the right, he move the Ford toward the curb and parked in a spot almost directly in front of the stairs leading down to his apartment.

Chapter 82

Food wrappers—McDonald's, Burger King, KFC, Taco Bell—littered the passenger side floorboard. Gazing at them he thought they were the perfect reflexion of his fucked-up life. Sitting here in the Nova for the past four hours plus, knowing it was certainly all but pointless, thinking the guy's a teacher and must have at least half a brain, enough surely to know that the last thing he should do was visit his own apartment. But what else was there to do but stake out this place from a block away and wait?

Short on sleep, he had caught himself dozing more than once, and now he sent a weary glance up from the wrappers to the guy's building.

And, behold, the raggedy black Ford Fairmont that Tina, the strung out dancer, had told him to look for, was parked right in front of the apartment.

Then he watched the young guy get out of the car and quickly disappear down the stairs.

"Thank you, Jesus," he said aloud and took one last look at the school newsletter photo of Giordano on the seat next to him. Reaching to open the glove compartment, he removed a small black metal box and climbed out of the Nova.

Down the sidewalk on the opposite side of the street from the apartment he walked until he was just past a point even with the Ford. Then he crossed the street and moved in behind the car. With one quick glance at the apartment's entryway, he squatted, flipped a switch on the box, and attached it to the frame near the underside of the rear bumper.

Chapter 83

Inside the apartment at his kitchen table John filled a shopping bag with three T-shirts and a worn pair of jeans, two library books — Elmore Leonard's *The Big Bounce* and *them* by Joyce Carol Oates — the two editions of the Free Press he had picked up off his doorstep, his toothbrush, a half-rolled tube of toothpaste, and the Minocycline pills he'd forgotten for his acne. It was amazing how carefully he had worked out every detail of his plan and yet was thoughtless about some obvious basics.

On the counter next to his phone he pushed a button on his answering machine. The tape rewound briefly, then played.

"Honey, it's your mother, calling from the great north woods. Just wanted to say hello and see how you're doing. Any job prospects yet? If not, I'm sure a good one will come along soon. I wish you would come up and spend a few days with us. It's so gorgeous up here, and we've got more than enough room in this cottage. Harry and I would love to have you. Well, dear, take good care of yourself and call me soon. Love you. Bye, bye."

The machine beeped and stopped. Shaking his head, he lifted the shopping bag from the table and moved to the door. When he opened it to leave, the large, imposing figure of a black man stood in his way.

"How you doin', John?"

His mouth puckered, and he swallowed hard. "Ah, okay. How about you?"

"I'm fine, John, just fine. Looks like you packed a few supplies. You goin' someplace?"

"Oh, just out for awhile." He paused, feeling weak. Finally he asked, "Do I know you?"

The black man smiled. "I don't know. Do you?"

"I don't think so."

"I don't think so either."

His nerves doing a violent hum, he tried to sound pleasant. "Then how do you know me?"

"That's my business, John. By the way, mind if I come in? It's kind of awkward here in the doorway." The guy pushed past him into the apartment.

"Well, I was just..."

The guy stopped and turned in the kitchenette. "You were just what?"

John took a breath. "I was just leaving. So I'll have to ask you to go."

The black man smiled again. "I'll be happy to go, John. Just tell me where you're keeping Megan Monelli."

Shocked and sliced with fear, he opened his mouth but couldn't speak. Until this moment he had clung to the hope that this strange, menacing guy was about something else. There was no possible way, he had told himself repeatedly, that anyone could connect him with the girl. Now, obviously, he'd made some kind of awful mistake. Finally he said, "Ah, I don't know what you're talking about."

"Yes, you do, John. And I'm ready to do whatever it takes for you to give me that information."

The guy had stopped smiling. John felt barely able to breathe. Somehow he managed to hold himself together. "Look, I told you I don't know what you're talking about. But you could do anything you want to me, and it still wouldn't help."

Saying nothing for a few seconds, the black man just stared and seemed to gauge the intensity with which John stared back.

Finally, the guy said softly, "Well, John, I'll tell you what. I want you to think real hard about what your life is gonna be like after tonight. Then give me a call before five o'clock." He slid a business card out of his shirt pocket and handed it to him.

Looking at it briefly, John put it in his jeans pocket and actually began to breathe again. "Okay, Charles, thanks for the advice. I gotta be goin' now."

The guy nodded and walked out the door ahead of him. As the two emerged from the stairway onto the street, John moved to the driver's side of the Ford. The black man gave him one last look.

"Think about it, John."

"Right. See you later."

"I hope so. For your sake."

John started the Ford, put it in gear, and drove off noisily as the black man stood on the sidewalk watching him go. In the rear view mirror, he watched the guy cross the street diagonally to a white Nova with what looked like a dented roof. Then taking his time, John made a right turn at the next corner and continued at a moderate speed until he reached an alley where he slowed to make another right.

Carefully moving the Ford up the alley, he glanced often at both the rear and side view mirrors. A half-block up the alley he stopped to one side, then turned to watch out the rear window, his hands damp, his pulse racing.

Biting the skin at the edge of the nail on his right index finger, he continued for a minute watching the street from which he had turned into the alley. But then after a while, he began to feel that somehow the black man was watching him, that he had magically found his whereabouts and was standing now right in front of the Ford, staring at the back of his head. John turned suddenly on the bench, but found no one in front. Then he turned back to the rear window, just in time to see the white Nova moving quickly past the alley entrance without the guy giving the alley a glance.

With the skin stinging next to the nail, John turned back to the wheel, put the Ford in gear and moved through the rest of the alley. At the next street he took a right and then drove with pace, his eyes moving quickly from the way ahead, to the side streets he passed, to what the mirrors showed behind.

There were only a few cars moving in this half-dead neighborhood, but the white Nova was not one of them. His nerves were still humming, but he was reasonably certain that Charles Watts, Private Investigator, traveling in the opposite direction on another street, had been given the slip.

Chapter 84

With the Nova idling at a red light, Charlie reached under the seat and pulled out another black metal box, this one larger than the one he had placed on the Ford. It had an antenna and a scope, and when he pushed the power button, the antenna extended and the scope glowed green, showing a grid pattern with two white dots, one blinking to indicate the relative position of the other box. This box also began beeping regularly as he made a tight u-turn to follow in the direction the Fairmont had traveled.

Glancing often at the green scope next to him on the seat, he continued to narrow the gap between to two dots until, far ahead he caught a glimpse of what he was sure was the Ford. Then he backed off a bit, and, satisfied with the configuration of the dots on the grid, continued to follow while staying far enough behind to remain out of sight.

When he knew they were approaching an entrance to I-94, he pulled over and watched the scope more carefully. When the lead dot suddenly began moving to the right, he guessed the Ford had entered the eastbound ramp. A minute later, nearing the freeway, he slowed but passed the eastbound access and continued for a block before stopping in the overgrown lot of an abandoned supermarket. Watching the scope for a few moments, he nodded to himself, then headed back for the eastbound ramp.

A minute later he had merged with medium and fast-moving traffic and was glancing at the dots every few seconds, grateful this cat-and-mouse game had started before the rush hour jams. When he finally hit Harper Woods, the first eastern suburb, the vehicles around him began thinning out. He glanced at his watch: 3:30 pm.

Fifteen minutes later he found himself on a mostly rural highway he had never seen before.

Chapter 85

With the outside door of the office locked again, he placed the shopping bag on a desk, turned on the lamp next to the couch and carried the Sears bag to the bathroom door. He opened the padlock and knocked. "You doing okay?"

He stared at the door and heard nothing.

"Megan, I got you a change of clothes."

Still no answer, so he knocked again. "Megan, how about a change of clothes?"

With only more silence he had the crazy thought that somehow she wasn't in there. Totally crazy but what if...? He opened the door, and there she was lying on the cot and giving him a frigid stare. Finally she said, "What kind of clothes?"

He handed her the bag. "Here, look for yourself. It's nothing special, but it should be more comfortable than what you're wearing."

"Sears?"

"What's wrong with Sears."

"I don't wear Sears, Loser Boy."

He turned away. "Com'on out when you're ready, and I'll make some hot dogs."

"Oh, goody." Her voice dripped mockery.

Saying nothing, he closed the bathroom door. Back at the desk, he snapped on the old portable TV set he had brought from the apartment a few days ago. After a moment, when the set had warmed up, it offered the last several seconds of a Depends commercial, followed by a stern-looking black woman who said, "Fourteen years as an abused wife." And after that came another woman's voice: "Next at 4 on the Oprah Winfrey Show."

Chapter 86

In the Cadillac's back seat, dressed impeccably in a black suit, gray shirt and a lighter gray patterned tie, Monelli sat alone with his thoughts as Robert turned the car into the entrance to the station compound at WTEM-TV. They stopped next to the gatehouse, and Robert lowered his window.

"This is Mr. Steven Monelli. He's scheduled to be on with Frank DeFauw."

The guard nodded quickly. "Oh, yes, sir. Just follow the road around to the back entrance, and someone will meet you there."

Raising the window, Robert accelerated past a Detroit Police car and its two officers parked inside the gate.

Two minutes later, carrying an attache case, he moved through the double doors to the reception area and held one for Monelli. In the lobby they eyed two more uniformed officers, one in an armchair, the other on the couch, both of whom eyed them back When Oprah Winfrey's theme music came on, a TV set built into the wall regained their attention.

As Robert was about to say something to the receptionist, a smartly dressed young black woman walked up with a smile and extended her hand.

"Hello, Mr. Monelli. I'm Fay Banks, Mr. DeFauw's producer. I see you found us all right."

"No problem." Monelli barely touched her hand and only glanced at her eyes.

"Great! Let me show you to our Green Room where we'll ask you to wait for just awhile before your segment comes up on the news."

Monelli nodded but didn't move. "Is there a phone I can use in that room? "

Fay's smile retained its wattage. "In the Green Room? Oh, sure. Use it as much as you want."

Chapter 87

With the jaws of the large cutting tool gripping the rusty chain, he grunted once and snapped it. Then he swung the creaky old gate open wide and moved back to the Nova, idling behind him on the highway shoulder.

Tossing the chain cutter in the back seat, he moved the Nova past the gate and up the overgrown road. The weathered old building he had glimpsed from the highway came slowly into view, and he was barely able to decipher the badly faded sign on its front wall: "Giordano Cheese."

As he spotted the Ford parked close to a door marked Office, the black box on the seat next to him was beeping like crazy. On the green scope the two white dots had merged. He hit the power button on the box, then backed the car out of sight from the office door and shut down the engine.

On foot he moved quickly to the building's cement block wall and followed it until he was close to the office. The window in its door had been boarded over, but moving closer, he saw a tiny crack of light coming from under the board at the lower left corner of the window. From inside he could hear Oprah Winfrey saying, "So tell us, dear, what he would do when he'd come home in that condition."

Moving back away from the door, he retraced his route along the wall, figuring there had to be other ways into this place. Turning a corner he came first to a large, drive-up opening, a loading dock covered with a rusted metal roll-up door. When he climbed up on the dock and tried to lift the door, it wouldn't budge.

Moving again along the side of the old plant, he gazed up at a bank of narrow windows, inaccessible at about 20 feet off the ground.

Chapter 88

Inside the office the hazy picture on the old portable showed Oprah, her large eyes full of deep concern, leaning toward a pretty woman in her mid-30s weeping and wiping her cheeks. "Just let it all come out, dear," said Oprah, as John stood at the desk and laid out hot dog buns on paper plates.

He started to look at his watch again and then stopped himself. Surely it had been less than a minute since he had last checked the time. And if he kept checking so often, this incredible thing he was doing and the time it was taking would only drag even more.

But his nerves buzzed, and his patience had frayed badly. His thoughts were jumping all over the place, from the girl's look when he had pulled the gun from under the seat, to that view of her father hurrying into the bus station john, to the desperate edge in the guy's voice on the phone, to his own strange elation—excitement, yes, but a weird kind of calm—when he had locked the girl for the first time here in the bathroom cell.

On the TV now Oprah was sticking a microphone in front of a young black woman standing in the audience. "And you say?"

Chapter 89

The large screen in the Green Room at Channel 5 offered the same image, brighter and sharper. The woman with a microphone in front of her was saying, "I say I'd never stick around long enough to let a man beat on me."

Monelli was not watching the set. Instead his gaze was locked on a telephone on a small table next to the chair in which Robert was sitting.

Fay Banks popped her head in the door with a smile. "Just as an update, Mr. Monelli, you're now scheduled to be on with Mr. DeFauw at 5:15"

Monelli barely glanced at her. "Okay, 5:15."

Fay lingered. "Oh, and I just wanted to let you know that we have found a way to accommodate your request to be right on the set with Mr. DeFauw."

"My request?" Monelli finally looked up at her.

"Yes, we don't normally do 'Up-Front' interviews that way, but I understand it was a stipulation from your people right from the first phone call."

"Okay, fine." Monelli stared back at the phone.

Chapter 90

At the far rear corner of the old plant Charlie finally came to a solid panel door along with a couple of windows that were only a few feet off the ground. Trying to look through one of the dirt-caked panes, he could barely see the remains of what appeared to have been a locker room. At the door he tried the handle and found it securely locked. Pulling out his small lock-pick tool, he inserted its two prongs in the keyhole, twisted it back and forth, flicked it a few times, then twisted again. And nothing.

He tried three more times, the last two with variations, but the lock refused to open, and he decided it was probably rusted closed. He tried shouldering the door, but there was no give at all.

Back to the window, he peered through the grime. It was locked. A quick look in the other window showed the same thing. So which sound would more likely reach the office? Breaking glass or pounding the door enough to snap it open?

He moved away from the door and, with a powerful three-step rush, slammed his left shoulder into it a foot above the lock. He felt it give and heard wood crack, but it would still not swing open. Listening closely in the silence between birds chirping in the trees around the old plant, he could just barely hear sounds coming from the TV set in the office. One more bull rush, with another thud and wood crack, and he was into the locker room. Standing stock still for a few seconds, he could still hear the TV set.

In this dust-laden room he looked around for a moment to get his bearings, then walked between two rows of lockers toward another door.

* * *

On the office TV Oprah was shouting to the heavens, "I don't believe this," as her audience roared and applauded. With the hot dogs finished in his old microwave from the apartment, John added potato chips to the plates and filled two paper cups with 7-Up.

"Megan?"

As usual lately there was no answer. He turned the volume down on the TV.

"Megan, you ready? How about a hot dog?"

Still no answer.

This time he yelled, "Megan, hot dog?"

Finally she answered. "Hold your little weenie, Loser Boy."

And after a pause: "Or maybe you'd like me to hold it."

"I told you to cut that out."

He turned up the TV volume again.

* * *

In the locker room at the rear of the building Charlie was confronted now by a simple push-through door. But when he tried it, carefully, it moved only a few inches before hitting something that blocked its way.

Looking through the narrow opening now at the door's edge, he could see that what was stopping it was an old card chair stacked with a pile of cheese draining tins almost four feet high. It looked like the arrangement had been placed there on purpose, to keep someone from coming through here in silence.

Again he pushed cautiously on the door and, despite the resistance provided by the chair and its stack of tins, he was able to move it a few more inches. Just a little more space and he might be able to put his arm through and secure the tins.

One more push, this time with a little more force, and the chair slid again. And then the stack of tins toppled to the cement floor with a loud metallic crash, several of them bouncing around to make the noise seem like it was lasting forever.

* * *

The girl finally emerged from the bathroom in her new jeans and top just as the crash at the rear of the plant sent echoes to the office. Startled, John nonetheless knew exactly what the noise was and where it had come from.

But had a rat eluded his traps and jumped on the chair or was there someone really in the plant?

He snapped off the TV and moved quickly to the girl, grabbing her roughly and turning her back into the bathroom.

She cried, Hey, stop it!"

"Sorry, you're gonna have to stay in here a while longer."

"Hey, can't you make up your damn little mind?"

He padlocked the bathroom and turned back to the desk. Opening the bottom drawer, he pulled out the .22 with his hand shaking badly. Then he moved to the room's other interior door, leading to the storeroom.

Unlocking and opening it slowly, he left the office.

Chapter 91

With the swinging door and scattered tins behind him and his .357 in hand, Charlie scanned this high-ceilinged space with its large round vats visible in the filtered light coming from the two banks of grimy windows high on each of the sidewalls. He could no longer hear Oprah coming from the office at the front of the building and knew that was probably not a good thing.

In the dark storeroom, John moved past the shelves to the doorway that would give him a view of the production room. When he reached the open door and peered around the jamb, his stomach flipped and churned as he spotted the black man about 40 yards away. The guy held his gun in both hands, sweeping it from side to side and stepping in his direction.

With his own hand shaking, John raised the .22 and aimed ten feet above the black man's head. For a few seconds he tried to steady his hand but finally gave up and simply squeezed the trigger. The gun's noisy crack and kick shocked him, and he nearly dropped it.

The bullet ricocheted off the cement block wall behind Charlie, and he dove behind the nearest vat. Crouching behind its three-foot wall, he tried to decide where the shot had come from.

Pressed against the inside of the doorway, John was out of sight from the production room. He looked at the .22 in his sweating, vibrating hand and quickly decided against trying to use it again. He gathered himself to keep his voice from quavering.

"Hey, Charles, that was just a warning. I don't want to hurt you or anyone else. So why don't you just go away and leave me alone?"

Charlie turned in his crouch behind the vat in the direction of John's voice. "I'll be happy to leave you alone, John. You just give me Megan Monelli."

After a pause: "I can't do that. The stakes are too high, and this is the only way to deal with someone like Monelli."

Trying to figure the exact location of John's voice, he cautiously raised his gaze over the top of the vat and said, "It won't work. He won't do what you want."

"How much is he paying you, Charles?"

Silence. Charlie bowed his head.

"It better be a lot, because what he's doing is destroying a whole generation of kids. Your people especially, Charles. A whole generation of your people. You sure he's paying you enough for all that?"

Charlie kept his head down behind the vat wall, quite sure now of John's location. "You overestimate his importance, John. Even if this whole crazy scheme works, tomorrow there'll be somebody else all set to take his place."

"I don't care about anyone else! I want Monelli." John's voice was more emotional now.

And glancing over the top of the vat again, Charlie saw the teacher move his head just a bit past the door jamb. He brought up the magnum and fired, and the bullet slammed into the jamb, exactly where he wanted to put it, about a foot from John's face.

The shot sent John reeling away from the door until he fell backwards over a small keg and sprawled in a heap amid empty burlap bags and old cheese tins. On the cement floor, he felt a wet warmth in his crotch and knew he had pissed on himself.

Following the shot Charlie moved quickly, running low to the next vat closer to the store room door, pausing briefly and running again to crouch behind one even closer.

The .22 still in his hand, John knelt in a corner with no cover between himself and the production room door. Finally, he realized he was only a few feet from another door, this one thick and airtight, leading to the refrigeration room adjacent to the storeroom. He grabbed its large levered handle and pulled it open. Looking into the dark refrigerator, he could see that its second door, leading to the production room, was standing open.

Moving cautiously into and through the dark room, he reached the open doorway, and with his heart slamming in his chest, he peeked around the jam into the production room. There, from this new angle, he saw the black guy moving to the edge of the store room doorway only fifteen feet away. John had a clear shot at his back.

Taking one cautious step out of the refrigeration room, he held the

.22 tightly in both hands and pointed it at the guy's broad back.

Charlie called, "Com'on out, John, and no one'll get hurt."

John summoned all the resolve he could muster to speak firmly, without a strain in his voice. "Don't move, Charles."

Charlie froze, his .357 pointed down, and John moved another two steps forward. "Now toss your gun into the store room and turn around slowly with your hands up."

After hesitating for a few seconds, Charlie did as he was told, the .357 clattering on the cement floor He turned to face John, then nodded toward the .22 and asked, "What do you think you're going to do with that thing?"

John almost glanced at his gun but stayed with the black man's deadpan eyes. "Use it, if I have to. Now move. Into the refrigerator."

Taking a few steps back to let Charlie pass, he motioned with the gun and waited for the black man to walk slowly into the refrigeration room. John followed, stopped just inside the door and said, "Okay, stop right there and don't turn around."

Holding the .22 in one hand, with the other John pulled on the heavy refrigerator door and swung it shut behind him. Charlie turned to watch John push against the door to make sure it was locked. There was no way to open it from the inside.

"I said don't turn around." John held the gun in both hands again.

Charlie lowered his hands. "I know what you said. But I don't think you'll use that thing on me."

"Don't bet on it." John was circling the black man, trying to get to the second refrigerator door, leading to the storeroom.

"I don't think you'd hurt anyone, John." Charlie took a step toward John as he circled.

"Stay away," screamed John as he backed into a rack in the dimly lit refrigerator and lost his balance for a second.

And in that instant Charlie leapt at John, grabbing the .22 with both hands and twisting violently. Despite a desperate effort, John was quickly on the floor without the gun.

"Charles, please!" John's voice and eyes were pleading. "Just let Monelli take his fall."

"Save your breath." Charlie quickly straddled him, pointing the .22 at his head and snatching the key ring from his belt loop. Then leaving him hopeless on the floor, Charlie stepped through the doorway into the storeroom and slammed the heavy refrigerator door shut, locking John in.

Shoving the .22 into his belt, Charlie grabbed the magnum from the floor and moved past the rows of shelves to the door standing open to the office. Peering into the room first, he entered and looked around more carefully. The two hot dogs and 7-Ups were sitting on the desk.

"Megan?"

In the bathroom, her ear pressed to the door, the girl was uncertain whether to respond to the unfamiliar voice.

"Megan Monelli, where are you?"

She hesitated, but only for another second. "I'm here! I'm in the bathroom!"

Charlie moved quickly to the bathroom door, glanced at the padlock, then looked at John's collection of keys. Shoving the .357 into his waistband at the small of his back, he looked at his watch. It was two minutes to five.

"Megan, you all right?"

"I'm fine. Just get me out of here."

"Hold on in there." Charlie looked again at his watch. "I'll have you out in just a few minutes."

Megan sounded on the verge of tears. "Please hurry!"

"Just hold on. I'll be right back."

Charlie had already crossed the office to the outside door where he tried two keys before finding the right one to open its lock. Ripping the door open he sprinted past the Ford to the Nova parked around the corner of the building. He climbed in the driver's side and reached into his pants pocket to come out with a slip of paper with phone numbers on it.

Finding the one for Channel 5, he grabbed his phone from the dash.

Chapter 92

In the Green Room, Monelli was still staring at the telephone, as if trying with sheer will power to make it ring. On the TV monitor Frank DeFauw, his brow deeply furrowed, was talking fast and pitching "an unprecedented live interview with reputed crime boss Steven Monelli a little later in the newscast." Fay Banks walked in with her big smile.

"Everything okay, Mr. Monelli? I'll be coming back for you in just about 10 minutes."

Monelli frowned at her smile. "Ah, I thought you said 15. I mean, the thing is, I'd like to stay here until the last possible minute. I'm waiting for a very important call."

Fay's pretty smile faded just a bit. "Well, I'll be happy to give you as much time as I possibly can, but we will really need to get you to the studio door precisely on time and make sure you're ready to go on set. We'll have less than a minute during a commercial break to get you in there and put a mike on you. Actually, I'll come and get you when we're only a few minutes away from that break."

Monelli said, "Okay, whatever you can do."

Fay left, and once they were alone again, he looked at Robert and asked for the second time, "You called everybody and told 'em the deadline's 5:15 now?"

Robert nodded emphatically. "Yes, sir." Then as an afterthought: "But what about that black guy? Didn't you hire that black guy? I don't have his number."

Monelli reached into the breast pocket of his suit coat and came out with a card. "Give me some privacy here. Go get me a pop."

Chapter 93

With the slip of paper on the front seat next to him, Charlie held the car phone in one hand and with the other punched in the Channel 5 number. Then his forefinger hovered over the talk button. Push it, he told himself. Nothing happened. As if he were paralyzed. Push it, he ordered himself. Push it! His finger didn't move.

He could not believe this was happening. Could he really not bring himself to do this? He held the phone in front of him, staring at it now, thinking this common device could simply change his life forever. And he just couldn't push a button?

Finally, with both anger and anguish he decided it was not going to happen. He snapped the phone back into its holder on the dash, crumpled up the slip of paper with the numbers on it and threw it in disgust at the windshield.

"Fuck!"

And then the phone buzzed. He looked at it, feeling suddenly even more nerve-wracked, then looked at his watch. He had called the official Greenwich time number and reset it twice today, and now his watch said 5 straight up. The phone buzzed again. And again. Why not answer? Because it might be Monelli. And if it was Monelli, what would he say, what would he tell him? On the fifth and last buzz, he picked up the phone.

"Yeah."

"Well, you got anything for me?" It was Monelli all right, but without this morning's rage.

He hesitated, wondering why he had answered.

Monelli barked, "Charlie, you there?"

"Yeah, I'm here."

"Well?"

"Well, not really."

"Not really! Either you do or you don't. Which is it?"

Charlie paused again, then finally said, "I don't. I'm sorry, I don't

215

have anything for you."

"Yeah, well, I'm sorry too. But listen, I got a little reprieve here. Another 15 minutes. You come up with anything in the next 15, you give me a call. You can still earn those 100 Gs, Charlie. Just find what I'm looking for and get back to me in time."

Charlie grabbed the crumpled piece of paper off the dash, opened and smoothed it with his fingers. "Yeah, right, I'll do everything I can."

For the next 10 minutes, actually almost 12, he glanced at his watch every minute or two. He sprawled and slumped and sat bolt up right in the Nova's front seat, trying to decide once and for all to call or not to call. Three times he had the phone in his hand. Twice he actually dialed the whole number and then, again, could not bring himself to send the call. Once he punched in the first four digits and then angrily tossed the phone in the back seat. He picked it up again a few seconds later to call Susan and talk this over one more time. But then he wondered, why the hell, would he do that, when he knew exactly what she was going to say?

He looked at the slip of paper on the seat next to him, with numbers for Catherine Monelli, for her husband's office and his portable and for Channel 5. The paper had been crumpled and tossed two more times, each time retrieved and spread flat again. He wondered if Monelli would call again. And wondered if he would answer.

Finally, Charlie spoke aloud. "You know damn well you can't fuckin' do this, so get out of the fuckin' car and get on with it."

With that he climbed out of the Nova and slammed the door.

Chapter 94

Monelli's attention was no longer fixed on the telephone. After all this excruciating waiting, he knew it would never ring as long as he was watching it.

Then Fay Banks walked in, this time with no smile. "Okay, Mr. Monelli, we're all set for you."

He remained seated. "Yeah, well, as I mentioned to you earlier, I'd like to stay here until the last possible minute, so I can take a very important call, if it comes."

Fay tried for a look that conveyed how serious this situation was. "As I explained earlier, Mr. Monelli, we really have to get you to the studio door and make sure you're ready to go on set during the commercial break that's coming right up."

She looked at her watch and then at a large clock on the wall. "Actually, we're only two minutes away from that break right now."

He raised one finger. "Just give me 30 seconds with Robert here. I have to talk with him privately."

Fay said nothing, pursing he lips. Finally, she turned and left, saying, "Olay, just 30 seconds."

When the door closed, Monelli balanced the attache case on his lap, opened the lid and removed two handwritten pages along with the zip-lock bag filled with white powder. He slipped the bag into a pocket in his suit coat. As he closed the case he looked up at Robert.

"If a call comes in for me about Megan, I want you to come into that studio and tell me, no matter what. Do you understand? No matter what."

"Yes, sir."

"And here, call this number and ask this guy Watts if he's got anything new."

Handing Charlie's card to Robert, he folded the handwritten pages and placed them in the inside breast pocket of his suit coat as Fay walked back in.

"All set?"

Monelli finally got to his feet. "I guess so."

"Great'. If you'll just come this way."

Nodding grimly to Robert, he the left room and followed the young woman down a short carpeted hallway and into a large, high-ceilinged storage area. Her high heels spanking the cement floor, Fay led the way to a spot not far from a huge pair of studio doors. There she turned to him, her smile back now.

"It'll just be a moment now, Mr. Monelli.'

And just then, one of the large double doors swung open, and a tall attractive black woman he recognized as DeFauw's co-anchor walked out. "Hello," she said with a pretty nod to Monelli and then paused, leaning close to him to say quietly, "When you get up there in my seat, just tell Frank the word on the street is that he's a flaming fag." He watched her smile and nod at him one more time as she walked away.

Fay ushered him through the door and onto the well lit set that looked much smaller to him than it did on TV. She told him with a grin, "Those two are always a barrel of laughs."

Monelli spotted DeFauw waiting behind the anchor desk, reading glasses tilted low on his nose as he looked over a five-by-eight card. As they arrived at the desk, the newsman glanced up and offered a big friendly grin.

"How are you, Mr. Monelli?"

"Okay."

They shook hands, and then Frank grabbed Mary Scott's two pillows off her chair and tossed them on the floor. "Here, you won't needs these."

Monelli sat unhappily in the chair just a few feet from DeFauw.

A technician quickly pinned a tiny mike on his lapel.

DeFauw said, "Hell, just relax and we'll have a great time. I guarantee this'll be painless."

Chapter 95

Back inside the cheese factory office Charlie closed the door behind him and secured the padlock. Megan immediately called from the bathroom, "Hey, how about letting me out of here!"

"In a little while."

"You said that an hour ago!"

"Yeah, it was 20 minutes. Just be patient."

"What happened to that other guy?"

"Don't worry about him."

"I'm not."

Moving back around to the desk to sit in front of the old portable TV, he turned it on. He moved the 7-Up and the hot dogs to get a better view of the screen and then adjusted the rabbit ears to improve the picture.

Then he turned up the sound in time to hear DeFauw's familiar, dramatic delivery.

"Tonight on our 'Up-Front' segment, something very special. Steven Monelli says he and his family are upstanding members of our community, their businesses legitimate and their contributions to society substantial. But certain law enforcement officials, those willing to talk, say Mr. Monelli could offer a rare look at the world of organized crime, a view inside a so-called Mafia family that has dominated organized crime in Metro Detroit for the past four decades."

On the Channel 5 news set, Monelli sat at the desk along with DeFauw, watching and listening as the anchor continued reading from a teleprompter.

"The son of alleged Mafia boss Michael 'Cigar Mike' Monelli, Steven Monelli has been called everything from a model citizen to the ruthless leader of a new, more sophisticated organized crime operation, which some say is every bit as vicious as the old gangland mobs of many decades ago. Tonight I'll talk with Steven Monelli, and we'll look for the truth about the man they call 'The Bank.' Mr. Monelli, thanks so much for being here."

"Yeah." From his inside coat pocket Monelli took the two folded pages. "But before we get started, I have a statement I'm gonna read."

"Well, Mr. Monelli, that is really not our format here on the 'Up-Front' segment and..."

Monelli interrupted. "It's very brief, Mr. DeFauw. I think it'll be of great interest to you and your viewers."

In the cheese factory office Charlie continued watching the old portable as DeFauw glanced quickly off camera and then said, "Well, all right, Mr. Monelli, but understand that if this turns out to be beside the point we're concerned with here, or it's simply a self-serving statement, I'll reserve the right to stop you and get us back on track. Also please keep it brief."

"Right."

Monelli unfolded his handwritten pages and began to read. "First of all, I want to make clear that no member of my family and no employee or associate of mine in any capacity is aware of what I am about to say."

Charlie reached for a 7-Up and took a sip. Then he got up, moved to the storeroom door, and headed for the refrigeration room. Opening its heavy door a crack, he said without looking in, "You wanna watch TV?"

Chapter 96

In the den of the Monellis' Grosse Pointe Park home, Cigar Mike watched his son on a 32-inch Sony built into a cabinet.

"No member of my family has any knowledge whatsoever of the activities I am about to describe, and my decision to talk about these activities is solely my own, undertaken of my own free will."

On the news set, Monelli stopped and looked up at the large studio doors, hoping against hope to see them swinging open and Robert charging through. He waited for five seconds until DeFauw finally said, "Mr. Monelli?"

With a quick grimace and a slight nod, he returned to his handwritten pages. "For the past seven years I have been responsible for buying and importing large quantities of both heroin and cocaine and supplying both to a major distributor in this city."

In the control room adjacent to the studio, the director, wearing a headset and watching a bank of monitors, screamed, "Whoa! Holy shit!"

The monitors showed him various camera angles on Monelli pausing for a moment to reach into his suit coat pocket and bringing out the zip-lock bag of white powder.

Flanked on one side by Fay Banks and on the other by an engineer working the switcher, the director screamed, "Three, get me a tight shot of that bag!"

"God Almighty!" said Fay, awestruck, her mouth agape.

"I don't fuckin' believe this," said the audio man in the back of the control room.

All the sets in the TV department of the Sears store at Lakeside Mall were showing a medium shot of Monelli, followed by a tight shot of the bag of white powder as a number of shoppers stood in a group to watch.

"This bag," said Monelli, "contains a kilo of uncut cocaine."

Back in the control room the director was screaming again. "Oh, yeah! Somebody get tight on Frank. He looks like he swallowed his freakin' tongue."

Fay was shaking her head, then glimpsed the VP-GM Alice Whitney and her News Director Jack Johanson entering the control room. Alice came to her. "Did you have any idea?"

"None!"

On his corner on Fort Street Jimmy Long squinted at the tiny screen of his Sony Watchman and listened as Monelli continued: "It's a small sample of what I've brought into this city over the past several years. When I leave this TV studio tonight..."

In Monelli's private suite at the Eastbrook Manor Motel, Marco and Albert were watching their employer on the 40-inch Mitsubishi.

"...I will personally deliver this bag of cocaine to the local offices of the federal Drug Enforcement Administration."

"What the fuck!" said Marco.

"I will cooperate fully in the Agency's investigation of my dealings in illicit narcotics."

Albert and Marco looked at each other and stood up simultaneously. They paused for one more disbelieving look at the TV, then headed for the door.

Curled in an armchair Susan watched Monelli on the set in her living room.

"And I will ask for the stiffest punishment permitted under the laws governing the crimes I have committed. As I said at the beginning of this statement..."

Catherine Monelli sat on the edge of her king-sized bed watching her husband on a portable color set on a roll-about stand.

"...no member of my family is involved in any way in these crimes or, to my knowledge, any other criminal activity. I have the deepest..."

With her head pressed against the bathroom door at the cheese factory, Megan strained to listen to her father's voice on the set in the office.

"...love and concern for my family, particularly my wife Catherine and my daughter Megan. And it is out of that love and concern..."

On the other side of the bathroom door Charlie and John stared at the portable as Monelli completed his statement.

"...that I am taking the steps I have outlined here tonight. Thank you."

At the news set desk, Monelli unclipped the mike from his lapel, dropped it on the floor next to his chair and got to his feet.

For one of the few times in his life, Frank DeFauw had been rendered speechless, but as his interviewee began to move away from the desk, he finally found his voice. "Well, I have to say, Mr. Monelli, that is one of the most extraordinary statements I've ever heard in all my years in broadcasting."

Monelli said nothing and moved between cameras through the unlit part of the studio to find his way out. DeFauw was standing now behind his desk shouting. "Please, Mr. Monelli, just stay with us for a few more minutes. I'm sure our viewers have a number of questions. I know I do."

"I'm finished," said Monelli, walking directly now to the large studio doors.

In the control room the director was standing now, barking instructions to his camera operators. "Stay with him, two, stay with him! Three, get me Monelli!"

On the large line monitor the picture was much darker now as Fay watched Monelli reach the doors.

DeFauw was still shouting. "Please, Mr. Monelli, just a few more minutes for some questions. I think you owe us the answers!"

The line monitor showed a dark image of Monelli shoving his way out the studio doors. He can be heard quite clearly saying, "Fuck you!"

"Go to black," screamed Alice Whitney. "Go to black."

Chapter 97

Feeling old and anxious. Cigar Mike Monelli thought that was one fucked-up combo. Chewing on an unlit Cuban at a front living room window in his son's home, he searched the empty street, then glanced at his gold Movado. It was 6:40 pm. Robert was due any minute in the Cadillac, and then it would be on to the motel.

Certainly his Steven wouldn't be needing a ride for a while. That blond guy on Channel 5, the one always waving his hands around too much, had said it on the news at 6. After what Steven had told DeFauw earlier in the newscast, he was not likely to be going anywhere on his own for quite some time.

The reporter had said Robert and the Cadillac were roaring out the front gate at Channel 5 when Steven was still stalking off the news set. In front of the Federal Court Building, the reporter had described how a Detroit Police cruiser had brought the "reputed, no, make that self-described crime lord" downtown, escorted by no less than five city patrol cars. Like everybody else in town, the cops had been watching Steven Monelli with Frank DeFauw.

"The fuck's goin' on, sir?" Marco had asked on the phone about a half hour ago.

"I'll tell you what's goin' on," Cigar Mike had barked. "Just get everybody together at the motel, and I'll come and say what's goin' on."

"You sure the motel's okay? Maybe he already told 'em about it."

"No, the motel is fine. Everybody's gonna be okay."

A little damage control. No, make that a lot of damage control, was what he needed to do now. Get them all together and tell them the threat against Steven's daughter had forced him to do it. All the more reason they needed to find Megan. Once she was safe, Steven would be out from under that hammer. Until then? He'd tell them Steven's plan was to stall and tell the cops nothing important.

Fact was, who the fuck knew what his son was gonna do.

Damage control. He had done a ton of it in his day. Tonight he'd certainly rather have been sitting on his new teak deck at the suburban estate outside Phoenix, eating artichokes and watching the sunset. But he wouldn't be there any time soon.

At least now he'd be in control here, and not have to bend to his weak-willed son. Like last night when the idea came to him to pop that fuck DeFauw. All they needed was time. More time and they'd get Megan back. So grab some the easy way, with a high-profile hit that would turn everything in this goddamn town up-side-down for a while and probably scare the shit out of those fuckin' kidnappers as well. But no, without even thinking about it, cock-sure Steven had pronounced the foolproof plan "too risky."

The phone rang in the den, and the old man, moving slowly with an achy knee, headed for it. Probably Robert calling from the Cadillac. After one ring there was silence, but he continued to the den and picked up the receiver on Steven's desk. Only a dial tone. He moved back out of the den and stopped at the foot of the stairs.

"Catherine."

With no answer he called again, louder. "Catherine, who was it?"

In her daughter's bedroom, Catherine Monelli sat, still shaking, on the edge of the bed. Her father-in-law's voice from below had prompted only one thought: never again trust a man named Monelli.

She steadied herself, then got to her feet and moved slowly to the bedroom door. With it open a crack, she asked, "What is it?"

She could no longer bring herself to call him Dad.

"Who was on the phone, Catherine?"

"It was nothing A wrong number."

Her father-in-law was silent for a moment at the foot of the stairs. "Okay. I'll be leaving for a meeting soon. Robert's picking me up. If you hear anything, call me at the motel."

"I will," she said, though she hoped never to hear his evil, rasping voice again. Closing the door she moved back to the bed. Instead of sitting again, she began pacing the room. Was she certain the voice on the phone was the same as the voice on the tape, without the phony drawl? What exactly did he say?

"Megan is safe, and she'll be returned to you soon."

Her voice filled with anger and hope, Catherine had asked, "When?"

The man on the phone had hesitated for a second. "Tonight," he

225

had said finally and then hung up.

Chapter 98

Near the factory wall in the Nova, John sat on the passenger side of the front seat still staring at the phone attached to the dash. The intensity of the woman's one-word question, "When?" reverberated in his memory. Charlie, sitting next to him behind the wheel, finally asked after a long silence, "Now, John, don't you feel better?"

Turning to look at the guy, he said, "No."

Then he turned away and gazed at the sun filtering though the thick foliage of the big old trees behind the factory. At least there would be more than two hours before darkness fell, and the black man would force him to return the girl home.

"I just don't see why it has to be tonight," he said finally. "Why can't we wait at least until Monday and give them a chance to get some useful information out of Monelli. The girl's fine, and nothing's going to happen to her in a couple of days."

"Look, John, I told you, they're already talking to Monelli. I used to be a cop. I know how they do things. The first thing they do is take a written statement from the guy and have him sign it. They're already doin' that. And you already got Monelli himself nailed. That kilo alone is going to send him away for a helluva long time."

"Yeah, I hope."

"But you've put that woman and her daughter through hell, John, and that's not goin' on a minute longer than it has to. Not to mention that every minute you hold Megan is another minute you make us targets for Monelli's thugs."

John glanced back toward the front of the property where the highway was invisible through the trees. "They'll never find this place."

"I found it. And they could very easily been tailin' me. No, John, as soon as it gets dark, you're gonna put Megan in your car and bring her home. And I'm gonna follow along to be sure you do it."

"Why don't you just do it yourself?" He glared sullenly at the

227

black man.

"Look, for a smart guy, you're not thinkin' very well. I told you, it's better for me, and for you, if I never found her. She hasn't seen me. She doesn't know what I look like or who I am. And we're gonna keep it that way. You understand?"

He nodded without looking at the guy.

"Anyway, that's what you're gonna do. And after that I only know what you should do."

Now John looked at him. "What's that?"

"Get out of this goddamn town for a long, long time. Go someplace far away where nobody knows you and start over. And whatever you do, don't tell anybody, especially your family, where you're goin'."

John nodded again.

"And one more thing, John."

"Yeah?"

"Lighten up, man. You're gonna get yourself and a lot of other people badly hurt doin' shit like this."

Chapter 99

Rolling the big BMW through darkness down the drive and into the street, Catherine felt sure she was forgetting something. Probably more than one thing, she thought, accelerating up the street. She was not about to take an inventory of the two suitcases she had packed and shoved in the trunk.

Certainly she was leaving behind life as she had known it. That had been clear almost from the moment she had hung up the phone with the kidnapper. And when her father-in-law had called from the bottom of the stairs that he'd be leaving shortly for the motel, her heart had begun racing with the thought that what she had to do might actually come easily.

Once he had left the house, and she watched him ride away in the Cadillac with Robert, she had moved directly to the den. Using the rhino and its little briefcase again, she had opened that big bottom desk drawer and found the audio cassette and the metal cash box still in place. Moving the cassette aside, she had opened the box and gazed in amazement at her luck. Five stacks of one thousand dollar bills, all but one of the stacks with their wrappers still intact. She lifted the loose stash and counted forty bills. The others must have fifty. There was nearly a quarter of a million dollars here.

She had taken the cash box, and for some reason, the audio cassette as well, closed the drawer and headed upstairs to pack. The only surprise had come when she was loading a suitcase in Megan's room. She looked up to find Anna, the old Italian woman who had been with them from Megan's birth, watching her from the doorway.

"What is it, Anna?"

The old woman had said nothing for a moment, her face so wrapped in sadness that Catherine had thought she was going to weep. "I go with you and Meggie. You all alone. You need me."

Amazed at what the woman already knew, Catherine had wondered what else Anna understood. And she had been touched by the offer. Moving to the doorway she had taken the old woman's hands in her own.

"No, Anna, I can't take you with me. Besides, Mr. Monelli may need you here."

The old woman's dark eyes had turned fierce. "No, no work for him, never no more."

"Well, Anna, there's just no way I can take you."

Suddenly stoic, the old woman had nodded and walked away.

What will happen to Anna, Catherine wondered now as she turned a corner fast enough to hear her tires squeal. That was just one of the many things she could not know or control. Like what would happen to the beautiful home she had just left without even taking one last look? Or what would happen to her husband? She was already having trouble picturing him clearly in her mind's eye. In fact, her most vivid image of Steven now was not what he had looked like on TV earlier, but instead her memory of his hands at the breakfast table that morning so many weeks ago when they had suddenly looked so cruel.

As she brought the car to a halt for a red light at the beginning of that upscale strip of stores and shops called the Village, she searched the two pay-phone stands on her right and found no sign of Megan. With her heart sinking she replayed the phone call that finally ended the agony of her wait in the big silent house.

"Mom, I'm at the pay phones in the Village. Come get me."

Like a hundred other calls before it when Megan had phoned for a ride home after shopping with her girlfriends. Only this call meant that enough of Catherine's shattered world would still be intact to forge a new life.

"Megan, baby, are you okay?"

"I'm fine, Mom. I just don't feel like walking home."

"Don't move, baby. Don't go anywhere. I'll be right there."

And now suddenly up the street on her left, in jeans and a top Catherine has never seen before, there was Megan turning in front of the bookstore window and waving at her. Catherine began to press the accelerator, then remembered the red light and slammed down the brake just in time to avoid a car crossing the intersection. "For Godsake, be careful," she told herself aloud. "All you need now is an accident."

With the light green she moved through the intersection, then swung the sedan in a quick u-turn and stopped in front of Megan at the curb. Her daughter opened the door, gave her a big bright-eyed smile, and climbed in. Her own eyes filling with tears Catherine grabbed the girl and held her tight.

"Oh, Meg, baby, I love you. I've been so frightened for you."

"Mom, I'm okay. Don't worry." Megan hugged her back with almost equal fervor.

"Oh, Meg..." Catherine enveloped the girl with a desperate joy, her relief beyond words.

With a small laugh finally, Megan said, "Mom, you're crushing me. Let me close the door and let's get out of here. That creep might still be around."

"Oh, God, yes." Catherine released her long enough for Megan to close the door. Then grabbing her again, she held her face in her hands and searched her eyes. "Meg, are you sure you're okay? Did he touch you? Did he hurt you?"

"Mom, I told you, I'm okay. He never touched me. Com'on, let's get out of here. I want to see Daddy."

Catherine kissed her daughter's cheek, then finally let her go and turned back to the wheel, moving the car carefully away from the curb. "Baby, some things have happened with your father, and we're not going to be seeing him for awhile. Maybe not for a long time."

"You mean what happened on TV tonight?"

"You saw that?"

"I heard it. Those guys were watching. They had me locked up, but I could hear it."

"Then you know what's happened." Catherine felt almost relieved as she turned right on Cadieux, a street that would take them right to I-94.

"I know what happened. And I know why Daddy said those things. They were holding me hostage so Daddy would have to do what they wanted."

Catherine felt her hands tighten on the steering wheel and told herself to stay calm. "Baby, the things your father said on TV are true. That's the problem. And that's why you and I have to go away."

"What do you mean, go away? I just want to go home."

"Megan, listen to me. I don't want to frighten you. But you and I are in danger because of what your father's said and done. We've got to go someplace where no one can find us and stay there until we're safe again."

"But we've got to tell Daddy that I'm okay, so he can tell everybody that what he said wasn't true."

"But, baby, I told you, what he said is true. And that's why we're in danger. Now I promise you, after a while, we'll make sure your father knows you're safe. But right now we've got to help each other and support each other, because we're all we've got."

Megan shook her head in silence as the signal light turned green, and they crossed Mack, the avenue that marked the Grosse Pointe limit.

Catherine said finally, in a softer voice, "I've packed a bag for you, darling, with some of your favorite things. We're just going to have to look at this as a kind of adventure."

"Some adventure." Megan spoke with a sullen air that promised many more difficult moments ahead. "I just get away from one kidnapper, and I'm kidnapped again—by my own mother."

Chapter 100

"That fuckin' DeFauw," said Charlie in the dark, his voice holding both admiration and disdain.

"I know," said Susan snuggling next to him in the bed, her head on his chest.

After his return to the flat that evening and his detailed account, prompted by her unending questions, of exactly what had happened, they had watched DeFauw at 11.

Off the top, calling this day "perhaps one of the most extraordinary in the history of journalism in this city," DeFauw had announced that Channel 5 was extending the newscast for an extra half hour. Then they had replayed in its entirety the "Up Front" segment featuring Steven Monelli's sensational admission of guilt. The newscast had also included another live report from the steps of the Federal Court Building downtown in which DEA officials were quoted as saying that Monelli had signed a statement and was cooperating fully. DeFauw had closed the segment with one of his patented, fervid commentaries, this one on the "marvelous contributions of Italian-Americans to our city, our state and our nation, from the hard-working guy pouring the cement for your driveway to the eloquence of Mario Cuomo to the extraordinary leadership of a captain of industry like Lee Iacocca."

"So what are you going to do with all that cash?" She shifted a bit to her side so she could move her hand down to Charlie's cock. And, yes, her suspicions confirmed, it was already huge.

He groaned with pleasure. "Ten grand ain't goin' very far. Not compared with what it woulda been, if I'd just made one little phone call."

"Oh, please, Charlie. You know you did the right thing." She stroked delicately, then played with his balls the way he always loved.

"Maybe...Oh, yes...maybe not. But I've been thinking, maybe I

233

should use the money to get me an office in the suburbs, Grosse Pointe or Birmingham maybe, where I'm more likely to draw the kind of cliental I need."

She propped herself on an elbow, still playing with him. "I think a new office location is a good idea. But not in the suburbs."

"Why not?"

"Charlie, if people like us, the much-maligned black middle-class, keep moving out of the city like whitey already has, that's going to be the death knell of this city."

"Hey, who says I'm middle-class? I ain't even near there yet, never will be if I don't start getting more business."

"You know what I mean. And I think you could probably do just as well downtown in one of the new buildings, or even in one of the older buildings where the rent is so cheap because of all the new space."

"I just can't believe you." He offered mock disgust as he turned her gently so he could slide his hand up under her nightgown. "My little do-gooder just never gives up."

"Oh, baby, I'm so proud of what you've done. I hope you know that."

Her nipples were hard, and he traced them lightly, the way that made them even harder. "Look, what I did, in the long run, ain't gonna make a damn bit of difference to anybody. It's just not going to matter."

"Well, there's one person it's always going to matter to." She smiled at him in the dark, then lifted her head enough to kiss him softly on the mouth.

"Yeah, I know." He sounded slightly exasperated. "You're proud of me and of what I did. And it's always going to matter to you."

"Well, that's all true, but I'm not talking about me."

"Who then?"

"You."

Chapter 101

A heavily bearded young man, his dark hair unfashionably long and curly, sat in the harsh neon of a small diner wrapped in the shadows cast by the huge cement stilts on which 1-95 stretched across downtown Miami. From his favorite corner table he worked on his Eggs Rancheros and watched the young Cuban girl who was the only waitress in the place.

In her tight light blue uniform she moved with an awkward grace behind the counter, running a damp cloth over the chipped and dented Formica, trying to look professional. Even though there were only two other customers, that meant acting as if she didn't know the bearded young man, as if he had not helped her get the job in this place two days ago.

He knew how she felt. He too had worried about looking professional that first night at La Veranda in Pompano Beach. He had taken the job a week after he had made it to Pompano with one last gasp from the old black Ford, finding the little ten-unit motel near the Intercoastal where he had stayed for a week with his mother and his stepfather a decade ago at the age of fifteen. The Ford had died shortly after his arrival, so he had walked to the restaurant that first night and had been nervous enough to drop a plate of linguini with clam sauce in the kitchen.

He had been honest with the manager about his lack of experience, saying he had held a couple of wait jobs in college and was an out-of-work teacher. And they had been patient with him, telling him to forget the dropped plate and generally making things easy. In fact he could have stayed on at La Veranda indefinitely, if he had wanted to, but frequently the place served what he thought were certain worrisome types, customers whose looks made him nervous.

Finally, one Saturday evening he had found a heavy-set fellow in a black shirt sitting alone and staring at him for most of the evening. And the next morning he had bought the Sunday Miami Herald and

235

searched the want ads. A live-in shelter on North Miami Avenue for run-away teens with drug and alcohol problems had caught his eye, and that afternoon he had taken a bus into Miami. He was surprised at how shabby the area around the shelter had been and how reminiscent of his own southwest corner of Detroit.

And he had been amazed at how easily he had secured the counselor's position without presenting any evidence of having done this kind of work before. Again he had been honest about his background, but the woman in charge had simply talked with him for an hour and then explained how difficult it was to find people who would live at the shelter and work with these children. Basically, he had been hired on the spot.

His salary had been minuscule, his room at the shelter hardly more than a closet and the meals there barely adequate, but at least he had felt safe and didn't need a car. Usually on Saturday afternoons, he had walked about ten blocks to a branch of the Miami public library and read a week's worth of his hometown papers, both the Free Press and the News.

Every so often he would find a story about Steven "The Bank" Monelli who had made a very public admission of his role in the importing of large amounts of cocaine and heroin to the city. But having signed a statement prepared by federal Drug Enforcement agents, he had then recanted his confession some days later and refused to testify against anyone he had previously named. His claim now? He had been coerced into making the statement by someone who had kidnapped his daughter and threatened her life.

"Monelli to Use DeLorean Defense" was one headline he remembered in a Sunday edition. The lengthy piece quoted the high-powered defense attorney hired by Monelli as saying, "Look, we all saw John DeLorean holding all that coke and saying it was better than gold. And we all know what happened when he said he only went along with the scheme because his 'business associates' had threatened his family. You're going to hear a very similar story from Mr. Monelli, and I'm confident you'll see a very similar result."

The prosecution wouldn't talk, but another criminal defense attorney in town, unconnected to the case and wishing to remain anonymous, had been quoted to the effect that since Monelli's 12-year-old daughter was apparently not available to testify, he might have difficulty proving his story.

"I think if I were on the case," the attorney had been quoted as saying, 'I might be trying to bargain down the time he'll get for possession of that kilo."

And apparently at Monelli's trial in Federal Court, the defense's inability to convince the jury that a kidnapping and coercion had actually taken place had, in fact, led to his downfall. A string of witnesses, most of them with credibility problems, testified that they had been out searching for Megan Monelli in the days preceding her father's public admission of guilt. A few of them claimed to have heard Steven Monelli say the kidnapper was demanding a false confession. But perhaps the most impressive defense witness, a private investigator named Charles Watts, had claimed that Monelli told him the ransom demand was simply one million dollars.

The most recent story the young man saw in the paper two weeks ago had said Monelli had been convicted of possession of one kilo of 92% pure cocaine and had been sentenced to seven and a half years at the Lewisburg Federal Penitentiary in Pennsylvania. With good behavior he would be eligible for parole in five years.

Earlier Detroit police officials had been quoted as saying they had seen some impact from the Monelli case on the price and availability of cocaine. More recent reports from the street indicated it was once again business as usual.

"Can I get anything else for you, sir?"

The young man looked up from the last of his Eggs Rancheros and gazed into the Cuban girl's pretty brown eyes. "How about a new life, Rosa?"

Chapter 102

Moving slowly with an old duffle bag into the row where Frank DeFauw sat was a young goateed guy who looked somehow familiar. Following him was a shapely black-haired girl, Cuban, he guessed. They ended up sitting directly across from Frank, and the young guy stared at him, saying finally, "You're Frank, right?"

"Yeah. I know you, don't I?"

"Yes, you do. You interviewed me once. Name's John Giordano."

"Giordano. Oh, right. We talked to you for the "Kids and Crack" doc. How you doin'? You were a teacher who lost his job."

Giordano smiled. "Good memory."

"So you found a teaching job down here?"

"No, right now I'm working for a small weekly paper. I'm writing profiles mostly about Cuban refugees, like my friend Rosa here." He put a hand on her thigh.

"Hi, Rosa, I'm Frank."

The girl smiled but said nothing.

After a pause, Frank said, "Well I'd like to read your stuff. How about sending me some stories? If I like 'em, I'll send them on to an old buddy of mine who's an editor at the Herald down here. I mean, if that's okay with you."

"Hey, thanks, that would be great. So you on business down here?"

Frank shook his head. "Pleasure. Coming back with my family." He gestured at Marci and Jen reading books and Bobby into his headset in a corner of the waiting area. "We have a place down on Providenciales in the Turks and Caicos Islands. How about you?"

"Going home to see my family. My mom really. It's been about a year and half. Hey, let me ask you something. I followed, as much as I could in the papers back there, that big story of yours about Monelli and his confession."

"Oh, right."

"Yeah, so whatever happened with Monelli's daughter. What was her name, Megan? They ever find her?"

"Nope. Story was, about a week after Monelli was on my show, the girl called her grandfather and said she was okay, but that her mother had kidnapped her, and she was somewhere in Canada. She didn't know exactly where."

"She said her *mother* kidnapped her?"

"Yeah. Of course, when Monelli recanted, his lawyers denied that story and claimed some enemy of the family had snatched the girl, and Monelli's supposedly false confession was the condition of her release. Which made sense, but without the girl or her mother they didn't have much of a chance in court."

"Yeah, that and the kilo of coke."

"Yeah, the coke was a little hard to explain."

Giordano shook his head. "Canada. So have the girl and her mother ever surfaced?"

"Not that we know of. Canada is a big place, and who knows if it's even Canada. We've sent a reporter up there to root around for awhile in a few cities—Toronto, Montreal—even some smaller places. Talk to cops, do some reports. Mostly it's just a ratings grabber. I can't imagine how much time and money the Monellis have spent on really searching. But so far, from what we know, mom and Megan have just disappeared."

Giordano stared off with a strange smile. Finally he asked, "So whatever happened to that documentary you were working on? Did it ever get finished?"

"Oh, yeah, got a great reaction. Lots of good comments about you, as I recall. I'll tell you what. You send me your stories, I'll send you the doc."

Giordano smiled again and put an arm around his pretty girl.

"You've got a deal."

###

Other Books by T.V. LoCicero

True Crime Books:
Murder in the Synagogue
Squelched: The Suppression of Murder in the Synagogue

Novels:
The Obsession
The Disappearance
The Car Bomb
Babytrick
When A Pretty Woman Smiles
Sicilian Quilt

Collection:
Coming Up Short

Word-of-mouth!
It's vital to any author. If you enjoyed this book, please consider leaving a review at Amazon. It may be only a line or two, but it could make a big difference and would be deeply appreciated.

Say Hello!
T.V. LoCicero offers info, thoughts, photos, videos and much more on his website and blog: www.tvlocicero
He'd love it if you come by and say hello. You can also get in touch on Facebook, or send him an email: tvloc1@netscape.net

Be the First to Learn of a New Release!
If you'd like to receive an auto email when the next book is released, please sign up at: http://eepurl.com/z26Vv
Your email address will never be shared, and you can unsubscribe at any time.

www.ingramcontent.com/pod-product-compliance
Lightning Source LLC
Chambersburg PA
CBHW020600180626
46810CB00007B/2578